Karl Erdmann Edler

Baldine, and Other Tales

Karl Erdmann Edler

Baldine, and Other Tales

ISBN/EAN: 9783337027377

Printed in Europe, USA, Canada, Australia, Japan

Cover: Foto ©Andreas Hilbeck / pixelio.de

More available books at **www.hansebooks.com**

BALDINE

And other Tales

BY

KARL ERDMANN EDLER

TRANSLATED FROM THE GERMAN

BY THE EARL OF LYTTON

NEW YORK
HARPER & BROTHERS, FRANKLIN SQUARE
1887

TRANSLATOR'S PREFACE.

Our novel-reading public is plenteously supplied by
its book - market with native productions and French
imports of every description; and for the lighter produce of German literature there is, at present, little or
no demand. To the *Dii Minores* of that literature
their own countrymen no longer accord the immortal-
ity so confidently certificated by Carlyle half a century
ago. But the Seer of Chelsea was not far-seeing in his
estimates of the relative importance of German writers
after Goethe; nor can he be altogether exempted from
the censure passed by himself upon Mr. Taylor, as an
expositor of German literature to whom some of its
most characteristic productions were "a sealed book,
or, what is worse, an open book in which he would not
read."

Upon Tieck, and Novalis, and Jean Paul Richter
Carlyle bestowed elaborate criticism quite out of pro-
portion to their permanent literary value; while Grill-
parzer, the most genuine dramatic poet of his time,
he contemptuously dismissed from notice as "a mere
playwright." The philosophy of Fichte and Schelling
found in him an appreciative interpreter; and his
miscellanies make respectful mention of minor German
poets whose names are now almost forgotten. But of

Schopenhauer and Heine he had nothing to tell us; nor of their transcendent influence in departments of German literature, which continued to engage his attention after the death of those writers, although both of them were his literary contemporaries; the one his senior, and the other not greatly his junior, in authorship.* .

Habent sua fata libelli! and no predictions are so often falsified as those of literary criticism. Countess Hahn-Hahn (that once popular novelist!) has gone the way of all flesh, and her works follow her. Of the later writers of German fiction, Gustav Freytag and Paul Heyse are not unknown to the English novel-reader; but they have certainly exercised no influence over English thought or sentiment. The illustrious author of "Wilhelm Meister" and "Wahlvervandtschaften" would perhaps have disdained the title of novelist. Regarded as works of art, however, his fictions cannot be placed in the category of good novels. To say the truth, the novel, whether of manners or of character, is a form of fiction so unsuccessfully cultivated by Germany, that in the department devoted to its production her imaginative literature scarcely deserves the attention it has failed to receive from the countrymen of Fielding and Richardson.

But, though I hope they may please our novel-reading public, it is not exclusively to it that I offer these specimens of the lighter workmanship of a German writer whose genius has created a type of fiction *sui generis*. Like some of Nathaniel Hawthorne's "Mosses from an Old Manse," or the "Märchen" of Hans Chris-

---

* Schopenhauer was born in 1788, and Carlyle in 1795. Heine, who jokingly called himself the first man of his century, was born on the 1st of January, 1800. He died in 1856, and Schopenhauer in 1860.

tian Andersen, though written in prose, they belong, in all essentials, to the province of poetry. They do not fetch their subject from the clouds, however, though they lift it above the common level. They are not abstractions of pure fancy, but ideal delineations of real feeling, with a definite core of human interest. In this respect they differ fundamentally from all such fictions as those of Lamotte-Fouqué, Arnim, Brentano, and Hoffmann. The world into which they admit us is neither supernatural nor grotesque, but thoroughly human. It is a world peopled by men and women—not by spectres, or sylphs, or abstract qualities in fancy costume. Some of their descriptive passages reveal an intimacy with the feelings of childhood and the significance of inanimate objects which will occasionally remind an English reader of the humor of Andersen. But between the genius of their author and that of the Danish poet the difference is also far-reaching; for where Andersen ends, this author only begins. His imagination hovers tenderly over the realm of childhood, but it does not rest there ; and what it seeks in the child is the father of the man.

Those to whom any work of original genius is always welcome, come whence it may, will probably be able to find some charm even in the clumsiest translation of it. But much of the peculiar charm of Edler's writings is, I fear, inseparable from their original form. Germanisms which are graceful in their native idiom would appear grotesque in ours. Colors delicately brilliant in one medium, become opaque and crude when mixed with any other. Each language, moreover, has not only an idiom, but also a cadence, special to itself. These conditions of his task sometimes make it impossible for a translator to preserve the spirit, if he maintains a strict fidelity to the letter, of the original. And yet even slight variations in the structure of a sentence or the position of an epithet may injuriously change the whole character of an original style; just as the addition of a pair of whiskers sufficed to convert the honest face of Sir Roger de Coverley into the Saracen's Head.

The author of these tales is a consummate master of the idiom of his own language. In his hands German prose, that generally cumbrous vehicle of expression, becomes a perfect instrument, and he plays it to perfection. His style is not put on, and therefore it cannot be taken off. "Edler," says one of his German critics, "combines great poetic gifts with a wide culture and an original mind; but these are merits which, though rare, are shared with him by other writers. What is peculiarly his own is the mastery of style which marked even his first appearance as an author; and it is this which renders his genius as captivating as it is original." Fortunately, however, the charm of this author's individuality, though enhanced by his style, is not wholly dependent on it. The depth and tenderness of his humanity; the accuracy of his touch upon the finer emotions; the delicacy with which he lifts the inner folds of feeling; the pensive sweetness of his humor, and an instinctive refinement of taste that never by inadvertence strikes a jarring note—these are merits which his writings may still retain, even in versions that lack the light, melodious movement of his style.

Karl Erdmann Edler was born in 1844, at Padebrod in Bohemia, and, whether of Slavonic or (as his name implies) of German parentage, he seems to have been born with a genius in which the characteristic note of both nationalities is curiously distinguishable. He commenced his university career at Vienna; and it was there, last spring, that I first became acquainted with his works, through Prince Philip Hohenlohe, a friend of their author. I began the perusal of them with reluctance, and in a sceptical spirit. I had been asked to read them with special reference to the question whether some of them, if translated, would have any chance of a favorable reception from the English public; and I expected to find them written in the style of Freytag's "Sollen und Haben." But I had not read many pages before I felt

> "As a watcher of the skies, -
> When some new planet swims into his ken."

I was conscious of being in contact with the mind of a new and genuine poet; and hence the present attempt to make some few of his writings known to those of my countrymen who are dependent on translations for their knowledge of German books.

Edler's first work, entitled "Koloritstudien," was published at Vienna in 1873. It consisted of two short romances, "Wilfred" and "Gabor;" the first a tale of the German Middle Age, and the second a story of the steppes. "Gabor," says an Austrian writer, "is a magnificent symphony, which has in it the very soul of the gypsy music." And here I may observe that, with rather less absurdity than is commonly involved in the prevalent fashion of applying to the effects of one art the technical terminology of another, the three little stories printed together in these volumes might perhaps be described as symphonies of sentiment, each in a different key.

Karl Edler's genius is psychological and dramatic.

All his works, whatever the form or the subject of them, are dramas of the inner life. But he respects the order of Nature, which has decently placed out of sight the inward organs of life, and his heroes and heroines are not continually turning themselves inside out for the purpose of self-examination. He works by synthesis rather than by analysis, and builds up his characters instead of taking them to pieces. In his style there is no flourish of the anatomist's scalpel, in his work no odor of the dissecting-room. His characters are alive, and we hear the beating of their hearts; though we hear them only through the fine atmosphere of those

"hohen Regionen
Wo die reinen Formen wohnen."

He has been justly praised as a colorist, but he does not aim at startling spectacular effects, and the peculiar merit of his coloring is in a subtle harmony between the pervading tone of the picture and the central idea of its design. That idea, moreover, is always beautiful, always graceful, and intellectually highborn. For Edler is not a literary photographer, but an ideal artist. Hence, in his slightest sketches we find a noble breadth of suggestiveness, and large proportions in small dimensions. His workmanship, however, is highly finished; and, unlike Jean Paul, of whom it has been well said that he gives us his brains instead of his thoughts, Edler's conceptions are never crude or confused.

The defect more or less common to the imaginative writers of Germany is an undefinable flavor of something provincial and *Kleinstättig.* Even the great Goethe is not wholly free from it. But of this no trace is to be found in Edler's writing. Nor in his humor is there anything disorderly or uncouth. All is select, symmetrical, reticent, refined. He is an essentially well-bred writer.

The romance of "Wilfred," published with "Gabor" under the title of "Koloritstudien," has been compared with Scheffel's "Ekkerhard," I suppose because it presents to us the image of a mediæval monk under the influence of a passion forbidden by his vows. But in nothing else do the two books bear any resemblance to each other.

Scheffel is a vigorous and racy writer. I am very far from wishing to speak of his remarkable talent in any spirit of depreciation. His "Trompeter von Seckingen" and his "Frau Aventura" are works of great force and spirit, which leave a lasting mark upon the memory; and the whimsical fun of his palæontological poems is delightful. But the difference between his writings and those of Edler is still a difference between talent and genius.

Scheffel goes to the Middle Ages for his materials, as a connoisseur goes to a curiosity shop to furnish his house in a particular *genre*. Whenever Edler reverts to a past age for the raw material of his romances, it is as a student of those human emotions which are common to all ages, and of which time only varies the external conditions. The predominant sentiment of all his writing is a profound compassion for the incompleteness and sorrowfulness of human life. In Scheffel's writings there is no compassion, nor in his view of life is there any cause for it.

The fact is, Germany is no longer a Prometheus Vinctus; and Scheffel's books reflect the justifiable contentment of a successful people, whose chief concern is to enjoy what it has so patiently and painfully acquired—its mental culture, its national importance, its picturesque past and promising future. All his productions, whether in prose or verse, are variations on the theme of *Gaudeamus igitur!*

Compare the mediævalism of Scheffel with that of Novalis, the difference between them is enormous. And it is historical; for it marks the progress made by educated Germany, in less than two generations, from aspiration to attainment. Edler is the reverse of all this; and, with nothing in him either of the mysticism of Novalis or the jollity of Scheffel, he stands in a totally different relation to German literature.

Scheffel was born at Karlsruhe, and educated at Heidelberg. Edler was born at Padebrod, and educated at Vienna. Scheffel was a young man, and Edler only a child, in 1848; and these facts go far to explain, not only the difference between the temperaments of the two poets, but also why Young Germany has accorded to the complacent conservatism of the elder a popularity not likely to be ever attained, in the present generation, by the wistful, questioning sadness of the younger.

The "Koloritstudien" were followed by the classical romances of "Ursinia" and "Artemis," the first of which appears to me one of the most charming of all its author's creations. In a German criticism of this book I find a passage which so correctly indicates the general characteristics of the author's genius that I cannot forbear quoting it. "What nobility," exclaims the critic, "in the conception, and what magic in the execution! This is not skill, but inspiration—a complete and unconscious surrendering of the artist's whole mind to a high ideal, and an unerring adherence to that ideal—the perfect embodiment of a beautiful mind in a beautiful form, by some process as mysteriously spontaneous as that of Nature herself, in which there is no perceptible trace of art, or effort, or self-consciousness of any kind. The fanciful, the humorous, and the tender find here an expression which not only satisfies, but transports us. I remember, in particular, that scene upon the Esquiline where Ursina is waiting for Eleanus. With what subtle strokes, in what living tints, does the author reveal to us the inmost motions of the girl's spirit, its rapidly changing moods, and its abiding undertone of unfathomable sadness! And all without a word of interposed description or explanation! With what witchery, moreover, in the attainment of this effect, does he contrive to impart, as it were, a human echo to the surrounding scenery! There is but one name for such writing. It is poetry of the purest and highest order."

To "Ursinia" and "Artemis" succeeded the three little modern idyls which make up the contents of the present volumes. Of one of them, "Notre Dame des Flots," a French translation, by Princess Hohenlohe, was, I believe, published some years ago in the *Revue de France*. In the list of Edler's works must also be mentioned a drama, of which, however, I know nothing except that it is entitled "Theodora," and has been acted at Hanover. His two latest productions are "Peire de Cinqtors," a troubadour romance, and "The Last Jew," which is generally regarded in Germany as its author's greatest work. The power of the book is indisputable, but I must avow a strong personal preference for his smaller idyls. Great historical novels are less uncommon than such literary cameos.

From this enumeration of Edler's works, the reader will see that the three translated here have been selected from the shortest and least elaborate of them all. They illustrate rather the delicacy of the author's workmanship than the full scope and variety of his creative powers. But I doubt whether, since Goethe's "Mignon," imaginative literature has produced a creation more novel in its beauty, or more touching in its pathos, than that of Baldine—the child who, reared in silence and solitude, with the dumb playmates, the dumb nurse, and the dumb god, has in her, all the while, a gift of surpassingly expressive song; a gift unknown to herself, and revealed only through an overwhelming sorrow. And the process whereby the great forlorn artist is at last redeemed from moral petrifaction, through the stimulus gradually given to that capacity of gratitude which, equally unknown to herself, had survived in her the loss of every other human feeling, appears to me a conception of wonderful subtlety and truth. The art with which the story is told is equally remarkable. There is not a single incident, however trivial, in the opening chapters, which does not bear, with steadily increasing significance, upon the whole development of the character of Baldine and the final solution of the problem it presents.

In the nature of its subject, "Notre Dame des Flots" approaches nearer than any of Edler's other fictions to the level of the ordinary novel. But it has, in common with them all, a certain spaciousness of spirit; and this is a supreme merit, considering how many long and elaborate works of fiction resemble large - scale maps of Little Pedlington. In these short tales the circumference of the actual story is small, but not so the scope of its suggestiveness. It is like a pinhole, through which the eye sees far. The field of vision swept by the gaze through so minute an outlet is of course restricted; but what we see is the segment of a vast orb; and, as the segment has all the qualities of the unseen circle to which it belongs, its significance is large. This far-reaching suggestiveness is not wanting to the story of "Notre Dame des Flots;" and it is specially potent in the closing picture of the happy daughter treading over the nameless grave of the devoted mother, on her way to inspect the monument she is raising to the honored memory of the utterly worthless father. The best judge I know of imaginative literature has said to me of this story, "It is very pathetic, but I cannot help wishing it had stopped with the adoption of Blanche's daughter by Dumont. The mind would have reposed in the hopes it would have formed for the child. To destroy this illusion balks us, and creates a feeling of disappointment." I should entirely agree in this criticism, if it were only an abstract statement of that principle of art which requires that at the close of the tragedy we should

> "With peace and consolation be dismist,
> And calm of mind."

But it implies that there is a violation of the principle, which I am unable to recognize, in the *dénoûment* of "Notre Dame des Flots." No principle of art requires that such a story as this should end comfortably in relation to the order of external fact; and the story would not end with greater comfort to the moral sense if it ended in the manner suggested. The illusion retained would, in that case, be a fraud upon the imagination; and it seems to me that its retention would have lowered the whole tone of the work. Nor do I feel that the author has disappointed any hopes for the daughter which can be legitimately excited by our sympathy with the self-sacrificing devotion of the mother. On the contrary, all such hopes are satisfied with exact propriety. The only proper reward of effort is the attainment of its aim; and no other can be admitted into the justice of ideal art. The mother's aim was to secure the daughter's happiness; and that object is completely attained, for the daughter is perfectly happy. Her happiness, moreover, in relation to its sources as well as its effects, is precisely of the kind which the mother would have wished it to be; for it proceeds not merely from her good fortune, but from a sweetness of disposition which bad fortune might have marred. We are told that, beautiful as she is, her chief beauty is in her smile; and the mention of this little fact is full of significance and purpose. The author must have meant us to understand by it the woman's whole character, for such smiles are the sunshine of the soul. We know, too, by the act of piety which brings her to the church at Havre, that she is not deficient in filial affection and gratitude.

But to win to *herself* the gratitude of her daughter, or to wean the child's filial reverence from the memory of a father who was unworthy of it, was *not* the object of the mother's life, or the wish of her heart. Such motives would have been incompatible with this woman's character; and equally incompatible with the daughter's happiness (which *was* the mother's object) would have been her knowledge of the truth about her parents. The *dénoûment*, therefore, does completely fulfil, and under the only conditions satisfactorily imaginable, the supreme prayer of the martyred wife, that her child might never be pained or shamed by a suspicion of the baseness to which she herself was a victim.

The distressing appearance of injustice is, after all, in its perceived relation to the infinite scheme of human life, only an *appearance;* which *disappears* as soon as we lose sight of the particular in the contemplation of the universal. So far from referring it to any erroneous conception of the nature of art, I admire in it a true reflection of the inevitable nature of things on their external side; and I think it ceases to be distressing when we regard it, as the author obviously intends us to regard it, in its relation to a mystery so vast and universal as to excite a sense of awful wonder which entirely transcends the fretfulness of hope and disappointment. To present to the imagination both the sorrowful and the terrible aspects of " the painful riddle of the earth," I conceive to be a salutary, as well as a legitimate, function of ideal art. It is, at any rate, the constant tendency of Edler's writings; but he also reconciles our imagination to the real sorrowfulness of the world by revealing to it the ideal loveliness of sorrow. The highest achievement of poetry must ever be in the ideal representation of the terrible side of life. Hence the high rank accorded to Tragedy in-the hierarchy of imaginative art. But injustice is a purely personal quality, and Tragedy knows no other justice than that which belongs to the impersonal order of the Universe; which, however terrible in many of its aspects and effects, has at least this consolatory quality — that it is inevitable. For, as no evils are harder to endure than those of which we think that they might have been averted, so is no consolation more effectual than that which springs from a complete recognition of unalterable necessity.

Of these three stories, the " Journey to the Grossglockner Mountain" best exhibits, perhaps, that peculiarity of its author's genius which gives tears to his humor and smiles to his pathos.

Karl Edler's writings belong to the literature of a sentiment for which Europe has adopted the name given to it by Germany. They reveal a profound consciousness of that *Weltschmertz* which has claimed so many illustrious victims, and given birth to so many great works. But perhaps what most distinguishes him from each of the writers who have successively contributed to the literary current he continues, is his freedom from the egotism common to them all.

Goethe has been called the physician, but he was rather the physiologist, of a malady which he did not attempt to cure, and which has long survived his diagnosis of its symptoms. Edler's relation to this *Weltschmertz* is that of the sympathizing friend, who would fain mitigate the pain of the sufferer in whom he recognizes his own kindred. During the *Walpurgisnacht* of 1848 he must have been asleep in his cradle, and safe from the spells of that Red-capped Sorceress whose wand transformed so many tolerably good poets into intolerably bad politicians. His writings are not polemical, like those of Heine and Börne; and there is no bitterness, perhaps because there is no egotism, in the humor of them. What apparently interests him in the world is its relation to *itself*, not its relation to *him*. Few poets seem more habitually capable of that intense but impersonal interest in man and nature which makes it all one to the contemplating eye whether the object it contemplates be seen by it "from the window of a palace or of a prison."*

---

* Schopenhauer.

Byron's writing is the passionate utterance of a be-wildered revolt, the cry of a wounded animal that suffers without understanding why, and resents it knows not what. Edler's is the thoughtful expression of intelligent resignation to a universal and inevitable condition of things—a resignation well assured that *"Everything has its Why, could we only understand it; though it is not everything that cries out when it is hurt."* Senancour's is a moan of despair prolonged in one monotonous note ; Edler's a voice of consolation speaking in many tones, but always proclaiming that *" Every human sorrow helps to bind together the whole human race, like a high and holy doctrine delivered unto all."* In him the *Weltschmertz* is absorbed by the *Humanitätsidee*, and has thus become impersonal. The subject of De Musset's lament is his own discomfort; the source of Edler's sadness is a deep compassion for a world in which the nobler the sufferer the greater the suffering. Leopardi contemplates this suffering without hope, and perceives in its conditions no possibility of relief ; Edler seeks, and finds, in a sympathetic study of those conditions the reconciling element of beauty. *" What is it in the human heart,"* he exclaims, *" which, when we search it to the depths, appears so unspeakably sad, and yet so unspeakably beautiful?"* And this is the key-note to all his writings.

The imaginative literature of to-day is not a literature of *Weltschmertz*, nor yet of *Weltfreude*, but of *Freudensucht*. The moral malady of the last generation had its source in the fretfulness of unsatisfied ideals. Our own age is a prey to the incoherence of a society which has no longer any ideals at all. The Revolutionary Gospel has ceased to be what it was even fifty years ago—a credited promise capable of kindling to enthusiasm men of strong and cultivated intellect. It is only a manual of clap-trap for the use of charlatans, who proclaim, not the freedom, but the sovereignty of the People, because they know that, during the endless minority of such a sovereign, the most impudent rogues and vilest flatterers will have the best chance of a place in the Council of Regency. The fervors which burned to a climax in 1848, consumed in that explosion a vast number of generous illusions; and we live now in a disenchanted world, whose strongest aspiration is towards a mere general diffusion of material comfort. Heine was the poet-laureate of the era which has come at last "to this complexion."

"O my friends," he sings, "I will give you a new song, and a better one. It is upon earth that we intend to establish the Kingdom of Heaven. We mean to be happy here below, and no longer beggars. The idle belly must cease to devour what has been acquired by the industrious hands. There grows down here bread enough for all the children of men. Ay, and roses too, and myrtles, and pleasure, besides green-peas in abundance! Yes, green-peas for all the world, and as soon as their pods are fit for shelling! As for Heaven, we leave that to the angels and sparrows."*

He called this song the epithalamium of the nuptials of Europe with the Genius of Liberty. But the epithalamium was composed in 1844, the year of Edler's birth, and many things have happened since then. The nuptials have been not only celebrated but consummated. The guests got intoxicated at the wedding-

---

* "Germania."

feast, and behaved uproariously. They hugged and
embraced each other all round, and toasted the bride
and bridegroom to their heart's content. But after the
embracing came the quarrelling, as it generally does
on such occasions, when people have drunk more than
is good for them. Many heads were broken; and some
lost their heads altogether, and have not recovered them
since. The Happy Couple have led much the same
life as all other happy couples—a life of little joys,
little sorrows, and little cares; scarcely one of transcendent felicity or splendid achievement. Their children have grown up with no exuberant satisfaction in
their lot, and no profound reverence for their illustrious parents. On the whole, these promising infants
have turned out rather dull adults. The poor old horn-
book of Liberty, Equality, and Fraternity has been
fumbled to tatters; but its most enterprising pupils
have not yet succeeded in satisfactorily solving a single
one of its elementary problems.

Yes! the mountains in labor have brought forth but
exiguous mice, and we live in a world disenchanted.
What wonder that we are sick of sentiment? It has
done so little for us! And so from sentiment we turn
to sensation, in the belief that we are thereby escaping
from illusion to reality—which is also, perhaps, an illusion. Meanwhile, we have done with the Unknowable,
and would be well content with the Comfortable only,
could we but get it. Green-peas and plenty of them!
That were a reality to be sensibly appreciated. Green-
peas in abundance, and as fast as they can be shelled,
for all the children of men! This is still the Gospel of
the New Philanthropy; and its apostles assure us that
the promise of it is to be attained automatically, without
painful moral effort on the part of any individual, by

the natural evolution of a society whose ethics are utilitarian, its æsthetics realistic, its religion a ritual, and its Kingdom of Heaven a political reform. *Gaudeamus igitur!*

Responsive only with a pensive sigh to these practical aspirations of an age whose disillusioned soul is to be saved, like Faust's, by industrial enterprise, Edler's genius has taken an unfrequented direction of its own. A shy and solitary stream, it diverges from the main current in which imaginative literature is now moving. But its narrow banks are haunted by the wings of bright fancies that hover among the blossoms of beautiful ideas; and in the lonely waters of it are fair reflections from old deserted altars of the Graces, and bowers where Eros is still a child.

LYTTON.

KNEBWORTH, *June*, 1886.

BALDINE.

BALDINE.

CHAPTER I.

In the forest clearing the sunbeams dance round an old pine-tree.

At the time when the other trees were felled to make the clearing, this one was so small that its largest boughs were no longer than the fingers of an infant's hand. The woodmen, with their threatening axes, passed it by; for the gentian lured their looks away from it to her own blue bells, and the wild strawberry covered with her leaves its tender limbs, and above its small green head the protective bramble spread her tangling hooks and spikes.

Thus the tree, surviving all its elders, has grown up alone; and now it looks down forlornly upon the solitude they have left around it. The sunbeams play about its dark pyramid, which they cannot penetrate. Nor can stem or branch peep out to them through the thick black layers of drooping fringes that enshroud the old pine from head to foot, giving it a sombre aspect — not, indeed, morose, but melancholy, as of a thing forgotten even by itself in its long loneliness. Only now and then, when the wind wafts to it faint greetings from its distant kindred in the forest, does a soft tremor stir the solitary tree, lightly rustling its heavy shroud.

In the shadowy circuit of the pine crouches a little girl.

She is examining a large india-rubber ball. The ball bears traces of better days, when it wore fine belts and was bright with all the colors of the rainbow. But of that extravagant foppery it is now happily divested; so far, at least, as little fingers have been able to scrape the colors off. The result, however, is clearly not worth all the trouble it must have cost; for the only secret revealed by the removal of the colors is a dull monotony of colorless gray, too insipid to satisfy even the moderate expectations of a mind easily contented. Deeper still within the ball must lurk the essential mystery of its being; and a wondrous seriousness deepens in the eyes of the little girl as she musingly examines it.

"Why do you jump so?" the child said to the ball.

He pretended not to have heard—or was it perhaps that he really did not hear that question? And again, putting her mouth close to him, she cried still louder, "Why do you jump?"

But he was even more dull of hearing than she had supposed.

Then the child's eyebrows went into a frown, her teeth shut fast behind her half-open lips, her small feet planted themselves firmly against the ground, and it seemed as if the whole of her little body were trying with all its might to concentrate itself into a single point. That point was the tip of her short forefinger, which she thrust hard into the ball. He yielded good-humoredly to the pressure, and made a shallow recess for the little finger which was not strong enough to pierce his tough skin. When he had had enough of this sport, however, he resumed his dignity, and jerked the little finger sharply back. He played the same sly trick upon the knuckle and the tip of the tiny foot, with both of which she tried to get the better of him; and, apparently quite resolved not to have a hole bored into him, there he lay upon the ground in a sulk, his fat gray cheek and plump lazy body swollen with pride and obstinacy. Worse still! when the child, pouting, spurned him aside with her little foot, he even sprang and capered about as if wild with pleasure.

The meaning of such conduct could not be mistaken; it was pure insolence.

She jumped up and kicked the ball angrily over the grass and moss of the clearing to the border of the forest. A push, a splash, and there he lay in the pool! She had meant to drown him; but his bath seemed to do him good, and he looked as if he thoroughly enjoyed it after his exercise. Up and down he bounded merrily on the water, hopped lightly across the ripples, dipped, and sprawled, and swung himself about, and looked saucily up at her. Then, refreshed by the romp, he swam comfortably on at a leisurely pace—round, gray, swollen, as before. It was intolerable.

The child now remembered she had once heard

the old wife of a glass-cutter in the village saying to a farm-servant, "That fellow is such a rascal, he deserves to be thrown into the water with a stone tied to his neck." She did not know who the fellow was, but she felt he could not possibly be a greater rascal than the ball. With one hand she picked up a stone, with the other she drew a string from her pocket, and eagerly she watched the saucy swimmer.

Suddenly, however, stone and string fell from her fingers. With both hands she seized her little frock (it was a frock of many colors, gayly patched and darned all over), lifted it up to her eyes, so high that her rosy knees shone bare beneath it, and burst out weeping bitterly.

He had no neck, not even a little one; and all out of pure spite!

So the ball kept his secret; and the child went sobbing back to her old place in the shadow of the pine-tree. There, upon the grass, all broken and covered with mould, lay her other toy — a little wooden jumping-man. He also had kept his secret. The headless body of him still commandingly stretched out its arm, and the bodiless head at the side of it was still grinning from ear to ear. But why he grinned so, and what important orders he was giving, the child had failed to find out, even after his destruction; for the sawdust, gushing from a gaping breast-wound, vouchsafed no satisfactory answer to her questions.

Then the eyes of the child, heavy with tears, wandered away from the dead jumping-man to the living ants that were building an elaborate edifice between two roots of the pine-tree. Farther on in the clearing the butterflies and forest-bees fluttered about the flowers; and in the midst of the flowers rose a shining stone, on which the lizards were warming themselves in the sun. Farther still, in the forest itself, the squirrels and sunbeams darted from branch to branch. And all of them the child had questioned, as she questioned the ball and the wooden man, and none of them had answered her. None!

Again she lifted her frock to her eyes, and ran weeping to the cottage on the forest border. There she stood still, and sobbed aloud,

"Zenz! Zenz!"

Through the little cottage window an old woman put out her head. In the old woman's face were a thousand wrinkles, and the sound of the child's voice crooked and bent them all into so many anxious notes of interrogation.

"He would not tell me, Zenz! No, oh—he, he—oh, oh!" sobbed the child, her words dying away in her sobs.

The thousand notes of interrogation deepened their lines upon the wrinkled face, and the old woman's eyes looked searchingly along the clearing.

The little girl understood the questioning wrinkles and the searching eyes, and said, "The ball, Zenz! Oh, the ball—"

Then the head disappeared from the window-frame, and a little old woman came, half hobbling, half trotting, out of the door. Without stopping, she went straight on across the forest grass; and

the child followed her, looking up into her face.
The woman's eyes were bent upon the ground, still
searchingly; but the little girl took hold of her by
the gown and drew her towards the pool.

"Look! look!" cried the child. "There he is,
sulking! the bad, bad, wicked ball!"

The old woman pulled a crooked stick from the
thicket, and tried to fish out the ball. But the girl
seized her arm.

"Leave it alone!" she sobbed. "I will not have
him now! No, never, never more! And they are
all just like him! The jumping-man has nothing
in him but sawdust, and the dragon - flies, and the
little worms, and the lizards, that only run away—
oh, all, all!—they are just the same! And you, too,
Zenz, you too! You say nothing. It is only grandfather that speaks, but he is always far away."

After a pause she added, "And the doctor—he
also can speak. Tell him, Zenz, to give me something that will make me die. The doctor can do
everything. Zenz, I should so like to die!"

Thereupon, all those interrogative wrinkles subsided into numberless fine lines of the tenderest
pity; and in the eyes now bent upon the child, the
restless gleam was softened to a quiet, loving light.
The old woman lifted the little girl from the ground
and carried her on her left arm, not without difficulty, back to the cottage. With her right hand she
talked to the child all the way as they went along.
With her lips she could not talk, for she was dumb.
But the little girl understood the old woman's dumb
language, and each of the crumpled fingers touched

a key intelligible to the child, whose lips replied aloud to their silent motions. All day long, however, no audible word had come to the ear of the little girl; nor yesterday, nor the day before, nor for many a long day before that.

When at last the dumb woman had laid the child safe in her poor little bed, the silent fingers consolingly announced to her that to-morrow the grandfather would come home. The grandfather! Ah, yes, *he* would talk with her to her heart's content; and so at that news she ceased weeping.

The little dumb dame sat by the bedside, and employed all her ten fingers in lulling the child to sleep. At last, when the moonlight, gliding through the casement, glimmered on their hushed fantastic movement, those flitting fingers began to seem to the child, as they gleamed and faded in the gloom beneath her closing eyelids, like the fitful sunlights playing far away in the dim forest. But they, too, kept their secret, and she fell asleep.

The evening of the next day the little girl was seated alone on the pathway skirting the forest border. Her fingers were stained with the black forest earth, for in it she had just been burying the ball, which the old woman had fished out of the pool for her; and with the ball the jumping-man. She did not bury them under the old pine-tree in the clearing, where she loved to sit, but some way off, in a part of the forest where she never went. What she had once rejected she would never, never more, have anything to do with; she would not even think of it!

The child had worked hard at her sexton's task; and now her tired hands lay resting in her lap, while her blue eyes looked dreamily into the blue distance.

Suddenly out of that distance came a faint, low, creaking sound. She sprung up and listened, turning towards the upland, over which a way led from the valleys beyond the mountains down into the forest quarter. This way wound along what had once been the fence of an old deer-park. The park had long ago been thrown open, and was now a clear, unenclosed space. The fence, however, or at least the ruins of it, remained, leaning crazily towards the forest, in one place half rotten, in another quite broken, with here and there wide gaps between the splintered planks.

The creaking sound grew louder. When at last it turned into a discordant shriek, the child sprung into one of the gaps in the fence and looked eagerly through the opening.

On the brow of the upland appeared, first a head, then by degrees a whole man.

The man was pushing a huge wheelbarrow heavily before him; and though his way was downhill, he seemed to find it hard and wearisome. The path he plodded—if path it could be called—was only a narrow furrow across the slope of a sandy potato-field. It was neither drained nor metalled, being entirely the work of the rain, which had displayed in its production a turn for picturesque effects; here scooping out the ground into holes, there heaping it up into hillocks; and in the washed-out soil between them laying bare a good many blocks of stone, some

pointed, others rounded in shape, but all of a considerable size.

The barrow staggered along like a ship on a stormy
sea, now rising high, now sinking deep, swaying
sometimes to the right, sometimes to the left, and at
every moment on the point of being capsized. Its
steersman, moreover, was old and feeble, and his
beard gleamed in the sun as white as snow.

When the wheelbarrow had got quite close to the
fence, the girl darted along the palings and hid herself behind them. Then she called out in a feigned
voice, "Featherhelm! Featherhelm!"

The man stood still; that call was to him. His
name was Wilhelm; the "Feather" was his profes-
sional nickname; and, by a combination of the two
words, he was called Featherhelm.

All was still. He listened for a while, but there
was nothing more to be heard.

The old man, however, went on no farther, but
began to make himself comfortable for a longer rest
where he had halted. He pushed the barrow against
a heap of earth, put down the handle, drew forth his
head from under the strap, and set a stone under the
wheel. Having completed these arrangements, he
took off his shaggy cap, wiped his dripping forehead,
and holding the cap with both hands before his face,
cried out, also in a feigned high voice, "Baldine!
Baldine!"

But the silence remained unbroken, and nothing
stirred. Then, out of the old man's clear blue eyes
a smile crept softly, round their wrinkled corners,
all down his face. But there it found no egress;

the face was so full of wrinkles and crevices that it wandered, quite lost in their labyrinth, here and there, up and down, like the barrow on its rugged way, till at last, not knowing where to get out, it crept back slowly, from wrinkle to wrinkle, and, with a brisk little leap, was safe home again in the eyes. Presently the old man said, turning round to his barrow,

"The sun is already below the Grünberg; we must go home, old friend!"

Just then, however, something behind him tugged at his coat-tail. -

"Baldine! Baldine!" he said, without turning, and speaking into his shaggy cap. The smile again descended the labyrinth of wrinkles, and settled round the corners of his mouth.

"It is I, grandfather! dear grandfather!" cried the child, as she flung her arms about him, laughing and crying all at once with exuberant delight.

After the grandfather had again set his cart going, she walked proudly at his side, and stroked now and then, caressingly, the coarse cloth of the old man's sleeve. The cart, too, she stroked sometimes, because it belonged to her grandfather. When they reached the cottage, she helped to unload the cart. The grandfather and Zenz pretended to be very feeble, and the child so strong, so extraordinarily strong, that she must herself carry everything inside. The two old people appeared only to help now and then, just a little. The shaggy cap Baldine carried into the room entirely without any help at all, and hung it on the nail near the door. Then she sat down beside her grandfather, and looked on with growing impatience while he ate his supper. This he did very slowly, for he had only a few teeth; but at last he managed to get to the end of his meal, and now he must talk to her—at once—with the last bit in his mouth. Eagerly she hung on his words—her ear caught every syllable. They were human words, such as she had not heard for many a long day.

By-and-by the old man rose and went to the cart-shed. He always brought home something for his granddaughter; gifts worth only a few pence, like the jumping-man, or found, like the india-rubber ball, by the wayside. For Featherhelm was very poor; but the scanty gifts of his poverty made the little Baldine very rich. To-day's gift was also a treasure which had cost nothing—a nosegay, which Featherhelm himself had gathered on his way home. Fatigued though he was by pushing his heavy cart, and weary from the summer heat, yet his old back had bent, and his tired arm been stretched, as many times as there were flowers in that nosegay. And there were a great many flowers in it, quite a big bunch of them; and all were blue—bluer than any flowers Baldine had ever seen before, bluer than everything but the sky.

She clapped her hands, and cried, "Give me them, grandfather! give me them, dear, dear grandfather!" Then she began at once to ask, "From what garden did they come, grandfather?"

"From a very large garden!" said the old man. "It begins on the other side of the Grünberg, and where it ends only our Lord God knows. The blue

3

flowers are called corn-flowers; they grow wild there, all about the fields. Here we have only woods, meadows, and potato-fields, but no corn; so that no such flowers grow in our neighborhood, nor can one find them without going far beyond the forest. But corn and corn-flower are always to be found together, like me and my cart."

He took a blossom out of the nosegay, and showed her the delicate petals round its calyx, and the little stamens inside. Then he went on talking to her about the villages in that large garden where the corn and corn-flowers grow; and of the town, with its tall houses and crowds of people.

Baldine held her nosegay very fast all the while, and she took it with her when she went to bed. Even then the grandfather must sit down beside her, and go on with his stories. That he might not steal away, she took one of his coat-tails into her bed, and held it there with one hand, while the other still grasped the flowers. The old man was tired, but he went on talking; though his talk grew slower, and his voice lower, and less and less audible, till at last he fell into a quiet doze.

But Baldine could not sleep. She mused awake on all his words, and how different they were from those which Zenz spoke with her fingers. She did not like to waken the sleeping grandfather, but lay quite still, and only kept looking at him with her large blue eyes, while he nodded in his sleep, and bowed over her, as the bearded corn bows over the nestled corn-flower.

Baldine awoke late in the morning. Long before she was up Featherhelm had driven his cart across the potato-fields to the glass-works, and home again. When she stepped out upon the threshold, the grandfather, already seated on his little bench before the cottage, was busily varnishing a large beech-mushroom. Baldine sat down at his feet, but he was so absorbed in this work of art that he did not speak. She looked at him musingly for a while, and at last she said,

"Grandfather, why have you no hair on your head?"

Featherhelm laid aside his brush, and held the shining mushroom against the sun.

"Well," said he, "in summer, you know, the sun is very strong, and in driving my cart I get very hot. Then I perspire. The perspiration soaks out the hairs; and in this manner all mine have been soaked away slowly one after the other."

"Ah, then, why don't you tell that to the doctor, grandfather, that he may make other hairs grow? The new doctor is like God: he can do everything; he can even make people live, if they are not already quite dead — you have often told me so yourself. Why don't you tell him, grandfather?"

"It is more comfortable as it is," replied the old man, quietly.

"More comfortable?" repeated the child.

"Yes, does it not save combing? You, for instance, have to let Zenz plague you with her comb every morning, and I have often heard you crying under the process; yet both the plaguing and the crying seem in vain, for in the evening no one could ever guess that Zenz had braided your hair in the morning. Nor could I ever remove all the little feathers out of *my* hair, when I had it, though I took great pains. Featherhelm would have had to be combing his head all day long; and for that he had no time. Now, thank God, it is no longer necessary. All is for the best!"

Baldine looked with mingled pity and vexation on the grandfather. He had really and truly not a single hair on his head, and it must have been out of pure perversity that he would not ask the doctor. Featherhelm understood her look, and, as he again took up his brush, he repeated,

"It is more comfortable as it is. All is for the best!"

Baldine sprung from the position in which she had been crouching near the old man's feet, and stepped up to him with a triumphant composure in her face.

"So!" she said, slowly. "And why, then, do you keep so many white hairs on your face?"

"That, too, is more comfortable," said the grandfather.

"Look, grandfather," exclaimed the child, "how wicked you are! and you are even telling a lie! I know why. It is because you are afraid. You fear the doctor will give you something bitter. Well, I also was once, you know, afraid of his medicine. I didn't like it myself. And when I upset the spoon Zenz put it into, she and you cried because you thought I would die. And so I would, too, rather than swallow the bitter stuff, if I could have helped it! But the doctor didn't let me die: he himself held the spoon to my mouth, and told me what I must do. You must shut your eyes, grandfather, and swallow it quickly, all at once. Then you feel almost nothing, and can have hairs on your head again. The doctor can do everything, and you know it. Why do you tell such a lie, grandfather?"

"I don't tell a lie, Baldine. If I did not like my beard, I should be obliged to scrape it off every day with a sharp knife, and should probably cut my face all over; like the clergyman in Oberau, who has to shave himself every morning, and cannot do it without scraping his chin to pieces. So, you see, it is more comfortable for me as it is. All is for the best. If you had a beard you would have to do as I do; but it were a pity that your milk-white face—"

"Fie!" interrupted Baldine. "Girls don't have beards." And after a little pause she asked, "But why is that? Tell me, grandfather."

Featherhelm smiled, and began to tell a story. He did this every time that he could not or would not answer a question. Baldine had plenty of such questions in store; but the stories Featherhelm could tell were even more numerous than Baldine's questions, and they were all delightful.

So the little girl sat down again at his feet and listened attentively. After a while, however, she tapped him on the knee.

"Grandfather," she exclaimed, "why is one of your boots pointed, and the other rounded?"

Featherhelm glanced down at his boots approvingly. "The left boot," he said, "of the pointed pair is torn, and so is the right one of the rounded

pair; and that is the reason. I gave both the patients to the boot-doctor; and meanwhile I wear the
sound one of each pair. By-and-by the right pair
will come together again. All is for the best."

As he said this, the old man rose and put his work
in the sun to dry. Then he took a large bag on his
back, and Baldine a little one in her hand, and they
went together across the clearing into the forest.
Baldine gathered up the finest of the fir-cones and
put them in her little bag. She also kept a sharp eye
upon the acorns, the beech-nuts and bearded lichens,
the catkin-blossoms of the hazel-trees, and the grass-
es that had feathery seeds; for all these things the
grandfather would afterwards glue together, and with
the scales of the fir-cones, make them into little
frames, boxes, and other pretty ornaments. Featherhelm searched meanwhile for the beech-mushrooms,
of which the Germans make tinder. Those that
were particularly large and fine he varnished, for sale
to the wealthy town-folks, who hang them on their
walls, and use them as brackets for little flower-pots
and knick-knacks.

The old man and the child returned from the forest heavily laden. At home they found Zenz standing by the hearth, where she had just finished cook-
ing their dinner; and all three sat down to a repast
of potatoes and a soup made of sour milk, which could
not have been more relished were they the greatest
dainties in the world.

The evening found the whole family again in the
clearing beneath the pine-tree. Zenz knitted a little
stocking for Baldine; Featherhelm carved away at

his little picture-frames. The old man was never idle. He was so old, and pence so hard to gain! Those which would be wanted by-and-by for the support of his orphan grandchild must now be earned quickly.

Baldine told him all about the wicked india-rubber ball, and the stupid jumping-man with the sawdust in his body; and how neither of them had answered her, though she had asked them hundreds of times, "Why this?" and "Why that?" The recollection of their spiteful obstinacy brought the tears back to her eyes, and she again began to sob.

Then the old man laid down his knife, took the child on his knee, and stroked her hair softly, saying,

"You are quite right, Baldine. Everything has its Why, but it is not everything that tells it when you ask. One must find it out one's self. Moreover, everything does not cry when it is in pain. And that, too, is for the best."

"Your cart cries, grandfather," said the child, "though nothing hurts it. Why does your cart cry so much?"

"It cries for me, Baldine. When I enter a village, it cries, 'Here is Featherhelm! He sells goose-feathers for the town beds!' When I come into the town, it cries, 'Here is Featherhelm! He sells goose-feathers, and buys glass pots for the glass-works!' And those whom it concerns understand its cry."

"Yes, but why does it cry all along the forest, where it concerns nobody?"

"Ah, there it cries more than ever for me, whom

its cry then specially concerns. But that you cannot understand."

"Why not, grandfather? Oh! you, too, are like
the ball—you will tell me nothing."

Featherhelm got up and went to the place in the
forest where the freshly turned-up earth betrayed the
grave of the ball. With a little stick he dug the ball
out of the earth, and carried it to Baldine. Then he
took out his knife, and stabbed the ball with it. The
ball emitted a faint sigh; the wounded spot deepened
inward, the perverse plumpness was flattened slowly,
and sunk and shrunk, till at last nothing was left of
it but a deformed gray rag. Baldine held her eyes
wide open, and fastened them on the thing.

"It is not always good," said Featherhelm, "to
speak, and tell one's Why; and therefore many things
are dumb. That is best for them. One has to find
out many things by one's self; which is good for us
also. You cannot do this yet, Baldine, but all is for
the best. Now go and help Zenz to peel the potatoes. You understand that very well, and they taste
much better when you have helped to prepare them."

After these words Featherhelm's head sunk upon
his breast. He was answering to himself the question
asked by Baldine, why the cart cried so specially for
him in the long forest, where its cry concerned no
one else.

The child had begun to walk slowly towards Zenz,
as the grandfather bade her; but she stopped abruptly half-way, paused a moment, and going back
to the old man, softly stroked his coat-sleeve, while
her eyes overflowed with silent tears. It hurt her

to see him so sad. When Featherhelm looked up
and saw her standing there, he did not send her away
again, but lifted her once more on to his knees, and
said,

"Has it ever happened to you, Baldine, to lose
something that was very dear to you?"

"Oh yes, grandfather—the little white cock! You
know, the rat caught him."

"Ay, I remember! When that happened, I found
you here beneath the pine-tree, lying on the ground
and sobbing. Well, you see, I once had a daughter.
When she was as small as you, she looked just as
you do now. I delighted in her—how much I cannot tell you—and my wife, your grandmother, also.
Then she grew up, and our joy grew with her.
When she was grown up, she married the glass-cutter, Sepp. He was the best man in the village, and
the most skilful cutter in the glass-works. These
two people were your mother and father, child.
Then you came into the world. But the Lord our
God was sparing at that time. To you he gave life,
and from your mother he took it away. Your grandmother could not live without her daughter, and she
soon followed her. After the burial of your mother your father began to cough constantly, and often
he clutched at his breast. He and others knew
what that meant. The surgeon spoke about the
lungs, but they call it here the glass-cutter's malady.
The splinters of glass which spring off in the cutting
fly about in the air by thousands, and the glass-cut-
ters breathe them in. That scratches and cuts them
inside the chest, but so finely that at first they do

not feel it. Later on, little by little, it begins to feel
like a thousand knives inside them, and they die of
it slowly. The glass-cutter, Sepp, he, too, was finally
delivered. But he did not look on death as a deliv-
erer; he suffered much; yet, in spite of his pain, he
was always sighing, ' Oh, that I might once more see
the furnace heated, and so lay up yet a little more
money for my child!' And he worked on till the
day of his death. He did not live to see a new furnace heated. Then there were only you and I. But
Zenz came to live with us, because she also had nobody in the world, and was alone like us. After
this, when I was driving my cart along through the
forest, I would have liked to lie upon the ground, as
you did when the little white cock died, and weep—
about many things. But meanwhile the cart would
have stood still, and that would have been a thousand pities. If the grandfather had wept for those
who were dead, his living granddaughter would have
cried for bread. So I restrained my trouble till the
day comes when it will throw me down entirely.
There will be time enough for it all when I can
never rise again. I kept it to myself, and laughed,
and made jokes with the people I met; for a pleasant face is best for trade. I let my cart cry for me,
and busied myself about the customers it brought
me, and the beech-mushrooms growing for me in the
forest. Sometimes, it is true, when the cart cries in
too heart-rending a tone for those beneath the earth,
the water comes into my eyes. That is not good,
because then I cannot see the mushrooms; and they
are precious to me, for I have bought the right to

gather them at the rate of three dollars a year. The cart soon finds this out, and it begins to cry in its sharpest tones, 'Baldine! think of Baldine, Featherhelm!' Then I take a firmer hold of it, and my sight grows clear again. All is for the best. Only one must learn to understand it, be it dumb, or cry it never so loudly!"

Thus the time passed away for Baldine in asking and hearing, till the day came when the cart again shrieked up the hedgeway. Then, after many long and longer days, it came crying back again. And so things went on variably till the summer was over. During the winter the cart slept its winter sleep. Featherhelm cut and carved and hammered and glued his treasure-troves together, and Baldine sat looking and listening. When spring came, the first cuckoo and the cart cried together in the forest quarter, but the cuckoo's voice was the soonest tired.

Baldine still hears the cart when the grandfather has disappeared below the upland, while the cuckoo has long been silent. She knows now that the good cart cries for the grandfather. She knows also that other dumb things have their language; only one must find it out, as the grandfather said. She no longer asks "Why?" of all the silent things and dumb animals. She looks at them a long time, and then she knows it of her own accord. She has watched the squirrels in the tops of the pine-trees; and since then she understands very well what the sunbeams are about. They play, just as the squirrels do. All the golden lights climb up and down the stems, spring for pure merriment from bough to bough, and hide themselves in the tree-tops covered with leaves, through which only a lurking sparklet peeps pertly here and there. Then they chase one another from one tree to another, and scamper like mad across the clearing.

But in their sport the sunbeams, like the squirrels, are shy of Baldine. They do not venture in to where she sits under the branches of the old pine. For them its aspect is too melancholy, and they only dance about it. There their choral revel glides round and round the maiden gayly, but never nearer to her than the length of her own shadow—a black phantom, blackest where the glory seems most bright, always present between the sunlight and herself, and always isolating her from the glittering Fairy Ring that flees from its approach, and fades beneath its touch. If she stretches out her hand, the sunbeams, like the squirrels, spring back frightened from the shade it throws upon them; and the dark image of that out-stretched hand, which is her own, rests sharply printed on the golden ground.

From Zenz, too, Baldine has learned so much, by watching her when she speaks with her fingers, that now she also understands the ants, and their whole system of house-keeping between the pine-tree roots. She studies them daily, and knows what trouble they give themselves to put all in order, and keep everything clean, as Zenz does in the forest cottage. They sometimes roll little round white things in the sun backward and forward; just as Zenz rolls the bread before putting it in the oven. Sometimes two of them approach each other, and converse by means of little threads upon their heads, which they move to and fro. They embrace and fondle and bow, and bid each other farewell with these threads, which are just like the speaking fingers of Zenz. But they quarrel also, and beat one another. Zenz never does that; it is only the bad boys in the village that do it.

The ants, the snails, the butterflies, and all the dumb creatures, are sometimes glad and sometimes sorry; and they all have fine threads on their heads, with which they speak without a word, as Zenz speaks with her fingers. Baldine knows all this quite well.

But at home she knows One who is also dumb, but never glad, always sorry. That is our Lord God, who hangs upon the cross in the corner of the room, high above the table. The cross is of black wood, and fastened to it is the white God. He cannot even speak with His fingers, for both hands are nailed to the cross. The drops of blood run down over His forehead and breast, from His hands and feet. His face is very pale and mournful; one cannot look at Him without weeping.

Once Baldine climbed upon a chair, and thence on to the table, to look at Him closely; but, when quite near, He looked even still more mournful. Then Baldine leaned her cheek against His bleeding arm, as at other times she used to lean it against the grandfather's coat-sleeve, and wept. She stroked the pale, worn cheeks, and said through her sobs,

"Poor God! be not so sad, dear God!"

But He remained still as sad as ever, and did not smile, as her grandfather always did when she stroked his sleeve. Then she grew angry at the nails, which hurt His hands and feet; and she tore and tugged at them till her cheeks were glowing, her curls all tumbled, and her little fingers bleeding. The grandfather once found her in this condition. It was a long time before she could be quieted; but he told her then that the good God heard all, even if He did not answer, and that He was only sad because He had taken upon himself to bear the sorrows of all mankind.

Since that time Baldine often climbs up on the table, and sits before the sad, pale face. The bloodless lips remain always dumb, the eyes staring, the fingers motionless; but she knows that he hears all. Everything which at other times she tells her grandfather is confided to the dumb God when the grandfather is not at home. Has she any sorrow? She weeps before Him. He is so good, the grandfather has told her. Has she any wish? Of Him she craves it — caressingly, or with a wild impatience. The doctor can do everything when somebody is ill; but the dumb God is yet more mighty than the doctor. All that the sunbeams, dancing round the pine-tree, or the moonbeams, hovering about her bed, suggest to Baldine's fancy — all she has ever thought or dreamed of — He can do.

One evening Featherhelm came home very weary; so weary that he could not get up the next morning. Baldine sat by his bed and talked to him, because he could not talk to her. The old story-telling had come at last to an end; the old story-teller was worn out.

Zenz went to fetch the doctor; and, when she brought him back with her, Baldine laughed and leaped for joy. Now all was well! To-morrow her grandfather would be able to get up and go with her into the forest to look for mushrooms. The doctor was there, and he could do all.

But the grandfather did not rise next day, as Baldine had expected, and he could scarcely speak.

When the doctor came again, a little hand convulsively clutched his own, and squeezed his fingers till they ached. It was Baldine's. She looked reproachfully up to him, and cried,

"Why don't you give the bitter water to the grandfather? When you gave it to me it made me able to get up. You can do all, and yet you do nothing! There you let grandfather lie—look at him—unable to rise or speak! Give him the bitter water, please!"

The doctor smiled, and said, comfortingly,

"Yes, yes, I will!"

She loosed his hand, and he gave Featherhelm a bitter water; but it could not have been the right one, for Featherhelm did not speak a word all day. At nightfall he said, smilingly, to Baldine,

"All is for the best. Only, to understand it—"

But what he was about to say remained unsaid, for he became suddenly silent. And so he rested— as the pine-tree outside in the forest, as the sunbeams playing round it, as the sad God above in the corner —dumb forever! The last audible human word in the child's world had died away.

The doctor came to look after the dead. Baldine threw on him a look of the most glowing hatred. Till he came, she would not leave her grandfather, but now she went out; nor did she enter the house again till the doctor had left it and was far away. From that time forward she avoided him, and whenever, in the after-years, they met by some untoward chance, not a word would she say to him.

For, oh the detected imposture! He could not do all—not even a little; he had let her grandfather die! His image in her soul was overthrown, shattered, annihilated—a thing collapsed and shrivelled up, like the ball stabbed by the grandfather's knife —nothing left of it!

And Baldine threw the doctor away forever— threw him to the deformed gray rag, and to the jumping-man with sawdust in his body.

CHAPTER II.

Years are gone by since then. Baldine has grown up alone with the dumb God and the dumb Zenz. But at last Zenz also has ceased to speak, even with her fingers. She is dead; and Baldine has taken her dumb God with her to the saw-mill high up in the forest.

There swift feet and young arms are wanted. The miller and his wife are old. They find it more and more difficult—sometimes quite impossible—to get through all the work there is to do in the mill, and about the stable and the house, and the forest meadow above, and the potato-field below in the valley. They have no need to go on working; for though the mill is not their own property, but belongs, like everything else in that part of the country, to the master of the glass-works, they have lived up there for forty years, and laid by an honest penny for a rainy day. They could, therefore, stop working and retire from business altogether if they pleased, but working has become to them like breathing: if it ceased, their life would stop.

The old miller is busy every day, from early dawn, in the saw-mill, and his wife in the house. Baldine lends a hand here and there, wherever she finds anything to do.

At dinner and supper all three sit together in the miller's parlor, but nobody speaks. The two old people have lived there for forty years quite alone, and what wonder if, by degrees, they have at last forgotten how to talk?

But there is also something to be seen in that whitewashed room which may have made them silent long ago. Against the middle of the wall, opposite to the window, stands an odd little bit of old furniture; it is a child's chair. By the side of it is a glazed cupboard, and in the cupboard a doll, a child's cap, and some little shirts and socks — all clean, but yellow from age. There is nothing else in all that part of the clean, bright, tidy room. From all the household fixtures, and all the furniture in daily use, the child's chair and the cupboard are set apart like an altar. The whole room itself seems

4

to be there only for their sake; as for their sake, also, the musing silence of the old couple, when the four eyes gleaming under their white locks are turned towards the little chair that stands there so still and empty.

Baldine thinks that, just as formerly the grandfather with his cart, so now the old miller and his wife let the forest brook cry for them, when it plunges loud over the mill-wheel, or murmurs low beside the floodgate.

Baldine had been accustomed to silence from her childhood. It had been her sole companion in the days when her grandfather was away with his cart, and in the years afterwards, when he was gone forever, and she lived alone with Zenz. In those days she did not often leave the lonely forest cottage, with its dumb God and the dumb Zenz. The people of the village she had long ago thrown to the ball, with the jumping-man and the doctor. They had taken no interest in the illness, death, and burial of her grandfather, nor in those of Zenz. Both were too poor to be objects of the least interest to those village folks who were so much better off. And at Zenz they used to laugh ill-naturedly, making sport of her, and mockingly imitating her finger language. The children especially were never tired of playing malicious pranks upon the poor, dumb, helpless creature. Baldine had not forgotten all this. She never forgot anything.

Later on, whenever she came to the village, the boys, now grown up, would nod and smile, and try to chat with her. They even left other girls to run after her and tell her—what was true—that she was the prettiest girl in all that part of the country. Everywhere, in admiring tones, the cry went after her, "Baldina!" "Paulina!" "Palina!" according as each accommodated her name to his own pronunciation. But it mattered not how they pronounced it, no response did any of them get from her. She did not laugh, she did not look angry, she did not even look up. Gravely and silently she passed them without notice, as if for her they were not.

Just as little did she notice the girls, who envied her for her beauty, and therefore made spiteful remarks upon her poor dress. And as, in spite of all invitations, she never joined the Sunday dance in the village, all the young men came by degrees to the conclusion that she gave herself insufferable airs; while all the young women asserted, on the contrary, that she was too ashamed of her poverty to look at her betters. Such as she had been before she went to live at the mill, she continued to be after she had taken up her abode there; and as she in her ways, so the villagers in theirs, remained unchanged.

For a while, indeed, many an enterprising lad would still secretly hang about the mill now and then, in the hope of a word with her, or at least a look; but at last they gave it up, and nobody tried any more to speak to her. Only, they stood still when she went past them, and looked after her. Sometimes, too, they followed her at a distance, so that Baldine could not see them, and listened to her song while she was cutting grass in the forest for the goats.

She had a singularly strange voice, with such deep tones in it that no girls in the village could imitate her song. It sounded almost awful through the forest, and nobody who had once heard it could ever forget the sound of it. It was also strange that she never sang any of the songs of the country; neither the tunes nor the words of them were ever heard from her lips. Not that her songs were foreign ones. To say the truth, they were not even songs at all. Her singing was a kind of song without words. All that was unspoken in her loneliness seemed to flow into a wild, wordless music from her otherwise mute lips.

Of whom could she have learned such song? It was a strange, many-toned sound, now as of birds piping on the branches, now as of the forest wind when it rushes athwart the multitudinous tree-tops with the moan of a mighty organ, and now like the low buzzing of wild bees.

Up at the saw-mill the brook and the mill-wheel keep holy the Lord's Day, ceasing from their labor; and in the afternoon the whole house is at rest.

The miller silently smokes his special Sunday pipe; his wife silently dusts the doll and the child's cap in the cupboard. Baldine leaves the mill-house and goes wandering through the forest. Fitful and faint, from the valley below, the music of the village dance comes trembling to her ear; but she does not stop to listen to it. The miller's black dog walks behind her, as usual; for wherever Baldine goes, that dog follows her like her shadow. Over moss and tree-roots go she and the dog together, till they reach the forest path and climb up it.

At the top of the path, close by the wayside ditch, an old, old, beech-tree rises from the lower wood. The trunk of the tree is not visible; for, slanted round about it, are rows of wooden planks, some of them only rough-hewn, with a cross rudely cut on them, others gayly painted and decorated.

These are the so-called "*dead-planks*" of the village. Church and church-yard lie far away from the forest, only to be reached with difficulty by rough mountain-paths in summer and isolated by snow-drifts during the long winter. For this reason it is the custom of the villagers, when any of them dies, to lay the dead body on one of these planks, and let it rest there till it can be put into its coffin and carried away to the distant graveyard at Oberau. It is thought that the plank is consecrated by the touch of the dead; and when the body has been removed from it, they take the plank to the forest and lean it there against the beech-tree.

Those who care to think of the dead, but cannot visit their distant graves, come to muse or pray beside the dead-planks on which their loved ones were borne to their long sleep. But to this place come also many others who are not concerned about lost friends or kindred; for it is impossible to get to or from the village without passing it; there is no other way across the mountains. Thus, nobody is suffered to forget the dead; for the dead-planks stand at the wayside, craving from every passer-by some recognition of their presence—a prayer, an uncovering of the head, a brief remembrance, or even only a pitying glance.

And if the rough-hewn plank of the poor man, and the polished and painted one of the rich, seem as emblems of their different ways through life—rough, hard, and joyless for the one; smooth, gay, and easy for the other—yet all the planks are made of the same wood, as all the lives of men have the same destiny—to suffer and to die. So that, rough or smooth, blank or colored, each dead-plank might with equal truth bear this inscription—

> "At my birthday as man
> My disquiet began,
> And it lasted till now.
>
> "Wouldst thou suffer no more?
> Follow me; when all's o'er,
> As I rest so shalt thou.
>
> "From the pining and striving
> Of the dying, called living,
> Here at last is release.
>
> "Be consoled: hap what may,
> Thou, too, treadest the way
> That hath led to this peace."

Nor is this all. The poor souls, say the folk of the forest, suffer in Purgatory just so long as upon earth their dead-planks stand; but the planks of the rich last longest, for the paint upon them retards the progress of their decay.

On the ground, about the bole of the beech-tree, lie the oldest of the dead-planks, crumbled and rotten. They who once cared for them have dealt with the remembrance of the dead as time has dealt with these, its fading tokens, letting it fall away and be forgotten; or else the mourners themselves are now dead, and their own planks already lean against the beech. Thus, one row of planks rests on the remains of those which stood there before it, as one generation rises above another.

Baldine likes to sit, on Sundays, upon the stone before the beech. The dead-planks of her parents have long ago fallen to the ground; those of her grandfather and Zenz still stand, but already they are beginning to give way at the base. The spirits of the old man and the old woman hover round the spot, and doubtless understand, without words, what Baldine is thinking and feeling and dreaming as she sits upon that stone. Without words, also, Baldine understands what the dead whisper to her, and what the brook murmurs, and what meaning there is in the song of the bullfinch and the cry of the sparrow-hawk, while she garlands the two dead-planks which are so dear to her with the wild flowers she has gathered in the forest. Then she begins, in that deep mellow voice of hers, the strange song without words, which no one can forget who has once heard it by chance; a song heard only when the singer is unseen; for, like the forest-bird above her, at the sight of a living face, or the sound of a living footstep, she is mute.

There came, as the days went by in this still way, a busier time, when Baldine ran to the dead-planks only to hang up the garlands she had woven on her way, and return, without loitering, to the mill. For

wheel and water enjoyed no longer their Sabbath
rest.

The master of the glass-works had long been med-
itating how he might turn to better profit the splendid old forest he possessed upon the Grünberg. The
timber there was magnificent, but the transport of
it to the nearest market was so difficult and circuitous that he could make nothing of it. After frequent consultation with some of his neighbors in
the town, he at last went off in search of more scientific advice; and when he returned he brought with
him a sunburnt man who, after one shrewd look at
the forest, was able to settle exactly what ought to
be done with it.

Signor Vico—that was the man's name—had a
well-experienced, sharp eye for cases of this sort;
and he could see at a glance things to which the
learned, looking through their scientific spectacles,
were blind. He was not learned himself, but he was
an old hand at such work. For years he had collected, every spring, at his home in Lombardy, a number of strong young men, whom he took with him
northward, wherever there were railways, roads, or
dams to be made, a rock to be blasted, a river-course
to be regulated, or a swamp to be drained. In all
work of this kind, the Italians displayed a remarkable skill; they laid hold of everything at the right
end, and they were diligent and easily satisfied. Leading, moreover, more temperate lives than their northern neighbors, they were able, every autumn, to bring
home considerable sums.

Signor Vico was the *Impresario* of this travelling

industrial company. He spoke the most horribly broken German, but it was just good enough for intelligible bargains with his foreign employers about work and wages; and his talent for languages made him, during the working season, the general interpreter on all occasions between his Italians and the people of the country. Moreover, he was chief staff-officer, commander-in-chief, commissary-general, inspector-general, and factotum universal of his army.

His wife, a lively olive-colored little woman, with sparkling black eyes, had a warm heart and a kindly hand. She adroitly tempered the stern despotism of her husband; diverted his angry grumblings from the culprit; gave, behind his back, here and there an advance of wages; healed the sick with home-made physic; tended the wounded; and patched the damaged coats with her own kind fingers. Having no children of her own, she regarded all the young workmen as such. To the supremacy of this motherly kind-hearted influence even her husband's energetic nature gave way. Signora Vico knew the ways and habits, the heartaches and love affairs, the hopes and cares, of all; and she chattered about them with each, under the large workmen's hut in the evening leisure hours.

Thus the hearts of all were drawn to her, and, it must be added, their stomachs also; for she it was who, over the open fire, in the enormous kettle which always accompanied the army, prepared for them their general meal—the daily-eaten, ever newly relished, and by all beloved, "*polenta !*"

She alone knew how to cook it exactly after the

home tradition, with plenty of the proper cheese in it, so that during the enjoyment of that repast every one of them could fancy himself at home again in beautiful Lombardy. The first who laid down his wooden spoon involuntarily began singing some sweet Italian song; the second in his turn took up the tune, and so on, till the whole group was singing in chorus, while Signora Vico beat time with her mighty spoon upon the polenta-kettle. Signor Vico upon these occasions sat throned, apart from his subjects, and smoked with great dignity his Cavour cigar. But even he could not refrain from humming a deep bass accompaniment, though he did it *pianissimo,* not to lower his dignity.

After a single visit to the Grünberg, Signor Vico entered the parlor of the master of the glass-works, and explained to him, in his dreadful German, the conclusion at which he had arrived. It was like the egg of Columbus. "The brook plunges down the side of the mountain. Why let it plunge to no purpose? Why use human hands and oxen, when the brook can do the work? Why should the brook only stroll and saunter for its own pleasure, instead of working like all the rest of the world?"

Signor Vico went on asking these very pertinent questions, till he had worked himself into a violent fit of anger against the idle brook; and clinching his brown fists, he shook them at it out of the window. Why make a tedious, fatiguing, circuitous cart-road in ever so many zigzags up to the brow of the Grünberg? Why go to the expense of employing oxen for heavy traffic on such a road? The brook has a ready-made road of its own, along which it takes its pleasure daily, without any useful object in view. Signor Vico will bring his workmen, who have just finished the railway-works in the town. They shall partly regulate and considerably improve the course of this idler, remove some bits of rock that obstruct it, establish a reservoir on the height with a floodgate, fell the trees, throw the collected timber into the standing water, open the floodgate, and—"*Fuori di quà!* Out with him! Forest and water move on; at first *adagio*, then *animo, coraggio!*—*più presto!*—then *prestissimo*, and—*via di quà!* Be off with you! *Bon voyage!*"

Signor Vico accompanied this animated harangue by imitative gestures, which represented the behavior of the wood in the water; now springing up and down the room, faster and faster, now stooping lower and lower, till he cowered upon the floor; which last expressive posture distinctly signified that the timber had arrived below at the glass-works. Thus convincingly explained, the feasibility and advantage of the project were so evident to the master that he willingly assented to it.

A few days later the Italians made their entry into the village, stared at by its astonished denizens as if they were a troop of wild beasts. Signora Vico especially, with her yellow face and sparkling eyes, was an apparition which struck terror to the hearts of all beholders when they saw her stirring the enormous polenta-kettle. They were not long in arriving at the unanimous conviction that she was a witch; but the first suspicions of that dreadful fact were excited by the strangeness of the animal that drew the little carriage, in which she made her entry into the village. This creature seemed half a horse and half an ass, and was only known to the inhabitants of the forest by hearsay, like the dragons and winged serpents of popular tradition.

Among the village youths the whole train provoked much scornful laughter, malicious looks, and significant shrugging of shoulders. They themselves wore the same sort of clothes as their fathers and forefathers had worn before them ; for the remote forest and its folk are tenacious of old traditions. But now there came, skipping and dancing among them, lads with high, broad-brimmed felt hats, and blood-red kerchiefs round their necks—some of them even wore red shirts! The village maidens, however, more tolerant of novelties, were only all eyes and blushes for the interesting strangers. The comely, bold brown faces, the black locks and beards, the bright, dark eyes, and the strong figures of these new-comers, presented a pleasing contrast to the sallow features of a race stunted by the glowing oven, the pounding-house, and the polishing-wheel of the glass-works.

Next morning the Italians were already at work on the Grünberg. Signor Vico, stationed on the brow of the hill, his chin resting on his staff, was giving his orders in a loud voice; while, by the open fire below, Signora Vico was watching over the polenta-kettle. Between these two poles of its diurnal motion the little new world was in full swing, and its brown people bestirred themselves as brisk and busy as an ant's nest. After four weeks they were ready to risk an experiment. The floodgate was opened. *"Fuori di quà!"* cried Signor Vico; and below the hill the signora greeted the arriving tree-trunks with a far resounding *"Evviva!"*

And this is how it came to pass that the forest brook which drove the saw-mill had no more rest than his brother of the Grünberg; for Signor Vico kept a sharp lookout on all idlers, and the brook was now forced, even on Sundays, to turn the wheel that kept the saw at work upon the loads of timber sent down to it from the mountain.

Nor was this all; for Toniello, who was the Italian *Impresario's* Jack-of-all-trades, found yet more work for the poor mill-brook. After a conversation with the master of the glass-works, at which Signor Vico performed his customary function of dragoman, Toniello constructed in the mill-brook, just under the large saw-mill, another water-wheel, which, by means of various leather straps, put in motion a third wheel with chopping teeth that, swift as lightning, cut into large logs for the glass-ovens all the spoilt timber that was unfit for boards and planks.

Toniello also came up to the saw-mill, and pointed out to the old miller many things in the machinery which were defective, as well as others susceptible of great improvement. Some of them the miller had already noticed himself, but he now became aware of faults which till then he had not even guessed. The explanation was carried on by means of gestures in dumb-show and various drawings, which Toniello sketched rapidly on the nearest board. If the miller could not understand it all, Baldine translated the gestures distinctly into words; for she understood the language of the arms and fingers, having learned it thoroughly from Zenz.

Toniello did not rest satisfied with disclosing faults, he also undertook to remove them. The master had an absolute trust in him, after his successful establishment of the second saw, and left all the improvements to his discretion.

In the evenings, when the wheel stood still, Toniello used to set about this work. On the hearth blazed cheerily the huge pine-wood fire; the miller helped Toniello as well as he could, and Baldine looked at the young man's eyes and fingers, interpreting their signals, ready to tell the miller what he had to do, and herself giving now and then a helping hand.

On these occasions, when the old miller lighted his pipe, he thought, as he smoked it, that his dead boy would have been just old enough to help him as the stranger at his side was doing. He contemplated Toniello with a musing eye, and wondered whether his boy would have looked like this young stranger. Then he shook his head. Such tall, slender figures were not to be found in the forest quarter; and if any of its native youths chanced to be as tall as the Italian, none had a frame so flexibly and finely built. The old miller thought that the great gentlemen in the town must move their feet and hands like this young Italian, whose graceful gait and gestures, small, well-cut nose with sensitive nostrils, curved mouth, and high forehead, had the charm of a refinement unfamiliar to the old man's experience.

So strange, indeed, to this patriarch of a flaxen-haired race was the blue-black color of Toniello's flowing locks, finely pencilled eyebrows, long eye-lashes, and small mustache, that again he shook his head despondingly. His son, he felt, would have looked otherwise; yet he would not have been sorry had the lad looked just like this stranger.

Baldine stood all the while between the two, hushed and thoughtful as was her wont, in the glow of the blazing pine-logs, and looked fixedly at the fingers, and into the eyes of the young workman.

When at last things were so far in order as not to hinder the mill from working on the morrow, Toniello sprang up, silently pressed the miller's hand, nodded to Baldine, put on his broad-brimmed hat, and wandered through the darkness down to the village. His clear song sounded from the forest path up to the miller and to Baldine, farther and farther off, lower and lower down, till at last all was still.

Baldine went up-stairs to her garret, and knelt down before the dumb God on the old, black wooden cross. She prayed her evening prayer, and then went to bed. It seemed as if something sang to her in the coming on of sleep, farther and farther off, lower and lower down, till all was still. And low to herself she hummed the tune of that distant song, singing it without words, till at last she fell asleep.

The miller stood, before going to bed, a long while musing in front of the child's empty chair. Then he murmured, shaking his head, "He would not have looked like that young man!"

Toniello went his way down to Signora Vico. He

was her great favorite; she always kept his supper
for him, giving him into the bargain a tidbit from
her own. Toniello requited the good little woman
with sincere attachment. She was the only one with
whom he chatted about everything. With his comrades he confined his intercourse to the business and
hours of their common work; for in his leisure
hours he preferred to sit alone, thinking out ingeni-
ous combinations of mechanism, sketching plans of
wheels and levers that could act upon one another,
or painting in bad water-colors flowers and animals
which looked wonderfully life-like. On Sunday he
usually sat an hour with Signora Vico, and then disappeared—nobody knew where.

The other Italians spent their Sunday at the inn.
They had there their own large table, played mora,
sang choruses, and made a great bustle; but did not
consume much, because of their inveterate frugality.

Beppo alone was the consolation of the innkeeper;
he consumed in food and drink all that he earned
during the week, and sometimes even more. But
he was also a cause of some trouble to mine host;
for he made such a noise, first on the table with his
fists, then on the ground with his heels, and lastly
with his throat, whenever he got a chance of exercis-
ing its powers of sound, that in his presence both
villagers and Italians were obliged to speak louder
and louder. If he succeeded in his endeavors to set
the whole room in an uproar, the noise he had provoked only furnished a deep bass accompaniment
to his own voice, which forthwith shrilled high and
loud above it. When he had thus out-bawled the

loudest, he began to feel tolerably satisfied, but not yet quite comfortable; his effervescence needed further vent in quarrelling and fighting, for which he did not even give himself the pains to find a plausible pretext. If the nose of a village lad did not exactly correspond to his ideal of noses, or the shape of a comrade's beard displeased him, that was enough; and however good-humoredly his sarcasms. might be taken by the object of them, Beppo thought himself deeply offended. To revenge his wrong, he forthwith resorted to acts of violence; and the victim, who had understood nothing of his taunts, was promptly admonished by a blow that he had unconsciously given offence to Signor Beppo.

This was of pretty frequent occurrence when heads, on hot summer days, had been heated by drink; and the single combat generally developed into a general scuffle, in which the combatants used as weapons the beer pitchers, chairs, and stools. In the midst of this hurly-burly Beppo moved about like a fish in the water. It was his element. But he was only perfectly happy when he could stick his knife into somebody.

These tastes of his, and the zest with which he indulged them, had subjected Signor Vico to many inconveniences. The *Impresario's* wife warned him every time to dismiss Beppo, whom she disliked for his want of heart as well as of temper. Signor Vico agreed with her that Beppo was a heartless, ill-conditioned fellow, and an incorrigible agitator and brawler, besides being the laziest workman and greediest guzzler and guttler in his whole troop; but then

5

Beppo was also his brother's son, and a Vico like himself. So the *Padrone* let Beppo stay on, and continue his disorderly life, till one of his tricks with the knife got him into trouble with the local authorities, who treated him to a short term of imprisonment. When he came out of jail, however, Signor Vico had the weakness to take his brother's son again into his employment; and the old life began anew.

Beppo's ambition was to subdue the men by his voice or his knife, and the women by his looks. His face, which had, to be sure, a coarse, bad expression, was disfigured by small-pox, and his stout figure and restless limbs were not attractive; but he thought himself irresistible. Whenever he caught sight of a village beauty, he kissed his hand and looked languishingly at her; nor could he pass by a young wench without chucking her under the chin, or putting his arm round her waist. He tried, moreover, to improve his appearance by wearing, on Sundays and Feast-days, a frock-coat which he had bought in the town, second-hand, from a dealer in old clothes.

When he contemplated his own image thus attired—on his head the broad-brimmed Calabrese hat, with a cock's feather stuck jauntily into it, and his crooked legs incased in high boots that came up to his knees; round his hips a blood-red kerchief, and round his neck an orange-colored one; a rosy waistcoat over his crimson Garibaldi shirt; and, surmounting all these adornments, the black frock-coat —he could only compassionately think of the women whose heads he was going to turn.

One of them, at least, should be made happy, one of them he would kindly notice; and she was the girl at the saw-mill. She was unquestionably the fairest maiden in the neighborhood all round, with her heaven-blue eyes and her golden tresses. When he came to think of it, he had never seen a girl like her; not even when he bought his frock-coat in the town. Yes, she alone was worthy of him; and, to say the truth, if he rightly remembered, he had bought that coat only for her sake.

Caparisoned in this fatal garment, he passed all his leisure hours prowling about the mill-house. There he had opportunities enough of seeing the girl, but she was never alone; the miller or his wife was always with her, and very often Toniello. He was convinced, however, that her heart had absorbed his amorous glances, and knew how to value them. To any other of his comrades he would have made it as clear as the point of his knife that he alone had rights over the girl to which all others must give way; but Toniello was the only one he never ventured to attack. Once, indeed, he had tried to draw a knife upon that young man, but Toniello had wrested the weapon from his hand, seized him with his nimble arms, and thrown him to the ground with a shock from which his head ached for several days after.

Beppo, however, understood the art of *espionage* and ambuscade. One afternoon, when Baldine was carrying a pail of milk down to the village, he suddenly placed himself, with legs astride, upon the forest path. As she approached, he began his wonted tricks: kissing his hand, tossing his arms towards heaven, and slapping that part of his body which he supposed to be the residence of his heart. Baldine went on without heeding this ridiculous demeanor, which she supposed to be meant for somebody behind her. As she drew nearer, however, she must have perceived that she herself was the object of it, for Beppo stood across the path, and barred her passage with his out-stretched arms.

She quietly turned aside from the path into the forest, and tried to continue her way between the trees. Beppo sprang after her, and seized her right arm. With her left hand she had to hold the full milk-pail steadily on her head, so that she had no other weapon than a haughty look; but for that Beppo did not care, and he tried to put his arm round her waist.

The girl drew herself up, took the pail from her head, and poured over him its whole contents. For a moment he was staggered, and nearly blinded, by the unexpected douche. But his wrath only increased his desire; and rushing upon Baldine, he threw his arms about her and clasped her close.

"Beppo!"

The sound of his own name rang sharp in the rascal's ear, and he looked up. But, in the storm of his passion, the glance he turned upon the speaker was purely mechanical; and whether or not he recognized Toniello, whose shout it was that he had heard — what was Toniello, what all the world, to him at such a moment?

The next moment, however, he lay sprawling on

the ground; and as he instinctively began to fumble at his knife, his wrist was clasped with iron fingers, and the knife wrested from him. In impotent rage he picked himself up, and ran off as fast as his heels could take him, without once looking behind him.

Toniello gazed for a while after the discomfited Don Juan, and then turned to Baldine, who was standing there, pale, with a strange, dark look in her deep eyes. There was something intricate in the expression of her brow; but it was an expression of visible pain. Her maiden pride had been hurt, and Toniello tried to console her. He pointed to the retreating Beppo, and laughingly lifted his finger to his forehead; Beppo was a madman, a fool; what he did was of no consequence. Then he approached Baldine, and softly touched the painful wrinkle between her eyebrows.

At once the girl's forehead grew clear and smooth as before, beneath her golden hair. She half opened her lips to say a word; but, remembering that he could not understand her, she closed them again, and only a smile stole gently into the curve of their sweet clasp. Toniello smiled also. Thus they stood a moment, both of them silent; then each nodded to the other, and Baldine returned with her empty milk-pail to the mill, and Toniello went downward to the village.

As he went, he sung again that melancholy national song which had found its way to Baldine's ear along the silence of the dark night air, when Toniello wandered home from the mill—

"Oh, were I slumbering deep
In death's eternal night,
My love would light my sleep,
And breathe the darkness bright!

"And when they lay me low
Upon my cold death bier,
In death I still shall know
That she is standing near.

"If o'er my grave she sighs
One little sigh of pain,
I soon shall ope mine eyes,
And smile on her again.

"But if, when I am dead,
My love her smile should keep,
Mine eyes will ope instead
To weep, and weep, and weep.

"Then, if she whispers low,
'My love, what aileth thee?'
My lips will ope, I know,
And answer, 'Pray for me!'"

That evening Toniello sat, as usual, in the saw-mill, and worked with the miller. Baldine watched, as heretofore, the speech of his fingers and eyes; and when he looked at her, she smiled. Her smile was meant to thank and assure him that she was no longer troubled or vexed about that madman, Beppo.

Nevertheless, ever after her encounter with Beppo, she made the miller's black dog run beside her as often as she went to the village; whereas, before, she had only let him accompany her in her lonely walks through the forest, where there was no fear of his falling out with the village dogs, with whom he was not on good terms.

Toniello continued his visits to the mill. After he had so improved its machinery that everything worked perfectly, he set to work upon a new piece of mechanism—a clock which was to be put in motion by the large water-wheel, with the help of smaller ones. Toniello bestowed much ingenuity and care upon this construction. When he had completed and fixed it against the wall of the saw-mill, the clock went extraordinarily well, and Baldine always regulated her work by it.

But Toniello was not yet satisfied with his master-piece. Every night he took it down and inserted into it new little wheels, which he skilfully connected with the old ones. For every hour he fashioned a little man who walked out on a board at the side of the dial, to announce the fleeting time. Then he constructed a dog, just like the miller's dog, and painted him black. At last he added chimes to the clock—and, in fact, it seemed as if his work would never be finished.

Sometimes, when he was at work upon something that did not require all his attention, he would begin singing with his fine, clear tenor voice the songs of his native land. While thus singing, he glanced across every now and then to the miller and Baldine, as though inquiring if they liked it; but whenever he came to his favorite song, the melancholy one beginning—

> "Oh, were I slumbering deep
> In death's eternal night,"

he always looked down, and never raised his eyes.

Before these later visits to the mill, he had heard
in the forest the strange, wordless song of Baldine,
with its deep tones so rich in variety of power;
sometimes suddenly swelling into a passionate burst
of thrilling sound, and then trembling away in faint
silvery notes along the stillness of the great woodland. He loved singing, as all Italians do; and he
especially loved the sound of an alto voice, because
that was the voice in which his mother had sung
to him the songs of his own land, and it is more
common among the women of Italy than in our
northern countries. Once (it was after the Beppo
incident), when he was leaning against a tree and listening to that wonderful wordless melody, its capricious variations suddenly glided into the soft sad
air of his favorite song—

> "Oh, were I slumbering deep
> In death's eternal night,
> My love would light my sleep,
> And breathe the darkness bright!"

It was the tune without the words, of course; but it
was sung in a voice as pathetic as the words themselves. Toniello stood and listened long after the
song had died away. But since that day he never
looked up when singing it himself; he was afraid of
betraying that he had listened, for he well knew
that the girl only sung when she thought herself
alone. And yet an irresistible longing to hear that
song once more from her lips continually tormented
and urged him, without clearly knowing what he
was about, to haunt the forest ways, where Baldine
used to wander by herself.

Thus it happened that he saw her standing, one Sunday afternoon, near the dead-planks. He was hidden in the thicket, and there he waited long to hear her singing. But she did not sing. She knelt a while before the planks, and then sat down upon the stone, with her face hidden in her hands, and her head stooping forward so that her golden hair streamed down over her fingers. In this posture she remained, till the miller's black dog laid a cautious, questioning paw in her lap, and looked consolingly up at her with his good, honest eyes. At this she rose, stroked the head of the dog, and moved towards the outskirts of the forest.

There she lingered a while, stooping down to pluck the flowers at her feet, or standing on tiptoe to strip off the lowest and slightest of the leafy branches above her head. With what she thus gathered she made two garlands, which she placed upon the two dead-planks; and then she went home again.

But all the way home she did not sing.

Toniello waited a little; and when she was out of sight, he went up to the old beech-tree. He examined all the planks, especially the two rough-hewn ones, with the fresh garlands on them; and that night he asked Signor Vico what was the meaning of the beech-tree and the planks.

Signor Vico explained it all to him; and why some of the planks were painted, and others only rough-hewn. "Rich — poor!" were the words in which he summed up his explanation of the matter; and, with his strong impulse to make everything

plain, he pointed, as he said them, first to himself,
and then to Toniello.

In a certain sense, however, Toniello was richer
than Signor Vico. The *Padrone* never gave himself an hour's relaxation from his survey work: but
Toniello the next morning renounced his wages for
that day, with a request for leave to go to Oberau,
where he had some purchases to make.

Signor Vico was reluctant to spare him, for his
general skill in all departments of the business made
him a trustworthy substitute for the *Padrone* himself in the supervision of many of its details. The
Padrone, however, said nothing, but in dignified silence scored out one day's work from the wages account. Signora Vico had meanwhile surreptitiously
slipped some victuals into the pocket of her favorite,
who was well upon his way a little after daybreak.

At noon Toniello reappeared upon the brow of
the hill, laden with a large supply of paint-pots; but
after this he must have stopped somewhere on the
road, for he did not reach the village before nightfall. And all the rest of the week, day after day,
he was off again before sunrise, while all the camp
was still asleep; returning, however, in time for the
beginning of the day's work.

When Baldine, next Sunday, made her weekly pilgrimage to the old beech-tree, she was greeted by
it with a wonderful surprise. No sooner had she
reached the tree, than she stopped and stood motionless before it; her figure turned into stone, and her
eyes fixed upon the bole of the tree. There were
her two dear dead-planks, leaning against it in their

accustomed place; but they were painted white, their edges adorned with black lines, and their crosses brilliantly gilt, and freshly decorated with little garlands of flowers.

Baldine crept nearer to them. Her lips were pale, her limbs trembling. She looked all around. There was no one to be seen. Long she knelt and prayed —longer than usual—at those reconsecrated shrines. Then she went slowly homeward, never lifting her eyes from the ground.

And the dog followed her dejectedly, for she took no notice of him that day.

Returning to the mill, she found Toniello already with the miller, who was smoking his Sunday pipe on the bench before the house. Toniello was hard at work on the construction of a mechanical cock, that was to spring out of the clock-door, and flap his wings, when the clock struck. When he saw Baldine, he only nodded to her, and then kept his eyes obstinately fixed on his work, while he went on singing to himself in low tones.

Baldine, however, went straight to him, and stood before him so close that he was obliged to look up. About her tremulous lips hovered the same smile which had sweetened their pensive loveliness after the discomfiture of Beppo's assault. Toniello feigned not to see it. He again took up his knife, but handled it so clumsily that he cut his finger. He tried to continue his favorite song, which the arrival of Baldine had interrupted; but the words stuck in his throat, the notes came false, he sung out of tune, and could not get on.

Then Baldine took up the right note, clear as a bell, and sung the air to the end. Her voice trembled a little, for it was the first time she had ever sung before any one; but she turned her back to the listener, as she sung, and looked far away, over the hillside, towards the beech-tree and the dead-planks. Still singing, with averted face, she went slowly into the house; and the last notes of her song came faintly through the open window to Toniello.

CHAPTER III.

Next evening Baldine does not sing, even to herself. She is sitting by the brook in the forest, below the mill; and the dog lies at her feet. He does not lift his paw to touch her knee and remind her that they must go home; he does not put his head into her lap, nor look up at her with his good, honest eyes, consolingly, as it was his wont to do when she was sad.

And yet this evening her sadness is heavy and sore. The dog does not care for it, however: he lies there motionless and callous, for he is dead. With difficulty he has dragged himself to this spot, that he might die at her feet. A strong poison must have been given him, for his agony was great when he looked up at her, with his dim eyes, for the last time.

And the agonized look in those poor dying eyes Baldine instinctively associates with her recollection of a strange, vindictive gleam in the glowing eyes of Beppo, whom she had seen a few hours before, prowling about near the mill.

When Toniello arrived at the mill-house that evening, the old miller and his wife tried to explain to him, by various signs, the fate of the dog. The miller imitated the barking, his wife the dying. Neither of them had much skill in mimetic art; but at last Toniello understood them, and hastened away in the direction they pointed out to him.

He found Baldine sitting motionless, and staring at the dog. Toniello knelt down, lifted the dog's head, and stroked him compassionately. The dog had been attached to him, too, with a touching affection; and till now had always greeted his coming with jumps and barks of joy.

To Baldine, who had borne her own sorrow silently, without a tear, the thought that Toniello also had lost a friend, brought fresh grief; and she began to sob. Moved by her tears, Toniello seized her hand, pressed it tenderly, and murmured,

"*Poverina!*"

To be sure, it was only for a dumb animal, a poor dog, that Baldine was weeping; but Toniello thought of how poor she was herself, and how lonely—of her own still, joyless life—and of how the dog at her feet had been her sole intimate, and her last; the constant companion and faithful friend of her seclusion; the trusty protector of her lonely forest walks.

"*Poverina!*"

He repeated the word so sorrowfully, that Baldine's tears flowed faster than before, in sympathy for his supposed grief about the dog. Then Toniello drew her softly to him, and stroked her hair, and wiped away the large tears that trickled down her cheeks. He leaned her head against his breast, and said nothing but *"Poverina! Poverina!"* and that each time in a lower tone.

Baldine looked up, and saw the tears standing in his eyes. She could not console him in his own language, much as she wished to do so; but through her tears she smiled on his. And, because it had comforted her when he had done it for her, she wiped his wet eyes and stroked his hair. Then he gratefully put his arm around her neck, and she felt that she must do as much for him; and when he softly pressed his lips to hers, still more softly hers returned the pressure.

Baldine had much to say that night to the dumb God, up in her little garret: and Toniello had a long talk with Signora Vico, who was an experienced woman, and loved him like a mother.

Next day the signora went bravely up to the saw-mill, though it was a hard and a long climb for such a fat, short-legged little woman. As soon as she got there, she asked for Baldine, gave the girl a hearty kiss on her cheek, and then began, in broken German, to speak to the old couple in the way she had seen her husband do it. After a good many bewildering mistakes, they understood at last that she had come to the miller, who was Baldine's guardian, with a matrimonial proposal from Toniello.

She also made known to them that Toniello possessed a little farm of his own at home, which he let out only because he had wished to see the world and satisfy his craving for information about foreign things and countries. As he had no parents, this way of life had till now been easy to him; but now he would return, with his wife, to his own land, and manage the farm himself. She and Signor Vico would miss him grievously, for Toniello had an excellent head on his shoulders, and was no common workman; but she rejoiced in his happiness, as if he were her own son. The miller and his wife felt how grievously they also would miss their Baldine; but, like the talkative little lady, they were glad of the maiden's good-fortune. The signora then took her leave, with two hearty kisses to Baldine; and all was happily arranged.

After their betrothal, Toniello and Baldine used to walk together to the old beech-tree and sit beside each other on the stone before the dead-planks.

As a blossom that grows out of a grave, was the growth of Baldine's love; and because he could not *tell* how he loved her, Toniello sung out all his heart to her in the songs of his own land. She accompanied these songs with the music of a voice whose strains were deep and soft and full as those of a violin. Words she had never sung, and those that Toniello sung to her she had never heard before; but she understood all they were meant to tell her, and her frank, fond eyes answered with loving looks the message of those loving words.

Sometimes, as thus they sit together on the stone by the dead-planks, she caressingly strokes his sleeve, as she used to stroke the sleeve of her grandfather when she was a child. But all this is not enough; and there is at least one little word, which she knows so well how to utter, in every conceivable tone, that it is forever on her lips. That word is "*Toni*"— the beginning of his soft foreign name.

To be sure, it is only one word; and that, too, a little one. But the birds that build their nest about her home in the lonely mill have also only one little chirp between them; and listening to them when they talk together in the leaves, Baldine has discovered that, with only this one sound, they can tell each other all they feel; and that according to the tone in which it is uttered, it means welcome or farewell, joy or sorrow, pleasure or pain, or even the manifold blissfulness of love.

So she with her "Toni!" What is there that this poor little word does not say for her, or say to him? How proud it sounds when she looks up at Toniello! How humble when she whispers it musingly to herself! How grateful when he brings her any little gift! How fond, when to him she gives a forest flower! How sweet, how inexpressibly sweet, when she is hanging on his arm and listening to his voice!

Meanwhile, the necessary papers had arrived from Toniello's home. Next Sunday, when he and Baldine passed by the dead-planks in the forest, it would be on their way to the church and the altar at Oberau. Signora Vico had prepared the wedding-feast, at which, of course, the indispensable *polenta* would not be wanting. The whole Italian colony wished to make it a splendid festival. Everybody planned

in secret some surprise for Toniello. The standard
of excellence was who should make the greatest noise.
Gunpowder played an important part in all these re-
joicings. Rusty old horse-pistols, and indeed all sorts
of old fire-arms, were hunted up; and on the heights
of the Grünberg various primitive preparations for
fireworks were stored in readiness for the occasion.

Beppo alone remained unsympathetic. But nobody
minded him, for it had been decreed that in a few
days his connection with the company was to come
to an end. Of late, his quarrelsomeness had increased beyond endurance; and he had even exhausted the forbearance of Signor Vico. Toniello he always shunned. Toniello had once spoken to him
about the worthless fellow who had poisoned the miller's dog; but he turned his back and hurried away,
grinding his teeth and clinching his fist, with an in-
articulate growl.

Toniello took no further notice of him, but Baldine, whenever the thought of him came back to
her, which it often did, was haunted by a vague fear
—not for herself, but for Toniello. It was for this
reason that, dreading a dispute between them, she
had never told Toniello of the many times she had
caught sight of Beppo's gloomy eyes peering through
a thicket as they passed, and felt that he was watching them when they walked together in the forest.

The last time this had happened was on the day
before their wedding, when Toniello came for a moment to the mill.

He only came to tell her, in their now familiar
sign-language, that he had something to do at the

6

Grünberg, and would not come again that evening,
so that she must go to bed very early, to be ready
next morning for the wedding walk to Oberau.
Which last injunction he explained by nodding as if
asleep, shutting her eyes with a kiss, and rocking her
head gently, while he sung to her in these words the
lullaby, *Vattene dormire*—

> "Sleep, dear, and be thy slumbers sweet!
> Of violets all shall be thy bed:
> Six angels watching at thy feet,
> Six angels at thy head.

> "Sleep, dear, until the morning-star
> Hath opened with his golden key
> That day, of all the days that are,
> The dearest day to me!"

Toniello went on to the Grünberg. Signor Vico
had been speaking to him about some obstruction,
which, he said, he had lately detected in the water-
course, and which he wished Toniello to have the
credit of removing. He would close the water-gate,
and shut off the water that evening, so that Toniello
might be able to examine the bed of the stream.

This, however, was only a pretence, suggested to
her husband by the signora, for getting Toniello out
of the way during the final preparation of the fireworks, with which the Italians intended to celebrate
the eve of his wedding.

They had all been racking their brains how to
manage it, till the signora hit on this notable plan;
and, although Signor Vico was at first reluctant to
join in her friendly subterfuge, which he thought a
little beneath his dignity, his wife had so effectually

talked him over that he ended by discharging his part in it with a zest which persuaded Toniello that the *Padrone's* whole reputation depended on the speedy removal of the pretended impediment.

So Toniello strolled leisurely up the bed of the stream. The water-gate was closed, the water-course dry, and empty of all but the confused heaps of stones that strewed its rocky channel. Toniello paused from time to time to examine the banks; and then, shaking his head, he climbed on slowly. No-where was a damaged place to be seen. At length he had got close under the floodgate, where the banks had been artificially raised; but here also he could find nothing wrong, though he carefully examined the spot.

Once he thought he heard a creaking above him. He listened, and looked up; but it must have been only the dull, angry sound of the imprisoned waters behind the dam; all around was still. He glanced up at the trees, thinking it might perhaps have been the flutter of some big night-bird in their boughs which had produced that strange sound; but no, the branches were motionless.

Then he thought of Baldine, who used to sing like the forest birds without any words, and wondered how her song would sound when she had learned the words sung by his own people in his own land —the songs of that home which would so soon be hers as well as his.

At last Toniello thought it was time to return; and he looked up to judge how far the evening was advanced. The narrow strip of sky above him rippled in and out like a rose-colored ribbon through the dark branches of the trees; and this set him thinking of the glow to - morrow upon Baldine's cheek.

Suddenly he was startled by a tremendous sound, like a mighty thunder-clap, just above his head; and through the opened floodgate, back into its old channel, came rushing and roaring the whole vast mass of the emancipated waters, which dragged along with them, fiercely tossed and jostled in their headlong course, all the logs and trunks thrown into them above the dam.

The Italians below in the valley, who had also heard this sound, supposed that Toniello, having discovered and removed the alleged obstruction, had opened the floodgates, in order to try the effect of his work; and they concluded that he would soon be back. All their preparations for his reception were now finished. Baldine, who had been summoned on some slight pretext, was sitting with Signora Vico in the workmen's hut; and Luigi, who was the swiftest of foot, had been sent to fetch Toniello, with a message that Signor Vico had something to tell him. They were only waiting for Toniello's return, and their thoughts impatiently followed Luigi up the Grünberg.

"Luigi must now be half-way up," they said to one another. And then again, after a little while—

"Surely by this time he has reached Toniello, and they must now be well on their way back. It is not too soon. Let us begin!"

And off went the fireworks! crackling, fizzing,

popping, blazing, banging, and merrily spouting into the dark heaven brilliant showers of colored sparks, while the drums beat, and the Italians shouted "*Eviviva!*"

But, on the height above, Luigi was lifting from the rocky bank a man stunned and crushed by the shock with which the whirling waters had flung him against it. The shouts, and the sound of the beating drums and bursting fireworks, were clearly audible in the still air upon the height; and the glare of the rockets and bonfires reddened the narrow strip of sky from which the faint ribbon of rose-colored light had long since faded. All these tokens of rejoicing rose up to the man who was lying there upon the wet moss. They were all addressed to him; they were all for his sake; but he neither saw nor heard them.

At last Luigi returned, breathless, panting, without Toniello.

The shouting and shooting suddenly ceased. There was a confused low buzz of troubled voices, and then all started off with a rush to the Grünberg. Baldine did not understand what was the matter, but she wrenched herself away from the hands of the signora, who, trembling, tried to hold her back.

When she reached the height, which the Italians had gained already, some of them were standing in a ring round something which she could not see; the others had lighted a fire, and were collecting about it a number of large branches.

Were these preparations for some special bonfire, she wondered. The Italians made way for her,

and she found herself at once inside the ring. In
the midst of it a wounded man was lying on the
ground, motionless. She gazed at him and bowed
above his face, lower and lower, till her bright hair
streamed over it. Then she glanced up, with a troubled look, to the faces around, as if asking, "Is this
really Toniello? For God's sake, say no!"

But the men remained silent. Some turned aside
to brush the tears from their eyes, while the others
bent still more busily over the litter they were making near the fire. Baldine knelt beside Toniello.
She did not weep, nor move, nor lift her eyes from
his face, till they put him on the litter. Then she
rose slowly, as if wearied to death, and silently
pointed out to the bearers the way down to the
mill.

They followed her directions; and as she walked
beside the litter—just as in by-gone days when, a
child, she used to walk by the side of her grandfather's cart—she sometimes stooped and touched caressingly Toniello's sleeve. The moon lighted the
forest-path, and no one spoke a word.

When they got to the mill-house, they carried Toniello, in obedience to Baldine's mute instructions,
up to her chamber, and laid him on her bed. Signora Vico was there, with her little medicine-chest.
She made them all leave the room, undressed Toniello, and then called Baldine to him. Life was not
yet entirely flown. He breathed faintly, but could
not raise his eyelids.

Towards morning the doctor and the curate arrived from Oberau; and with them many people

from the village. Baldine's chamber was entirely filled. The people outside the house were talking in low tones, and those inside spoke only in whispers, while the doctor examined Toniello's wounds; but all were asking the same question—

"How could the accident have happened? How was it possible? Could Toniello have loosened the sluice-gates, without knowing, while he was examining the bed of the watercourse?"

Baldine had turned from the bed, when the doctor approached it. She heard, as in a dream, the whisperers round her discussing all these possibilities, as she stood by the open window staring at the forest— where, all at once, she seemed to have seen something in the distance, for, with a loud cry, she stretched forth her arm, and exclaimed, "Beppo!"

All shook their heads. Beppo was a bad fellow, but not so bad as that! Moreover, he had left the neighborhood the day before, and taken leave of all before he went away.

But Baldine did not heed these incredulous protestations; she repeated several times her emphatic exclamation of "Beppo! Beppo!" and when the doctor, turning to the assembly, shrugged his shoulders, she smiled bitterly. She had known it—ah yes, long, long ago!—that he could do nothing for those who are at death's door. He had let her grandfather die; and him and his science she had long ago contemptuously dismissed, as since then so many other things, to the limbo of detected lies.

One, however, she still knows, in Whom there is help at all times, and for all. That is the dumb

God on the black cross. She had learned to speak to Him without reserve or doubt, when He still looked down on her from the corner of her little room in the forest cottage; and she had done so, day and night, ever since He had been hanging above the table in her garret at the mill-house. All that she had borne and suffered so silently, all that was hidden away in her young breast—its great heartsore, its humble joy—all this she had trustfully laid bare to His sad eyes; and He, that could do everything, knew all. His lips are mute, and His hands are motionless; but His love and power are not as human lips that lie, and human hands that fail, and He will save Toniello.

So she stands before the crucifix with lifted looks and supplicating hands, and lips that murmur unintelligible words.

A faint sigh reached her ear.

She ceased to pray, and ran to the bedside. Toniello had opened his eyes and was looking at her. She sunk on her knees beside him, and softly stroked his arm in her old childlike way. The one poor little word she had so often said to him before, meekly, humbly, heartily, was all she could say to him now, in the anguish of her last hope.

"Toni!" she whispered, bending over his face, and smiling.

He must have heard that word and seen that smile; for he too smiled and whispered,

> "Oh, were I slumbering deep
> In death's eternal night,
> My love—"

But there the whisper died away. His eyes closed again, and a shadow passed across his face.

The doctor signed to the curate to come forward.

Baldine started up, rushed to the table, sprung upon it, and stood before the crucifix.

"Save him, O God! dear God!" she murmured, fervently.

The curate, at Toniello's bedside, was muttering the prayers for the dying.

"Save him, O God!" cried Baldine, with a heart-broken wail, which she repeated again and again, louder and louder, wilder and more wild. She did not pray any longer; she stormed, she raved, and threatened.

"He is gone!" whispered the doctor to the curate; and the other murmured calmly,

"Lord, be merciful to the poor soul, and receive him into Thy heavenly kingdom!"

Then Baldine furiously tore the crucifix from the wall, and held it close, with both hands, before her face. Her eyes looked deep into the eyes of the image on the cross, and once more her lips repeated that piercing wail.

It was a dreadful and a terrible cry, and for years and years afterwards it haunted the ears of those who heard it.

With the cross still in her hand, she rushed to Toniello. Now at last he must recover! The dumb God was not like the worthless doctor, and He would make all well again!

"Toni!" she whispered.

But he did not look up, and on his face the shadow remained unchanged.

"Toni!" Baldine repeated, and clasped her arm about his breast, and laid her head upon his heart; but it beat no more.

Toniello was dead.

Once again that dreadful cry!

And then, after a silence which no one dared to break, Baldine rose, with tearless eyes and a bitter, disdainful smile upon her lips. All the melancholy softness of her features was turned into the hardness of frozen ice.

She deliberately lifted the crucifix high above her head, and dashed it against the wall, from which the broken wood flew splintered in all directions.

The priest covered his head and hurried out of the room. The villagers hastily followed him. Their religion had been insulted, their superstition alarmed; and around the house uprose, upon a hundred voices, the ominous cry of ancient days, "Stone the blasphemer! stone her!"

The popular indignation extended even to him for whose sake the sacrilege had been committed. No villager accompanied the funeral procession of the Italians. The dead-plank of Toniello, placed according to the usages of the place against the beech-tree in the forest, was removed the next morning. And the curse ran backward, excommunicating the preceding generation; so that with Toniello's dead-plank those of Zenz and Featherhelm likewise disappeared.

Baldine, amid execrations, was carried away by Signora Vico.

The miller's people had loved her well; but they belonged to the old forest race, which clings fast to its old reverence for its old God, and they would not harbor the blasphemer another night beneath their roof.

The priest preached next Sunday at Oberau a moving sermon on that strange event, and the Church condemned her with deliberation, as the people had already condemned her with haste. If the signora ever suffered Baldine to be seen at the door of the little house where they now lived together, every one crossed to the other side of the road, as if flying from an infected person; and the village boys had always stones in their pockets, ready to throw if they caught sight of her.

Baldine, however, was utterly callous to all these demonstrations. She did not even perceive them. Even of what was said to her by the friends with whom she lived, she seemed scarcely conscious. She was not ill, but she looked like a person who had gone through a long and wasting illness. In her face there was a waxen hue, and in her eyes a glassy stare.

Signora Vico was kindness itself to her, and so was the signora's husband. With his assistance Toniello had, after his betrothal to Baldine, so arranged his affairs as to secure to her his little property in Lombardy, in the event of his death. But as Baldine could not manage this property, and was unwilling to live there, Signor Vico exerted himself, through friends of his upon the spot, to dispose of it advantageously on her behalf; and the produce of the sale, which he handed over to her, was sufficient for the modest requirements of her future maintenance.

She learned the success of his efforts with apparent indifference, and signed, without reading them, the papers which Signora Vico put before her.

The signora, however, had devoted her whole heart to this poor girl, and it was her wish that Baldine should accompany her and her husband back to Italy. The villagers of the Grünberg, who were stupid and pitiless, would be the death of her if she remained. The signora herself, moreover, childless as she was, longed to have some one about her whom she could love as her child.

Baldine, to whom she explained all this, nodded silently. Baldine would have given the same silent assent had they proposed to lay her living in the grave; it was her way of answering everything.

Meanwhile the autumn was far advanced, and the Italians were preparing to return to their own land.

It was rumored about the village that Baldine would go with them, and the villagers were glad of it. Bad harvests, sickness, and fires were less to be feared when the taint of sacrilege was thus removed from among them. All the children had their pockets full of stones, and the grown-up folks their mouths full of maledictions, for the departure of the Italians.

But the signora was not only kind-hearted, she was also prudent, and before daybreak had contrived to get Baldine away on foot. Signor Vico, smoking with wonted dignity his Cavour cigar, was the only person seen beside her, as she sat, with her polenta-kettle, on the little wagon, drawn as before by the

unnatural beast which had so greatly excited the
suspicions of the villagers on the day of her arrival. This was a bitter disappointment to the boys
with stones in their pockets, and the mule had to
pay for it.

The Italians followed behind the wagon, shouting
and singing louder than when they first entered the
village, whence they were now joyfully returning,
with their hardly earned wages, to their own beautiful country.

Only two of them were missing, who at their entrance into the village had sung with them—the bad
Beppo and the good Toniello.

CHAPTER IV.

"*Il Cartellone!   Il Cartellone!*"

The news-venders roared it in the streets and
squares; the loungers in the *cafés* cried out for it
till they were hoarse; and in all the saloons of Naples the word went round from mouth to mouth.
Crowds collected at the street-corners, whispering,
murmuring, shouting, about the gigantic placard in
which the *Impresario* announced all the operas selected for the *Stagione*, and the names of his artist
troupe.

This was "*il cartellone*," the greatest event of the
day.

Among the artists mentioned on its list were some
whose names, like stars of the seventh magnitude,

gleamed only in a pale phosphoric light, when looked at through a powerful telescope. Others were discernible through spectacles, and some even visible to the naked eye. Then came a few whose place in the operatic firmament everybody knows; and, finally, the sun, round which all the other stars revolve.

This sun was Signora Iduni.

Her name was written on the *cartellone* in letters three times as big as all the others. But on the stage she had, as yet, been seen by no one. One does not begin all at once with the sun. When he rises, the dazzled gaze can see no stars; the eye must get accustomed by degrees to the increasing brilliancy. For which reason, only the little telescopic stars appeared at the beginning; and at these the public hissed with an energy belonging only to the South. That was, in the opinion of the *Impresario*, exactly what the public ought to do. The sooner he threw a victim to its satirical propensities, and the more mercilessly that victim was mauled and mangled, the sooner would the public get tired of its sport.

The *Impresario* had this time every reason to be satisfied. All joined in the whistling and hooting; the public was full of life, agitation, and interest. When the greater artists made their appearance, it had grown weary of whistling and hooting. So it rested its lips, and began to feel a pleasing restlessness in the palms of its hitherto inactive hands. The applause increased, the large opera-house grew more and more crowded, the *Impresario* rubbed his own hands, and felt that the world was going all right, though the sun had not yet risen.

He held that luminary hidden under the horizon
with great secrecy, nobody knew where. In other
respects excessively communicative, on this question
he remained as silent as a fish; and the expectations
of the public were raised to a pitch that, for nervous
temperaments, was quite intolerable.

Then, one fine morning, symptoms of the dawning
of the mysterious sun began to appear in the journals; little revelations, that steadily increased in intensity, like the glow before the sunrise. At first,
the shades of night yield to the disturbing glimmer
of twilight; then there appears in the east a streak
of pale splendor, across which a rosy flush begins
to hover; forthwith, a sudden fiery beam leaps up;
then a second, then a third; then a full sheaf of
brilliant rays, till at last the whole heaven is set
alight, though the sun still lingers under the horizon and bides its time.

The first disturbing glimmer of twilight was sent
forth by a newspaper which announced the discovery that this long-expected sun, in spite of its Italian
name, was not an Italian sun.

The discoverer was a man of national spirit, and a
stanch protectionist. He coupled his announcement
with an elegy on the neglect and suppression of native talent, and a bitter philippic against the impor-
tation of foreign products. The *Impresario* had
perpetrated an act of treason to his country, and
Signora Iduni was the *corpus delicti.*

This at once compelled the opposition journals to
preach a crusade against the Government. And they
started it with very spirited and eloquent leaders

upon the gross financial mismanagement, the outrageous growth of the public burdens, the depression of trade, the impoverishment of the people, the increase of emigration, the bankruptcy of the towns, the starving condition of the agricultural laborers, the frightful *Pellagra* - epidemic in the north, the eighty per cent. of crass ignorance in the south, the *Massia, Camorra,* and *Brigentaggio* — of all which things the sole cause was Signora Iduni!

Soon afterwards came the second discovery.

The *Diva* was not only not an Italian, she was even a German; though whether she was born in Austria, or in Germany, had not yet been ascertained.

The organs of the "*Italia irredenta,*" however, decided that she must be an Austrian lady, who had made her escape from that land of hideous tyranny, where she had been threatened with the most painful death. This view of the matter was copiously illustrated by thrilling romances about underground dungeons full of water and rats, with hangmen, and sworn tormentors, torture - chambers, and the most horrible tortures. The romances, naturally, ended in the wonted cry for the deliverance of the brethren who, in Trieste, the Tyrol, and Dalmatia, were languishing under the same tortures.

Nevertheless, the other journals asserted that the *Diva* was from Germany proper; where the children, as soon as weaned, swallow every morning a ruler for breakfast. By that interesting piece of information the Italian public might adjust its expectations of the plastic grace and dramatic *brio* of this lady's acting; and as for the art of singing as practised in Germany, it was well known that one end of the ruler always remained in the German throat.

People who did not write for the press were beginning to ask, with a titter, " Have you read?" And before long the question was, " By - the - bye, have you seen ?" For the comic papers had opened a complete course of illustrated lectures on the German system of swallowing the ruler.

But all this was only the twilight and glimmer of dawn.

The fiery glory came later. It began with a dry statement of fact in one of the morning papers, to the effect that the voice of Signora Paolina Iduni was an *alto*.

A host of astonished readers spelled out that paragraph slowly, over and over again, open - mouthed, and with eyes round as a plate, to assure themselves that they were really and truly under no hallucination. But it was no hallucination, it was not even a typographical error; for there it stood, plainly printed : " She is certainly a contraltist."

Few could swallow their chocolate, that morning, unchoked by just indignation. Here was a coarse outrage upon all the proprieties, a clinched fist shaken in the face of the public, and of each individual — a thing unheard of! And what unprecedented insolence, to have announced on the *cartellone*, in letters thrice as big as usual, the appearance as *Diva* of a person whose voice, it now appeared, was only fit for the parts of old mothers, elderly confidantes, crones, witches, gypsies, enchantresses,

7

and fortune-tellers! Even the least sensitive souls felt that the *Impresario* had practised a sorry joke upon them, and were outspoken on the subject of his shameless insolence.

An enterprising tradesman, who was up to the spirit of the day, immediately advertised for sale a new sort of whistles with an exceedingly loud and shrill note in them, which were made of tin, lead, pinchbeck, silver, silver-gilt, and even gold, for every rank and condition of purchasers. They were a great success, and he drove a roaring trade with them; while the very poorest portion of the population practised at home upon all the keys they could find, with a view to the discovery of which gave the shrillest whistle.

That was the morning glow.

The sun, which was the cause of it all, still lingered under the horizon, and knew nothing about it; but the *Impresario* kept his eyes and ears open to the signs of the times, and was well on the *qui vive.*

At first he had been frantically delighted at the manner in which the journals occupied themselves about his *Diva.* It was just as if he had paid them for it, and yet it had not cost him a penny. But now he perceived that all was lost. The thing had gone too far; and he presented himself as a broken man before Signora Iduni, with chattering teeth, for the purpose of duly impressing upon her the extremely precarious nature of the business, and the ticklish state in which it stood.

Signora Iduni smiled.

The *Impresario* had drawn a smelling-flask from

his pocket; for the situation was one of which he had long experience, and he knew that the announcement he had come to make was invariably followed by a fainting-fit on the part of the lady concerned. Now, however, he stood staring at the *Diva,* with eyes greatly surprised, and even a little frightened. The disdainful tranquillity of her smile disconcerted him, and at last it put him fairly out of temper.

"Ah," he exclaimed, "you are able to smile, signora? Smile! Good heavens! Do you know that Iduni whistles are being bought by the thousand, every day, to welcome you?"

"Childish playthings!" said the *cantatrice,* contemptuously.

"How? Childish playthings? You make a jest of it, do you?"

"A jest!" she said. "That would have been the first jest you have ever heard from me. But I have noticed that, among a number of children, if one child laughs or cries, or pouts or throws stones, all the others often do the same without knowing why. You, signor, I should think, must have observed a like tendency in the conduct of your theatrical public. Such things do not in the least affect me."

"But they affect *me,* signora—for your sake, of course!"

"What is the drift of these fine phrases?" said she. "I don't like them. I know, and so do you, that what excites you is not sympathy, but self-interest. You fancied that by your manner of announcing me to the public you were doing a clever thing, and had made a lucky move. Had I known of it, I would not have allowed such a proceeding; but now the thing is done, and cannot be undone. The golden mountains you hoped to gain have fallen visibly flat, and this is what upsets you. Had you not interrupted me, I would have told you before what may now be of some comfort to you. As for myself, you have already had my assurance that things of this sort never disturb me in the smallest degree; and as for you, you have only to reflect that children soon tire of one plaything, and take to another."

"Yes, I know that!" groaned the *Impresario.* "After the whistling comes the drumming with fists and feet, and then—"

"*Et cætera!* Well, then, let us dissolve our contract! I release you, unconditionally, from all your obligations."

"No, no! Never! What do you think of me? Can you suppose that my word—no, your word—no, I mean my word—is to be broken in this way? That I would take advantage of your generosity? That I am capable of cheating you in so unheard-of a manner? That would be . . . unconscientious!"

"You mean imprudent. I like to look at things as they are. Let us come to the root of the matter. Why this continual draping and posturing? To state matters plainly, your real meaning is that my so-called generosity would certainly be very inconvenient to you just now, when no celebrated singer happens to be disengaged; and that you want me to help you to find a vein of gold where your shaft has hitherto only struck barren rock. Well, then, I can give you back your word. I never take back mine."

"But what do you propose to do? We are in a terrible fix. You will be hissed and whistled off the stage. They are all provided with whistles. Even the boxes will whistle; among the thousand Iduni whistles there are at least ten of pure gold. Just think of that, signora! The Iduni whistles have become articles of fashion. They are all the rage. People wear them as *breloques*. The whole theatre will be filled with whistles. They'll whistle you into fits before you know where you are. You'll infallibly falter and break down. That's what always happens. You stop—choke down a sob—try again—no use—whistling louder than ever—burst out crying—go into hysterics—swoon away—carried off feet uppermost—and then—general confusion, uproar, revolution, universal smash, and the devil to pay! I see it all. I've seen it dozens of times before, and this time—"

"This time you will *not* see it. They will go on whistling, and I shall go on singing. For a moment, perhaps, the whistling may drown my voice—the orchestra does that sometimes. But 'tis not I that will first be out of breath."

"You don't know! They will compel you to stop singing. This is not an ordinary occasion. No means have been spared to make you hated and ridiculous. Some threaten, others scoff, all are against you. Do not reckon either on your art or your indifference, consummate as they both are, to win you a fair hearing from such an audience."

"I do not," said she.

"Upon what, then, can you rely?"

"Their injustice, and my own scorn of it. I am not afraid of what I despise. When the injustice of anything has been publicly exposed, the thing itself becomes ridiculous, and soon drops. Now, to convince these people of the injustice, and make them ashamed of the absurdity, of the proceedings you anticipate with such terror, there is one very simple means."

"And that is—"

"You shall learn it, and it is perfectly easy."

Hereupon followed a long conference between the *Impresario* and the *Diva*, at the end of which he fervently kissed her hand.

All the way home he ejaculated to himself in unabated ecstasy, "Angelic conception! heavenly idea! infernally clever! d-e-v-ilish good!"

The people he passed in the street looked after him with a smile, thinking how cheap wine must be this year.

Several days after this interview the play-bills for the evening announced the performance of the "Muetta di Portici."* At noon, however, these bills were covered by a fiery red placard, which informed the public that the first dancer was prevented by a sudden indisposition from appearing in the part of Fenella; but that the *Impresario* had succeeded in procuring a competent substitute.

----

* "The Dumb Girl of Portici." An opera better known in England as "Masaniello."

"Substitute? Competent substitute! But of what kind?"

This question occupied everybody; and throughout the first three scenes of the opera the audience remained in a subdued fret, exhibited only by a low humming.

At the end of the third scene Elvira starts up suddenly from her throne to ascertain the cause of an approaching tumult. The thousand heads of the public are simultaneously turned, with lively curiosity, in the same direction. The humming stops. All eyes follow those of Elvira with an interest incomparably keener than any which the singer is able to simulate; and when she asks "What is that?" the question appears as if written on a thousand astonished faces.

What is it, indeed?

Has a daughter of Palma loosed herself and her golden locks in all her enchanting beauty from some old picture-frame in which her father's hand first set her? Yet, no—this is scarcely a daughter of Palma, with that ever-beaming smile of hers, in which Giorgione, Titian, and the Veronese once sunned themselves. The look with which Fenella, flying before her pursuers, rushed upon the stage, never visited the face of Palma's daughter; had she once looked thus she could not have so smiled again.

The girl's deep-blue eyes are opened wide, with a feverish glare in them; her desperate look appeals in heart-felt anguish to the whole public, craving help of all and each, till it rests suddenly fixed on Elvira. In an instant the out-stretched hands are clasped with a convulsive clutch upon Elvira's garment; and as, clinging wildly to the feet of the princess, the dumb girl's passionate gestures depict her love, her incarceration, her flight, the whole audience is hushed and breathless. It is as if each spectator were not only looking, but listening intently, and afraid to lose a syllable. The eyes of the dumb girl, every muscle, every nerve of her, pour forth intelligible words without sound, which powerfully express all she is feeling, in a silence more poignant than the most thrilling song. The whole body vibrates and speaks in every tone of emotion, like some perfect instrument under the hand of a great *virtuoso;* and when, at the sight of Alphonso at the nuptial altar, the woman's image appears— miraculously transported, as it were, in the flash of a single infinitesimal moment, to the threshold of the chapel—it is impossible to say whether her feet have carried her there, or her arms been changed into wings.

Then again, in the succeeding scenes of rapidly increasing passion—the meeting with her brother, and the tent scene—her acting is an incomparable presentation of love, anxiety, jealousy, hatred, struggle, despair—a marvellous alternation of intense emotions—visible in every glance of her eye, every feature of her face, every finger of her hand, every changing outline of her noble figure. Each fresh movement is a distinct external revelation of the innermost life; and the whole effect is like a glorious picture - gallery, through which the spectator must hasten with a rapid foot — too rapid, indeed; for there is no time to study each successive masterpiece as one would wish; one can only feel, at every step, increasing astonishment at the wonderful faculty which has produced them all.

The audience could no longer restrain its enthusiasm; and an applause such as never before had been heard in that house at last burst forth from every part of it.

Already, after the first act, the spectators had sent out in all directions for flowers and garlands. Nobody had been prepared for this, nobody had brought a single flower, but now the stage was changed to a flower-garden, through which Fenella needs must pass in response to the innumerable and vociferous calls for her which greeted the close of the performance.

She came forward quietly, as if taking a walk, turned her eyes with indifference towards the thousands of crowded heads below, just as if they were so many stones in a pavement, and then bowed slightly, as a lady might do out of her carriage to a distant acquaintance in the street.

Such conduct was as entirely new to the audience as the performance which had preceded it, and it increased their admiration. They had been accustomed to see the strangest affectation in the acknowledgment of their applause; the archest coquetry simulating the most mincing modesty; the folding of the hands, the pressing of the heart, the imploring looks and deprecating gestures; and finally, the usual die-away retreat, in humble gratitude for so much unmerited favor. But on the present occasion all

such customary demonstrations of humility were con.
spicuously absent; and with the totally new and
strange behavior of this equally strange and new
apparition every one was enchanted.

As soon as the performance was over, all the *jeun-
esse dorée* crowded about the stage door, resolved to
carry their applause into the streets, and to take Fenella's horses out of her carriage and draw her home
in triumph.

The ripest of these gilded youths, who indeed were
over-ripe, took the entrance of the stage by storm,
and lined it like a hedge. At last the greenroom
door was opened; but the lady who came out was
not Fenella. It was a little elderly woman, with a
good-humored smile on her face.

Encouraged by that smile, they besieged and be-
sought her not to deprive them of the pleasure of a
supplementary ovation. She had not the least objection, and threw the door wide open. The room
within was empty. Fenella had long ago escaped
by a side door. Only the countless garlands and
flowers lay about in gay heaps upon the floor.

"Fenella, then, has not taken home with her these
tokens of her triumph?" they all exclaimed.

"No," said the little lady, putting on her bonnet.

"True," said they, "it would have been impossible. Here are flowers enough to fill a wagon—but
she will send for them afterwards?"

"No," said the little lady, buttoning her gloves.

"Then what will she do with them?"

"Some one will put them away. My niece does

not like flowers," said the lady, with her kindly smile, as she bowed and went off.

The gilded youths were left alone with the flowers, at which they stared dismally through their eye-glasses.

"She does not like flowers? *Cosa stupenda!* Not like flowers? But that is not to like what every artist dotes upon—applause, fame, honor, triumph! Well, they would go their ways, and discuss at the Club what other outward and visible expression of their homage it were best to select for a lady who does not like flowers. Strange, but truly interesting phenomenon! And, in any case, decidedly *chic.*"

Then they remembered that they had ascertained neither her name nor her lodging. The *Impresario* had excused himself, pleading indisposition, and to the whole staff of the opera company Fenella was quite unknown. So, at least, they had all declared, in reply to the countless questions about her with which they were plied. Some of them, to be sure, had smiled significantly, with an air of superior knowledge; but none of them had vouchsafed a particle of information.

The next morning the newspapers treated their readers to a fresh surprise.

They announced that the artist who, on the previous night, had unexpectedly appeared in the part of the dumb girl of Portici was herself a born mute.

This information furnished the public with a perfectly simple explanation of the startling naturalness of the performance; which, thus explained, ceased to

be wonderful. Any person to whom mimetic action
was not merely the special accompaniment, but the
single habitual and only possible vehicle of expression, would of course employ gesture as naturally and
easily as words are employed by those who possess
articulate speech. The muscular and facial flexibili-
ty of the performance was clearly the product not
of art but of custom; just as, by mere force of habit,
the person who can speak knows how to choose his
words instinctively, without the troublesome prelim-
inary of a conscious intellectual effort every time
that he uses the organs of speech. Those, therefore,
who had yesterday fancied they were contemplating
an achievement of ideal art, might now lower their
too exalted conceptions to the level of a pleasing
reality.

It was not till several days afterwards that the
long-looked-for sun, which had lately been quite forgotten in the unexpected triumph of Fenella, rose
at last above the horizon.

"Aïda" was the opera announced on colossal plac-
ards, and at the head of them, in no less colossal
letters,

Amneris . . *Signora* PAOLINA IDUNI.

Forthwith Fenella was forgotten in the renewed
excitement about the German contraltist said to have
been reared upon rulers.

This singer was not, it seemed, to make her first
appearance in the character of an old woman or a
witch. So much the worse for her! As the young
daughter of Pharaoh, such a creaking angular incar-

nation of Teutonic rulers would be all the more ridiculous. The boxes and pit had brought their whistles with them in their waistcoats, the gallery had their keys in their breeches-pockets, and all were ready for the signal of revolt.

Excitement was at its highest pitch. Every place had been sold for five times its ordinary price; and half an hour before the doors opened, not a seat was to be had for love or money. The whole world and his wife had resolved to be present at the "execution." For in the breast of the public this occasion revived a passion which had slumbered for a century and a half — the savage blood-thirst that, in ages gone, rushed up in the hearts, and surged through the veins of the old Italians when a Christian maiden was exposed to the wild beasts in the Amphitheatre.

The ancient classic drama of martyrdom was now to be re-enacted as of old; and again, as of old, the lion, panting for blood, stretched his huge limbs at ease in the arena.

The first scene of the opera passes uninterrupted, unnoticed. The house is ominously still. The lion awaits his victim; motionless, but on the watch, and ready for a spring.

At length Amneris appears upon the threshold of the scene.

The lion stares at his victim—stares and glares, yet makes no motion. His eyes are sparkling, his limbs strained for the leap, but he does not move. He is petrified.

The Amneris of to-night is the same as the Fenella of last week.

Those deep-blue eyes of hers have already spoken
to Radames. Her inward agitation at his aspect is
already revealed in the delicate tremor of the whole
frame, and every eloquent ripple of the glorious
hair, before she has yet opened her lips. But now,
from those opening lips pours forth the first pure
note of a voice that goes ringing, full and rich,
through the wide theatre to its remotest corners.
Like a stream of electric fire, the strong sweetness
of that sound passes, with an instantaneous thrill,
through all the thousand hearts of the astonished
multitude.

There is a charming poem by Hartmann von der
Aue, taken from the Arthurian legends, of Sir Iwein
and the lion. Iwein delivers a lion from the jaws
of a dragon, and from that time forward the grateful beast becomes the knight's devoted companion,
following him with touching fidelity.

In the present case the old Arthurian legend is
pleasantly revived.

The dragon has for weeks been vomiting fire and
venom; and the lion, inebriated, stupefied, and ob-
fuscated by those poisonous fumes, is unable to ex-
tricate himself from the foul jaws of that ravenous
monster. All at once, however, an heroic woman appears, and delivers him from this position, with as
much composure as an ordinary woman would
smooth her hair or tie up her tresses. The liberated
lion, who, in his blind distemper, had been crouching,
ready to spring on the approaching heroine, thereupon suddenly recognizes in her his intrepid deliv-
erer, the dauntless slayer of the dragon; and as of

yore for Iwein, the noble knight, so now for this noble woman, the grateful beast becomes all eyes and ears, following with touching fidelity every motion of her hand, every sound of her voice.

Nor was it gratitude alone that touched and subdued the lion's heart. He was transported to rapture by the irresistible magic of that woman's voice.

The few words—"*Come, O beloved, enchant my soul!*"—communicated to the whole audience the enchantment they invoked; and eyes and ears alike were spellbound by the pathetic scene, in which, while the priests below condemn, Amneris above forgives, and passes mute through all the tortures of a broken heart.

This time there were no storms of applause, but only paroxysms of convulsed emotion; trances, spasms, surges of sobbing sound that rolled round the theatre with a suppressed but unappeasable passion, till the calm blue eyes looked down with tranquil indifference, and their glance was followed by a slight inclination of the stately head.

There are eyes of which it is said that they can subdue madness better than a strait-waistcoat, and these are of that kind. But scarcely is their look withdrawn than the delirium begins anew. Is it that the spell of their power is so soon broken, or that the instinctive longing for the sweet subjugation of their glances is so strong?

And so it goes on again and again—a continual wonder! No one is willing to leave the theatre—though Signora Iduni herself has already left it, as the *Impresario* finally announces, stepping forward instead of her.

The dragon, who for weeks had been disporting himself in every conceivable color, was dead.

The journals had now not another word to say about rulers or witches. The serious connoisseur, the experienced judge of music, the well-bred author, stepped at once into the gap previously occupied by the dragon. They analyzed the performances of Fenella and Amneris; but even the masters of both arts found it difficult to decide whether Signora Iduni was greatest as an actress or as a singer. One thing only was certain, that the ideal of a dramatic singer was attained by this wonderfully harmonious combination of both.

It was characteristic of the disposition of the public that nobody any longer spoke of the opera as "Aïda." All, as if by common agreement, called it "Amneris." Verdi's work was rebaptized.

CHAPTER V.

THE little lady with the pleasant smile had already given the *Diva's* adorers to understand that her niece did not like flowers. They consequently prepared in her honor a serenade and a torch-light procession. But the serenaders were told, when they arrived, that Signora Iduni had driven that evening into the country; although, from the information given them by their scouts, they had every reason to believe her safe at home.

The costly gifts—gold ornaments, diamonds, and magnificent antiques—daily despatched to the signora's lodgings, were invariably returned, with the unanswered letters that had accompanied them. Visitors were received by the aunt, with the well-known smile, but by her alone, and so dismissed. All invitations, without any exception, were declined.

The aunt's face was never without that good-humored smile, except when the bolder spirits expatiated on the princely fortunes with which they were willing to purchase a smile less constant from her niece. Those gentlemen the little lady promptly sent home with a flea in their ear. To some who seriously added to the offer of the princely fortune that of an illustrious name, she smilingly returned her customary answer—"My niece doesn't care about it."

It was heart-rending! What in the world *did* she care about?

"*Niente,*" replied the little lady, with a cheerful smile, as if she were telling them the most natural thing in the world; and, so saying, she dropped a short courtesy and disappeared.

But what really went beyond all bounds was that the aunt appeared to be as incorruptible as the niece was indifferent. No sort of bribe could obtain from her admission to Signora Iduni, nor even a promise to mention the suitor's name to the signora.

The aunt and niece were of the same impenetrable stuff, and "*Niente!*"—Was that all that either of them liked?

Impossible!

8

Thus arose the second all-important question—
"What was the aunt's weak point?"

And this question proved exceedingly difficult to
answer. It was no use to assail her with nicknames
behind her back, and call her Cerberus or Argus, or
the Colchean or Hesperian Dragon; the truth remained unshaken, that this aunt was an outwork
which must be taken before the besiegers could
hope to get a sight of even the finger-tips of the
niece.

The *Impresario* also, to the question, "What does
Signora Iduni like?" returned the stereotyped answer, "*Niente!*" and to all appeals for his inter-
vention, he replied, with a shrug, that it would be
utterly fruitless. The signora, he said, had her pe-
culiarities, which the gods themselves could neither
bend nor turn by so much as a hair's-breadth; and
as for the aunt, she was a virgin fortress.

Nevertheless, this apparently impregnable breast-
work was at last insidiously carried by a surprise.

One day a card was presented to the inexorable
aunt, and the name upon the card was—

Conte Gaetano Armoneta.

The good lady sighed compassionately as she glanced
at it.

"One more to the many!" she muttered. "Well,
let him enter!"

The count was a handsome, distinguished-looking
man; but so, alas, had been not a few of his pred-
ecessors in this Forlorn Hope. He looked a little
more serious than the others, and that made her sor-

ry for him; for she saw at the first glance that he would be harder to get rid of, and might take his dismissal more to heart. There was a certain earnestness in his features which rather distressed her on his account, and a melancholy expression in his eyes which a little softened her motherly heart to him.

But she soon discovered, to her great relief, that he was not of the tribe with which she had so long been dealing. He did not inquire after her niece, nor even allude to that lady by so much as a single word.

"Allow me, signora," said he, "to ask you if you can give me any information concerning a young man named Antonio Bardi?"

"Toniello," cried the little lady, springing up in spite of her corpulence.

"Yes, Toniello," replied the count. "He was my foster-brother, but I loved him like a real brother; and like a real mother was his mother to me. She it was who brought me up when my own poor mother died. In my young days I was a great traveller, and during one of my absences from Italy my father died also. He bequeathed to Toniello, by his will, a little farm, with the intimation that this was not to stand in the way of Gaetano's intentions on his behalf. For my father knew how much I had at heart Toniello's welfare; and he approved of my intention to intrust him with the management of all my estates as soon as he had learned to manage his own little farm. On my return, I was informed that Toniello had let out his inheritance and gone with

a party of workmen northward, to see the world.
Later, the news reached Lombardy that Toniello
had perished abroad, and his little property was pur-
chased by the tenant to whom he had let it. After
many fruitless inquiries, I was directed to you, Signora Vico; and I have come directly from the station
to your house."

Signora Vico was seized with a fit of her old volubility. She indulged in a detailed account of Toniello's life and death, mingled with ejaculations, sighs,
and sobs.

The count drooped his handsome head, and was
silent for some time. At last he said, looking up
with moist eyes,

"And his poor bride? Does she still live?"

"She does," said the signora.

"Where? What can I do for her?" cried the
count, with eagerness.

"*Niente!*" said Signora Vico, sadly. "Come this
evening to the Opera. There we can speak of this
again. But, for Heaven's sake, no more just now!
I am beside myself with all these cruel reminiscences.
Eight years have passed since then, and to me it appears as if it had all happened yesterday. Go now,
Signor Conte! You cannot stay here any longer. I
am every moment expecting my— No matter! somebody who never receives visitors.

"*Addio, Contino!*" she added, as the count withdrew.

Contino! He was already adopted by her motherly heart, as years ago it had adopted Toniello. Those
moist eyes had bewitched her.

Once again "Aïda," or as it was now called, "Amneris," was performed.

Signora Vico sat in her box near the stage. The count had seen and saluted her as he entered the theatre, but he never came to her box. He must have forgotten all about her; he did not even once look towards her during the performance. Indeed, he did not look either way, to right or left, but kept his eyes immovably fixed upon the stage; and, during the *entr'actes*, he looked at the curtain as if his gaze were trying to pierce through it. Signora Vico supposed, at first, that this abstraction was entirely due to his admiration for Amneris; but she dismissed that idea when she noticed that he did not move a finger to join in the repeated rounds of applause.

The opera appointed for the next evening, in compliance with the vociferous demand of the public, was "Fenella;" for so also was the "Muetta di Portici" now generally called.

The count sat in his previous place, and conducted himself just as before.

And so on for several evenings.

At last, one forenoon, he paid a second visit to Signora Vico's house. He was pale, the earnestness of his features appeared more pronounced than on the occasion of his first visit, and his whole face was pervaded by an expression of profound melancholy.

"I come," he said, "to take leave of you, signora. I am going in search of Toniello's bride. She is to me a holy legacy."

"Don't, Signor Contino!" cried the signora. "You can do nothing at all for Baldine. Pecuniarily, she is very well off; she possesses more than she ever possessed before, much more than she requires for her support. And mentally— Dear Mother of God, what's gone is gone! You cannot bring her back. You cannot restore to her what was once hers—the love of man and beast, and bird and blossom, the kindly human trust in human kindness! They are gone. And ah, Signor Conte, worst of all, gone with them is the comfortable Christian faith—the faith in the Madonna, the faith in God and His holy saints! What is left to look for? *Niente! niente!*"

And Signora Vico shook her head sadly.

"Nevertheless," said the count, "I will bring Baldine here."

"Here! And why? For what purpose?"

"For what purpose? That she may once see Signora Iduni as Fenella. Fenella suffers deeper pain than that poor girl. She also loses her lover—loses him, moreover, by base treason, yet she finds a refuge in her love for her brother. Baldine, too, has a brother—myself—and I will accomplish my task. I will find her, even if I lose myself in the attempt."

"What do you mean, Contino? How can you lose yourself in the attempt?"

"Did you never hear, signora, that what is an antidote for one may be a poison for another? Addio, signora! I must be gone, for I leave in an hour."

"Blessed Madonna! how hot your blood is, Signor Contino! Who would have guessed it? You look so cool! But Baldine is no longer in the forest quarter of Oberau."

"Where is she, then?"

"I don't know."

"Then I shall seek her out, wherever she be. Till now I have wandered purposeless about the world. Henceforth, at least, my wanderings will have an aim. Addio, signora!"

Signora Vico grasped his arm.

"You must not go away, Signor Contino, to wander about the world again at random. Wait only a few days, till I myself have made inquiries about her. Promise me this! What, you will not? Then, at least, one day! No, I do not let go of you thus! Presently my — niece — will be coming home from the rehearsal. I will speak with her — that is, I shall— She would be anxious if I went out without telling her."

"Your niece? Ah yes, Signora Iduni!" said the count, looking down.

And then, as if following out a long train of thought, he murmured to himself,

"They say nobody has seen her off the stage; they tell strange things of her."

"As of you, too, Contino!" put in Signora Vico. "How in the Indian jungles you have stalked wild tigers; how in Africa you have hunted lions, and elephants, and unicorns; how you have been engaged in conflicts with the slave-traders, and have thrust yourself everywhere into the most dangerous places, where death is ever at hand; how you—"

"Good God! yes, signora, one runs away, and wanders through the whole world, to be anywhere happier than at home. That is an illusion. Nowhere have I felt so well and glad as at home, in my childhood, while Toniello's mother, the kind-hearted Maruccia, sat on the bench before the house shelling chestnuts or stripping maize, and Toniello and I lay on the lawn at her feet, listening to the homely songs she was never tired of singing—the songs of our own people. Ah, those dear old songs!"

"Yes," sighed the signora, "dear old songs! Toniello inherited them from his mother. He sung them so beautifully! And there was one in particular—his favorite song, which I think I shall never forget. Let me see, how does it go?"

And she hummed softly the beginning of the melody, but presently paused. She seemed unable to continue it.

The count rose and opened the piano. He touched the keys dreamily, and then began, in a soft barytone, Toniello's favorite song—

> "Oh, were I slumbering deep
> In death's eternal night—"

While he was thus singing, his eyes fell upon the mirror on the wall opposite to him. In the frame of the mirror appeared the image of the woman he had seen as Fenella and Amneris. Her eyes were staring at him, and her arms hung slack at her side as she stood, leaning slightly forward through an opened door, beside which sat Signora Vico, watching her with a face of great anxiety.

The count's voice failed him.

His fingers for a while went on moving the keys automatically, but suddenly they struck a discord as he sprung up, and, with a face which had been

rapidly growing paler, bowed in silence to Signora
Iduni.

"This is Toniello's foster-brother," said Signora
Vico, in a suppressed voice.

The *Diva* looked a long time silently and keenly
at the count, but she said nothing.

In a tone still more broken, Signora Vico went
on—

"Conte Armoneta has called on me to learn the
fate of Toniello; and now he has set his heart upon
going in search of Baldine, that he may bring her here
—to—"

She stopped suddenly.

"To what?" said the deep, soft voice of Amneris.

"To find in him a brother, because to him she is,
as it were, a legacy from Toniello. And he wishes
to bring her here in order that Fenella may show
her how a brother's love can be a refuge from despair."

Once more Signora Iduni looked fixedly upon the
count.

"A brother's love!" she said, slowly. "But the
love of a sister brings no good to Masaniello. He
dies by sword and poison. For Fenella, too, perhaps
the happiest end is to warm herself at last from the
world's chill in the fire of Vesuvius. A brother!
and wherefore a brother? But why all these mysti-
fications, which seem to be to the taste of my *Impresario?* You need look no farther, count. It is
I who was Toniello's bride. I am that Baldine you
wished to find and fetch. Be assured, however, that
Baldine died long ago, and that you have only found

a person who can tell you, perhaps, more of Toniello than any one else.

"*Mamma mia,*" she added, turning to Signora Vico, "Toniello's foster-brother may come again, if he wishes to hear of Toniello. He is an exception —he does not come for *my* sake; it is just to him that I, too, should make an exception."

Thenceforward the count occasionally availed himself of this exceptional permission.

Signora Iduni told him all she knew of Toniello. She was always perfectly tranquil, indifferent, and cold; and she spoke without betraying any feeling in her features or her voice, as if she were reciting some old legend of by-gone ages. There was not a lyric note in the whole narrative: not a single colored thread did she suffer to entwine itself with the monotonous gray woof of her recital. It sounded like an ancient epic, whose rhapsodist entirely suppresses his own personality—exhibiting no emotion, and interposing no comment, in the course of what is given him to tell, but standing aside from his theme, as it were, a passive listener to all that he relates.

There was no lack, however, of glowing lyric and blooming idyl in the tales narrated by the count. His talk always reverted to the childhood of Toniello and his own, and the unforgotten foster-mother, the good Maruccia. In the intervals of conversation on these topics he would sit down to the piano and sing some song of Maruccia's, while Signora Iduni stood behind him, and he could see her staring eyes and drooping figure in the mirror. Sometimes also he told her stories of his later life, of its restless wanderings in distant countries, and of outlandish folk, and their strange ways and doings.

Then, as Signora Iduni sat in the sofa corner, listening with bent head, an old, sweet, by-gone dream returned to her. A loudly creaking cart came laboring up a mountain - path; behind it appeared a head with a snowy-white beard—an old man's head —and then, by degrees, as from depths of mist, the whole figure of the old man. Nearer and nearer he staggers on his way to her, and begins to relate to the listening child stories of strange lands beyond the mountain-brow, and of distant folk, and all their doings. And clearly and distinctly at last the words come to her, in the accents of a well-known, long-lost voice—

"*All is for the best, and everything has its Why. Only one must find it out!*"

She passed her hand across her eyes, to sweep away the dream-picture.

"Find it out?" she mused — "find out what? What is there to find where nothing is? Most probably the old man meant that into all things one must put something. A something that may perhaps benefit for a while, or comfort those who have not the courage to look open-eyed into the terrible emptiness around them. Yet this, too, is nothing worth! What comes of it all, at the utmost? Illusions, fictions! and beyond them — a bottomless abyss! *Niente! Niente!*"

One day the count entered in a state of painful agitation, ill-suppressed, and wholly unlike his habitually quiet melancholy. He stepped hurriedly forward, as if he had something of pressing importance to communicate to Signora Iduni, but suddenly checked himself, paused in evident confusion, went to the table, turned over the leaves of an album, then opened the piano, struck a few chords, closed the instrument again, and finally sat down silent in the recess of the window.

The actress looked at him inquiringly.

He felt her keen gaze resting on him, rose abruptly, walked to the *fauteuil* in which she was sitting, and said, with a trembling voice,

"I have in the course of my life wasted a good deal of foolhardy courage upon nothing; and now, when I most want it, my courage forsakes me. I have learned to know what fear is, and I feel it at this moment. Will you not help me, signora?"

"What is the matter with you?" she said. "Tell me."

"It was once Toniello's wish to make you happy," he replied. "His wishes are holy legacies to me. I cannot fulfil them all. I am not Toniello. I cannot make you happy, but I wish, at least, to see you less sad; and I believe that I can make you more cheerful. Fate and men have wronged you. For that wrong I would make amends; and I feel in myself the power to achieve what I desire more than all things in the world, loving you as I do unspeakably. Be my wife, Paolina!"

"And *you*, too!" she said, sorrowfully; "you, too, then, are like all the others! But they, at least, did not know me. To them my manner must have seemed a strange caprice, which might, perhaps, change any moment, like the weather. *You*, however? You, who, for Toniello's sake, have been admitted to stand inside my life; you, by whom I thought it possible to be understood!"

"It is because I understand you," he answered, quickly, "that I have faith in my own power to make your life less sad. Only in the strength of this faith could I have told you all I feel. Be my wife! I love you fervently, but I would have crushed into everlasting silence the cry of my heart if I did not feel that it was the voice of a prophetic faith."

"And yet," she replied, "it is only the voice of a twofold superstition. Both your faith in what you deem your love for me, and your confidence in its power to effect the smallest change in either my life or my character, are pure illusions!"

"I swear by God—"

"God?" she interrupted, almost fiercely; and then, eying him coldly, she added, in a hard tone,

"You have been very piously brought up, count?"

Both compassion and scorn seemed mingled in the tone of this question. He did not reply to it; but she, who had learned to interpret mute expressions better even than uttered words, could read in his looks and features the pain it had caused him.

She gave him her hand, and said,

"I am sorry. Forgive me if I hurt you. I know you mean it well, but you are deceiving yourself about me, and about yourself too."

"About myself, no!" he answered, earnestly. "I

once knew a girl who is no more. We were little
neighbors in childhood; and as children our souls
grew together in a thousand ways, like young trees
whose branches interlace as they grow up, till they
have but one foliage between them. She became
my wife. A few weeks after that she died; and it
was her death that drove me abroad. My spirit,
longing for escape from a life that was only the consciousness of suffering, dragged my body with it
through the pestilential air of the Indian swamps
and jungles, under the murderous climates of Africa, and into the company of wild beasts and wild
men. But, wherever I went, my grief followed me
from place to place, and the death I sought evaded
my pursuit. Thus I returned to my own country
the same as when I left it, a man with no hope or
purpose in life. The rumor of Toniello's unknown
fate eventually led me to this town. But here I
have discovered that my heart is not yet dead. A
single look of yours, Paolina, has quickened it to the
core. A spark, still smouldering under the ashes,
leaped up when I saw you. Then you sung. Yours
is a voice which does more than charm the ear with
a sensuous delight; it penetrates the depths of the
heart. On mine its influence was like the breath
of spring, thawing the laid-up ice, moving the foun-
dations of the deep, and awaking what till then lay
still and dead. It swept the withered leaves from
the loosened soil, and revealed the liberated bud-
dings of new life. I felt my heart begin to move
once more. It beat feebly and coldly, then stronger
and warmer, and at last, little by little, loud and glow-

ing, as now, with all the love you have taught it to feel for you!"

"For *me?*" she said. "No, but for the *artist!* You have yourself proved, better than I could have done, the truth of what I tell you. I did not discourage your enthusiasm for my art, because I saw that it was for you a source of happiness. But now that I see you deluded and ensnared by it, I must speak out. It were no kindness to prolong a dangerous illusion. You talk to me of my singing and my acting. Neither the one nor the other has ever been to me a matter of feeling. Both are entirely the products of acquired skill."

"Skill?" he exclaimed. "You speak thus of a performance so profoundly touching, in its truth to Nature's deepest feelings and highest forms, that every time I behold it the applause it elicits from others seems to startle me out of a deep dream! I feel something like a physical pain whenever I hear that applause; and I cannot but imagine that to you, also, the shock must be painful when the reality of the effect you have produced thus shatters and scatters, like a brutal blow, the inspiration that has enabled you to produce it. To yourself, no doubt, the intoxication of such applause may perhaps partially soften what—"

"You are doubly mistaken," she interrupted. "The applause cannot intoxicate me. I am absolutely indifferent to it. Nor does it snatch me out of dreamland, for the simple reason that I have never quitted the firm ground of reality."

"Impossible! You? No, Paolina, I do not believe it!"

"Ah, it troubles your illusions," she said, sadly. "Once I, also, had illusions of the same kind. Like you, I supposed that on the stage, in order to move others by the representation of the passions, one must, one's self, really feel, or at least be capable of feeling, love, hatred, anger, ecstasy, despair, and so forth. In this belief I invariably replied to all the exhortations of my masters that I knew myself to be unfit for a dramatic singer; I could not simulate on the stage what I was incapable of feeling off it. When they assured me that this supreme self-composure was just the mint-mark that stamped me for a genuine artist of the rarest quality, I entirely disbelieved them. Then, to the place where I was living at that time, there came a great tragic actress, a woman, such as one sees only once in a century, with power to stir the most stagnant spirits to their deepest depths. She roused my own from its long apathy. Like you, I felt again a movement in my soul. Once I saw her as Desdemona. I shall never forget it. I sat as if I were petrified, and could have knelt to her, as I saw her standing there before me on the stage. On either side of me I heard a growing trouble of soft sounds. I looked up; the women were sobbing, the men had tears in their eyes. To me it is not given to weep, but with dry eyes I stared again at Desdemona. Then I saw that mighty mistress of the emotions of others, just at the conclusion of a scene the most passionate and affecting that you can possibly conceive, lightly turn and nod and smile at some one in the side-scenes. I rose and left the theatre. That one look convinced me that I was fit

to be an artist. I never again beheld the great tra-
gedian. I threw her image to the rest of the rubbish
I had so often before mistaken for truth. Call all
that refuse 'Lost Illusions!' This one was my last.
But do as I did, count! Throw the *Cantatrice* Iduni
to the great rubbish-heap of discarded fictions and
shattered faiths. For *you*, at least, other illusions,
fairer, and perhaps more lasting, still remain. For
me there is nothing left."

"In you, Paolina," cried the count, "the capacity
for deep feeling is only asleep. Your ordinary life
does not disturb its slumber, and therefore your ordinary self is unconscious of its existence. But on
the stage it awakens with Titanic, because unex-
hausted, power; and then it is the existence of your
ordinary self that becomes effaced. Between the
two extremes there is no intermediate stage of consciousness. The life that informs the ideal image is
your own, and it is the only life that is truly yours.
You do not see this, any more than one sees one's
self. You are not conscious of the process, for process there is none. It is not you that gives life to
that image, it is the image that gives life to you."

"That is so," she replied. "But why? This image, as it shapes itself out, displaces nothing in my
inmost self. Nothing there need give way to make
room for it, for there all else is empty. In such a
desert every form finds space enough for expansion.
Once I knew an old man who let his cart moan and
cry for him. So I, who cannot do it for myself, let
these creations of the great masters cry and moan
for me. And if I sing, and sometimes laugh, upon

9

the stage— Well, I once possessed, when a child, a ball, from which I tried in vain to learn the cause of all the irrepressible gayety and wild delight with which it was always springing about. The ball would not reveal to me its secret; but at a single stab of that old man's knife the thing shrunk, and collapsed into a wretched gray rag. The secret of its buoyancy, and all that deceptive gayety, was—air, nothing but air! Art remains. Yet even to Art I owe but little. By far the greater portion of all you admire in me is only the product of an acquired skill. I lived in my childhood with a dumb person, and afterwards with those who seldom spoke; so that, without conscious effort, I have learned to understand the language of mutes and dumb animals better than spoken speech."

"And your song, Paolina?" said the count. "That wonderful interfusion of words, gestures, and melodies! that song which sets vibrating every heart-string, now touching softly the tenderest chords, now sweeping into storm the whole diapason of feeling!"

"It is all the same," she replied. "Words have ever been a burden to me. There was once a time when I could sing true song, though it was a song without words; a time when my own thoughts were as harp-strings, and my heart was a lute on which all things played. Now, the song draws the reluctant words along with it, as a gang of prisoners is drawn along by the chain to which they are fastened."

The count let his head sink on his breast.

"What does this woman love?" he thought. "Not

even the art she has brought to supreme perfection! not even her own superlative genius! Does she, then, feel nothing, believe nothing, care for nothing, hope for nothing, wish for nothing in this world?"

And he put these questions to her.

"You ask what is my faith, my hope, my love?" she replied. "I have none. What I feel? I know not. I only know it is neither love nor hatred. Call it indifference, apathy, hebetude — what you will! And this is why I cannot become your wife. A phantom is no wife, especially for a man like you, who has yet a heart and a faith—a man who hopes and loves."

"It was the belief of the old times," said he, "that a phantom gets life by drinking the blood of a living person. Take my heart's blood, Paolina—I give it willingly. You seem to yourself a phantom, only because there is nothing in your life for the sake of which you care to live, nothing in the present that points to the future."

"And you naturally wonder," she replied, "why I live, and how I contrive to live, with nothing to live for? But do not suppose, count, that I could live, even thus, without a purpose in life. I have one. From childhood the main-spring of my life has been an inveterate and inflexible sense of justice. This is a cold motive, but, in my case at least, it is a firm one, and it moves me like a spring of steel."

"You have looked deep enough," she continued, "into the very simple mechanism of my life to guess the direction in which it is kept going by this motive. The Vicos have dealt by me, she as the tenderest mother, her husband as the most careful father. Cursed and rejected by my own people, I found with them a new home. The signora's brother was the *Maître de Chapelle*, Iduni. He was my first music-master, and it was he who afterwards procured me others whom he deemed greater than himself. But to him I owe more than to all of them; and to him, too, I owe even my name, for he adopted me. My German name, he said, was impossible for the *cartellone;* and rejecting 'Baldine' as barbaric, he always called me 'Paolina.' When he had done for me all he could do, and before I had yet been able to do anything for him, he died.

"Signor Vico, meanwhile, had risked and lost all his hardly gained fortune on an enterprise which, not being in the way of his own business, turned out a dead failure. He has been compelled to resume his old labors, and every year he migrates northward with the swallows, while his wife remains with me. It were a great injustice did increasing years bring no rest to this excellent couple. What they have so richly merited on my behalf it is now in my power to procure them; nor can I rest till I have done enough.

"As for my *Impresario*, I look upon him only as the cashier of the Vicos. Whenever my thoughts turn from them, it is to wander back to my former home. The people there have cruelly wronged and injured all I loved in my childhood. My grandfather was poor, the old woman who reared me was dumb. That was their only crime, yet these people illtreated them! Me, whom they cursed and outlawed, they had perhaps some right to punish, for I had insulted their Faith. But what had the two old people done to them from the grave, or what the dead Toniello, on whose desecrated ashes fell the bitter ban of their anathema? I say that this was an injustice which is still to be redressed.

"My dead ones shall be righted. The *Impresario* here is my cashier for Signor Vico; but I have another in America, who is my agent for the purchase of the whole forest quarter of Oberau. Every house and field there belongs to the master of the glass-works; the people are only his workmen. Every house and field there I intend to buy, and for work and home those people shall go elsewhere. The old beech-tree, with its dead-planks, shall go with them, and in its stead I will make a graveyard in the valley. The first three monuments erected there will contain the dear and injured ashes of those whose dead-planks they have banished from the place.

"My dead shall be righted! In the forest valley my Lombards shall live at ease, where of old they worked with Toniello, whom they loved. There shall every Lombard colonist have a little house and meadow of his own; and the sole lord of the manor-house, the forest, and the glass-works shall be a Vico!

"One only of that race and name still lives as to whom I cannot yet tell you my intentions, for my present thoughts of him may be unjust. As yet they are only surmises; and as I never trust to appearances, so I have never acted on suspicion. But could I see this man with my own eyes, I know that

I should read in his, and at once be able to say, whether justice demands his death, or sanctions the continuance of his worthless life. To the police of the province where he still prowls and plunders I have offered a sum of ten thousand lire if they bring this man to me, alive. Not one of them has yet been able to gain the reward. But I shall find other means; it would be unjust to leave any untried. Have you heard, count, of the notorious robber, Beppo, the captain of a gang of banditti as ferocious as himself? That man is also a Vico, and he is the man I seek."

The count had listened to all these words in unbroken silence.

What did they reveal to him? Was it nothing but the frigid impulse of the steel spring, to which she had likened the sole motive power of her life? Were there not here, at least, glimpses of feelings warmer and more far-reaching than those which are exclusively dictated by an abstract sense of justice? Was her heart really so empty as she supposed? In this threefold aim of her life, was there not something like attachment, gratitude, and hatred?

Such were the count's thoughts while she was speaking. But when she ceased he rose without a word.

Paolina approached him, gave him her hand, and said,

"You understand me now, and what you understand can you not forgive? As for what you spoke of before you knew all this, you will not think any more of it, will you?"

He bowed, but did not answer.

Then he took his hat, and made a few steps to the door.

"We meet to-night at the Opera," she called after him.

"No," he said, half turning, "I cannot come to-night."

She looked wistfully at him.

It would be the first time that he had missed her singing.

"To-morrow, then!" she added, with a little disappointment in her tone. .

"I start to-night," he replied, "to look after my estates."

Once more she looked at him wistfully, and then, with a bitter smile, bowed her head, and turned away.

He went out.

She leaned against the window, and watched his carriage disappearing down the street. The bitter smile still lingered on her face.

This was the man to whom she had told all, before whom she had opened her whole soul. To cure him of his passion she had conquered her pride; and now he had gone away in a fit of wounded vanity and egotism—unjust to her, yea, more unjust than all the others!

The carriage disappeared round the corner; the bitter smile died about her mouth; and the count was thrown away — with the stabbed ball, and the broken jumping-man, and the doctor, and the dumb God, and the old home—to the great rubbish-heap of "Lost Illusions."

CHAPTER VI.

THE great *Diva* continued to live her lonely life, celebrated on the stage, unknown in the world, and invisible at home. When the Italian season was over she went to England, where she won new triumphs. A short time before the end of the English Opera season she received a letter from Lombardy. The handwriting of it was unknown to her, but the words and signature were as follows:

"SIGNORA,—You were right. Justice *did* demand the death of Beppo. He lives no more. It was not possible to bring him, as you wished, alive before your eyes, but he has made a dying confession —that, impelled by jealousy and hatred, he opened the floodgate at Oberau, and thus accomplished the murder of Toniello.   GAETANO ARMONETA."

The letter bore no address, neither was it in the handwriting of the count, which was not unknown to Paolina.

Whose were the hands that had slain Beppo? To whom had the robber made that dreadful confession?

On these points the letter contained not a word of information.

She telegraphed to the chief of the police, and received from him, after some delay, a detailed account of the affair.

From this it appeared that Count Armoneta, a personal friend of the chief, had organized, at his own risk and cost, a powerful expedition for the capture of the notorious robber. The whole band had been surprised and surrounded by a force which the count himself commanded. Some of the robbers perished in a desperate struggle; the rest were taken prisoners; but their leader, Beppo, had fallen in single combat by the hand of Armoneta. Of any special confessions made by the dying robber to the count, the police had no knowledge. The count had ever since this event been living in great privacy on his estates in Lombardy.

Thither Paolina hastened, accompanied by Signora Vico, as soon as she was able to return to Italy, and one afternoon in autumn the two ladies arrived at the Villa Armoneta.

They were informed that the count was at home, but too unwell to receive visitors. On learning their names, however, the count summoned the physician who was staying at his house; and he, after a short conversation with his patient, conducted Paolina into a chamber from which every ray of light had been carefully excluded.

Through the darkness of this room, which was as black as midnight, the doctor guided the *cantatrice* to a sofa, and requesting her to sit down, immediately withdrew. Presently she felt a hand upon her own. It was the count's, who was seated at the other end of the sofa. He said, cheerfully,

"This is just like some grewsome old ghost story, is it not, signora?"

"Don't laugh, count!" said Paolina. "*Mamma mia* at once assailed your doctor with her usual volubility; and he, with of course the oracular ambiguity of his profession, has told her of the inflammation in your eyes. I do not believe in doctors, nor in the airs of sagacity they give themselves, but I do know that these affections of the eyes are no laughing matter."

"Why not?" said the count, still cheerfully. "This inflammation is only the result of an ophthalmia I once had in Egypt. But you did not come here to talk about my eyes, and you must be impatient to hear the confession of the robber Beppo."

"No," she replied; "you are mistaken. I came because I was haunted by a consciousness of injustice in my own conduct. I have wronged you, count. When we last parted, I thought you a vain egotist, who had requited the openness with which I laid my whole soul before you by simply turning your back upon me. I know now that you went to risk your life for my sake."

"Holy Virgin! what an idea!" said he. "You have not been at all unjust. I went away because I could no longer endure your presence. I had need of distraction from a great inward trouble; and, instead of hunting wild beasts, as formerly, I took to hunting robbers, out of pure dissipation. Besides, was it not my duty to pursue the murderer of my foster-brother?"

"Count, did you even guess, when you went away

to set your life against the life of that man, that he was Toniello's murderer? No; you have no talent for lying! You set out only for my sake, and you imperilled your life, only for something which you must then have regarded as one of my caprices. That was foolish—very foolish! But I thank you for it. I have wronged you, but I am glad that I have a wrong to confess, and that it is to *you* this confession is due."

"Allow me," interrupted the voice in the dark, "to tell you of Beppo; how he—"

"No; we will talk of all that by-and-by, when you are well again. For then you will come to see me at Naples, will you not?"

"Yes, I will come."

"Soon? How long will you be obliged to lead this life of darkness, my poor friend?"

"Oh, only a short time—a few days."

"But do you not find it very tedious? Are you well taken care of here? Who waits upon you?"

"The old Baldassare, my father's valet. He cannot reconcile himself to the change which time has made, and would like to carry me about in his arms as when we were children, Toniello and I—Toni on one arm, and I on the other. He spoils me, as a mother her baby. The butler, too, is an heirloom from my father, and so are the other servants. The old folks here have known me since I was a child. I am only too much spoiled by them all."

"So much the better! And now somebody else wishes to enter. *Mamma mia*, to whom you are greatly endeared, is waiting outside. Be kind to her, and make haste to get well again! *Addio, a pronto rivederci in Napoli!*"

While Signora Vico was sitting with the count, Paolina, in the adjacent saloon, leaned against the window, and gazed in a soft reverie upon the gay colors in which autumn had painted the vine-garlands hanging round the elms. While she was thus absorbed, a gentleman, conducted by Baldassare, entered the room, and at once began a conversation with her about the master of the house.

"It is a sad case," he said—"a very sad case!"

"What?" asked Paolina, startled.

"Well," said the stranger, "the loss of the one eye is a misfortune easily endured; for after a little while a man sees with one eye as well as with two. But, in the abnormally depressed condition of the patient, I greatly fear that he will also lose the other eye. There is a dangerous want of nervous energy and rallying power—"

Paolina had risen and approached the stranger.

"How?" she said, falteringly; "what do you mean? That one eye is lost?"

"Oh yes, the robber's bullet fortunately destroyed only one eye; but, my dear signora, the eyes are like the Siamese Twins—the one always participates in the suffering of the other. Add to this the count's profound dejection of spirits, which in turn affects the physical stamina. There is in the constitution, or, at least, in the disposition of the organs, no natural healthy resistance to the development of the mischief; for body and soul are also Siamese Twins."

Signora Vico came out, and the stranger was conducted by Baldassare to the count's room.

Paolina asked Signora Vico to wait a little before they left the house. She turned again to the window, and stared at the gay vine-garlands, but without seeing them. She thought of the half-blind man there, in the adjoining room—how cheerfully he had laughed, and how much he had concealed from her! An old saying, heard long ago in her childhood, was sounding again in her ears—

"Not everything laughs when it is glad, but neither does everything cry when it is hurt."

Baldassare came out of the room, and she asked after the name of the stranger.

It was a famous oculist from the capital, who had twice before been at the chateau for consultation with the local doctor. If any one could save the *padrone*, it was he.

Paolina cast a disdainful look at the door through which the famous oculist had disappeared, and the old bitter smile played about her mouth.

Then she had a long conference with Baldassare and the butler.

When the famous gentleman had departed, shrugging his shoulders, Baldassare guided the count out of the room where the physician had examined his eye back to his wonted seat on the sofa in the dark chamber.

But to-day the count sat down in the other corner of the sofa, where Paolina had sat before, and sent Baldassare away. He wished to be alone.

All was still in that room, and all was still outside. Nothing was audible to the sufferer, in the darkness where he sat alone, but the throbbing of his own pain in the sore eye-socket. Nothing, till suddenly a voice, a hand, and—oh, what a rushing welcome glowed in the darkness to that voice and hand! It was the voice of Amneris, the hand of Fenella. The voice which had taken possession of his whole being with its mysterious charm, the hand which could give such deep expression to the keys of the commonest piano!

And the song—ah, that was the dear old song that Maruccia used to sing in the days of their childhood to Toniello and to him—

> "Oh, were I slumbering deep
> In death's eternal night—"

But the song could go no further. At the feet of her who sung it lay a man, with his face buried in the folds of her dress, sobbing like a child.

She lifted her hand from the keys, and laid it soothingly on his head.

"Gaetano, these tears are injuring the other eye which Beppo has left you!"

"Paolina!"

"Hush! I now know all. Will you suffer yourself to become quite blind, and never see me again in this world? You used to like to look at Fenella, and now—"

"Ah, *now*, Paolina!"

"Yes, now," continued the sweet voice, calmly, "is it not just that she should help to while away the dark, tedious hours you endure only for her sake? You like music. I shall play and sing to you. Is it not natural that my eye should fill the place of yours, which suffers thus for me? Henceforth, therefore, it - is upon my arm that you will take your daily walk in this dark room. I shall read to you by a dark-lantern; *Mamma mia* and I have already settled ourselves in the other wing of your house. This is only simple justice. What do you find strange in it?"

Gaetano had risen.

"It is impossible, Paolina!" he exclaimed. "It would be the ruin of your reputation, and I cannot allow it. You must go away to-day—at once!"

"My reputation? Surely," she said, "you cannot seriously suppose that I care for such things? What is to me the opinion of the world?"

"You must carry out your engagement to the Opera. I shall never—"

"Signora Vico has already sent my resignation to the *Impresario.* Baldassare posted the letter just now. Child, have you any other objection to raise? Hush! give me your arm!"

And she led him back to the sofa-corner. Then she returned to the piano, feeling her way to it through the darkness, and sung to him all the national songs she knew.

Presently Signora Vico came in, and chatted away to him with such incessant volubility that at last she fairly sent him to sleep.

Not a single moment was Gaetano ever left alone. By night the old Baldassare remained with him, and by day one or other of the two ladies.

Signora Vico possessed the gift of indefatigable chatter. Paolina sung to him by degrees her whole Opera *repertoire*, or she read aloud for hours by the light of a lamp specially constructed for the occasion. With Dottore Corri, the count's physician, she never exchanged a word; but Signora Vico talked with him all the more, and many a disquieting remark escaped her before Paolina. Such remarks, however, could tell Paolina nothing about the contino which she had not observed for herself.

As for Gaetano, his days of tediousness were over. There were moments when he appeared even happy, but they were brief, and always followed by long hours of deep melancholy; and the inflammation of the eye increased more and more.

Once, when Paolina had ceased singing to him, and was sitting quite still, he imagined himself alone, and murmured,

"Always night! never more to see the light of day! And yet how easily could I bear it, were she always here!"

All at once he felt her hand upon his own, and that deep, sweet voice of hers answered him quietly,

"And why should she not be always here? If it makes you happy, Gaetano, I will always stay by you. I will even become your wife if you wish it."

Again he was sobbing at her feet, and again she laid her hand soothingly upon his head.

Then she left the room softly, and Gaetano remained alone with his new felicity.

Several days after this occurrence the famous oculist came again, and was agreeably astonished by the changed condition of his patient. The count laughed and jested, and seemed in irrepressibly high spirits.

The great man, after a careful examination, declared that his patient's room might at once be partially undarkened. The inflammation in the socket of the lost eye was already healed. The safety of the remaining eye was now assured; and if the admission of light were judiciously adjusted to the progress of its recovery, the cure would be completed in a few days.

"It is useless," he continued, "for me to come again; and in taking leave of you, count, I may now tell you that I had at first but very little hope of your case. You were threatened with entire blindness. By-the-bye, may I ask who was the interesting lady I met in your drawing-room on the occasion of my last visit?"

"My bride."

" Ah, I congratulate you, and—understand !"

"Understand what, dottore ?"

"Signor Conte, I understand what has banished the wretched dejection in which I found you some time ago. When I tell you that this greatly increased the inflammation, you, too, will understand who has been your real oculist. Not Dottore Corri —not I, but your bride. Remember me to my amiable colleague! I lay down my arms before her. Addio, conte !"

*　　*　　*　　*　　*　　*　　*

From the subdued light Gaetano was at last led out into the full daylight.

10

It had been his wish that Paolina should be his guide on that occasion. Her eyes must be the first sight that met his own.

In the quiet look of those eyes did he find what he sought?

He said nothing; but the ardent gaze with which his own solitary eye long searched their depths sunk slowly to the ground.

"It will come," he thought, "by-and-by!"

But it did not come—neither in the days of their betrothal, nor on the day of their wedding. Once only a warmer glow—warmer, but not with the warmth he longed for—kindled those sad blue eyes of hers: when she found among the wedding-gifts the deed he had completed in her name for the purchase of the forest valley of Oberau. Silently she pressed Gaetano's hand in gratitude for that gift.

The wedding was celebrated, according to her wish, in private and with great simplicity. Their honey-moon was passed in visiting the various chateaus and villas belonging to the count's extensive property. Paolina had no wish either to travel or to go into the world; and it was in compliance with her request that Gaetano now undertook the personal management of his large estates. By degrees he found an interest in the occupation.

All the while Paolina would sit at home playing on the piano, singing, reading, or listening to the chatter of Signora Vico, whose husband was now, through Gaetano's recommendation and help, at the head of a great enterprise. Or else, she walked alone under the elms, and watched the horizon with her old listless look. Every evening when Gaetano came home her eyes greeted him with the same soft but indifferent tranquillity; yet every morning he went out to his business, hoping for a change which never came in those quiet eyes. Her demeanor towards him was always that of a tenderly devoted sister.

He sought to surround her so completely with the evidence of his love that at every step she must notice something he had done for her. And how difficult it was to know what he could do to please her! She never asked for anything, and ever since her wedding-day she had been very sparing of words. But Gaetano was learning to spell out her face as a child spells out its lesson-book; and by degrees his love was able to read and understand the thoughts working behind her smooth white brow, as clearly as if it were made of glass.

Thus he read there, distinctly, the reasons why she became his wife. It had not been from love, but from the wish to redress an injustice unconsciously done to the man who had risked his life for her. And she remained kind and good to him, because that also was an obligation of justice.

So long as his illness and helplessness had claimed her constant personal help, and filled her hours with fatiguing tasks, a warmer stream of blood had seemed to run through her body, and a brighter light to gleam in her soul; but it was only as if she again were standing on the stage, and animating some ideal image with a life not given to her own habitual self. And again, as of old, he, the spectator of her performance, had mistaken the ideal image for the living woman. The motive power of the whole performance was only a strong, clear, coldly clear, impulse of justice. And now that he was well again, and could see with one eye as well as formerly with two, her task was finished, and justice satisfied.

The eyes in which Gaetano read his dreary lesson were not those of Fenella or Amneris. They were the tranquil, indifferent eyes with which the great *Diva* used to look down upon the passionately agitated public when she had finished her part.

He said nothing about it; but all night long he lay awake, silently invoking from Heaven some star-beam to rekindle in Paolina's eyes the light that was gone out of them; and all day long he wandered about, searching a wild world of troubled thoughts for something to recall to Paolina's lips the smile that seemed fled from them forever.

And he searched in vain !

Eye and lip retained their cold tranquillity. Yea, there even came a time when the woman he adored avoided him more and more, as if the sight of him afflicted her.

He suffered silently, and bore his torment without showing it. He even rode away to the farthest farms upon his property, and remained absent for days together, perceiving that his presence distressed her. It was as if he had done her an injury of which she was too proud to complain.

Then came days more anxious still, and full of torment, each one of them a horrible eternity, when Paolina was lying ill and would not see him.

Nor was even the Dottore Corri permitted to approach her. By her orders the doctor was refused admittance to the house. Signora Vico was her sole companion.

At last, one day, Mamma Vico smilingly called her Contino into Paolina's room.

This is a strange surprise to him, for he has not seen a smile for many a long day upon any face in the whole house.

He enters softly. Paolina's face looks like a faint white rose; but glowing like a little red rose, and fast asleep in its cradle beside her, is her baby. Gaetano stands still, between the bed and the cradle. He is quite upset, and does not venture to look across to Paolina, fearing to aggravate her recent aversion to him. He is grateful that she allows him to stay near her, and to look at the child. Only, as often as he thinks she does not notice it, he glances towards her bed; and when she closes her eyes, he hovers round it in distant circles. Her eyes remain shut; so, ever and anon, he looks at her from afar; then he steals hesitatingly forward on tiptoe, and looks passionately upon her, a little nearer, and ever nearer still. There are the beautiful long golden tresses floating loose over the white pillow! Long and adoringly he gazes on them; then, stooping low, he kisses them cautiously—*that* cannot awake her!

But she opens her eyes, over which the lids had fallen only from exhaustion, and smiles at him.

There is a melancholy, but sweet, softness in this smile.

He only says, "Paolina!" and goes out quickly. She lets him go, and does not call him back.

She has noticed how tenderly his voice trembled in that fervent utterance of her name, and that the tears were standing in his eyes; and half closing her own, she looks again upon the cradle. A strange rosy flush rises, slowly suffusing the mother's pale face, and mingles with the smile about her lips. Her blue eyes open suddenly, large and wide; and in them is glowing a celestial splendor. It seems to have streamed into them from the cradle on which they are gazing, and they are filled with the tender radiance of it.

This is the star-beam which Gaetano, in his sleepless nights, had invoked from heaven.

The child there in the cradle has brought it down with him. And the celestial splendor glows in Paolina's eyes every time that she looks upon her child.

Once Gaetano was blessed with a gleam of it for himself.

That was when, returning from the baptism, he put the child into her arms. She had left to him the choice of the infant's name.

"What is thy name, little one?" she asked the baby when it was brought back to her. But the baby did not seem to appreciate the new dignity conferred on him, and he only cried lustily.

Then Gaetano said, smiling, "Don't you understand, Paolina, that he is trying to say to you, 'My name is Toniello?'"

In spite of the cheerful tone, and in spite of the smile with which he said it, his voice trembled.

Paolina stretched her hand to him, and clasped his own.

She said nothing, but her husband saw the star-beam from her eyes, resting, this time, on himself.

The little Toniello was the incarnation of injustice.

He seemed to think that the whole world was made to wait upon him, and that the universe existed only for the reception of his commands, and the prompt satisfaction of all his wishes. He cried, at first, for the mere sake of crying; he cried, afterwards, for nourishment; and then he cried for Heaven only knows how many different and incredible reasons. The capacity of noise contained in that little lump of rosy flesh was inexhaustible. Whenever the poor mother fell into one of her habitual reveries, and began to think of old days and events, her little tyrant immediately set up an intolerable howl. By night his shrill small voice left her no sleep, and by day it vouchsafed her no repose. For her the daily reverie, the nightly dream, was over.

All this was exceedingly unjust.

But she hugged the incarnate injustice to her bosom, and refused to part with it by day or night. She said cheerfully that no one but herself could understand the child's cries, and that the short intervals of broken sleep, which were all those cries allowed her, were the most refreshing she had ever had, because so sound and dreamless.

Toniello already possessed a remarkable power of making his will respected. He disdainfully rejected his nourishment when it was given to him, and roared for it all the more vehemently the next moment. He insisted on having light about him when it was dark, and *vice versâ*. He was intolerably querulous till his cradle was rocked, and then he was not to be pacified till they made it stand still. In the shortest possible time, and with the greatest possible ease, this baby had reduced to abject subjection his father, Signora Vico, and the old Baldassare. They became his slaves, but the infatuated mother had been, from the very outset, the unresisting instrument of his capricious despotism.

That was unjust.

Yet although the innumerable whims and insatiable exactions of her little tyrant left the poor woman no time to breathe, they were all welcomed and extolled by her with the liveliest satisfaction, as singularly promising indications of a resolute and manly character. She was proud of her slavery. It was one of Toniello's amusements to thrust his little fingers into his mother's eyes, which gleamed with grateful pleasure while they winced and watered under the operation. He also took a special and ferocious delight in pulling her golden tresses, and trying to tug them out.

This also was unjust.

But his patient victim wiped the tears from her eyes and smiled when the tiny tormentor had got a good handful of her beautiful hair plucked out in his little clinched fist; for then it was evident to her that her boy was thoroughly enjoying himself.

Nor was it less than a gross injustice that Toniello, in spite of his poor mother's increasing tenderness and boundless devotion, greatly preferred being in the arms of his father; that the father's harsh beard pleased him better than the mother's soft hair; that he crowĕd louder on the father's knee than in the mother's lap, and liked no plaything half as well as the paternal forefinger.

But the poor mother only smiled, and said nothing.

And so in this way the injustice went on. Ay, and in many other ways too!

A path stretched straight from her present life to the earliest childhood of this woman. It was the Path of Justice; but of that severe Justice that walks with bandaged eyes, into which compassion may never steal, lest the hand of the executioner tremble, and the sword of judgment falter as it falls. Narrow as the sword's edge is the path; and thus far, the woman had walked it without staggering, without stumbling, without looking to the right or to the left; strict in love as in hatred—an eye for an eye, and a tooth for a tooth! Now, however, had come a day when Injustice clothed itself in flesh and blood and became a child—her own! With its little hands, that baby has softly diverted her from the narrow path, and even without her knowing it!

Whither the child leads her now, thither had a graybeard once pointed out the way to her.

"*All is for the best, only one must find it out,*" the old man had told her.

She did not understand him then, did not find the way he spoke of; but now she follows the child step by step, further and further, far beyond the old man's purpose; for even there, where she finds nothing good, she believes all just.

In this process, the incarnate injustice thrives bravely, and grows apace.

Its first experiments on human speech are but awkward stammerings of its little tongue. The stammerings are utterly senseless, but the mother detects in them a rare precocity of thought. They are not melodious, but the great singer thinks that the most sublime masters of music have never composed or conceived anything so enchanting.

The little creature's first articulate word is not "Mamma," but "Papa." And the mother says,

"Of course! how intelligent! 'Papa' is so much easier to pronounce!"

The woman who had been so sparing of words ever since her wedding-day, and indeed throughout her whole childhood, now chatters all day long. Toniello wishes it; and words must come, even when ideas fail.

The child wants to know the name of this and that, in such a hurry! He insists on knowing at once what the people are doing down there in the garden.

"They are weeding," says the mother.

"Weeding," he repeats, with a grave face. Suddenly he laughs aloud, and repeats the word ever so many times—"Weeding! weeding! weeding!"

The sound is the main point with him; he enjoys the word, he does not trouble himself about the idea. What "weeding" is, concerns him not, but so is it called; and the word sounds well.

The mother never gets tired of producing for him all day long such wonderful artificial sounds. One day the little tyrant makes the discovery that the singing of his mamma is no bad thing. And so she sings to him; not at the piano, not from notes, not what she sung on the stage, not what the great masters have taught her, not words at all! She sings as she sung in the days gone by, when she herself was a child; as she sung in her girlhood, to herself, unheard in the lonely forest. A song without words, that rises in her heart from the long-silenced depths of far-distant years, sweet, solemn, mysterious, sounding like the flutter of the birds, and the breathing of the wind, in the forest branches.

Gaetano leans, in the adjoining room, against the door, and listens.

The phantom has come to life, he thinks, the empty spirit has found a joy to fill it, and the aimless days a purpose. But it is not *his* heart's blood that has given life to the phantom, or joy to the life restored. One Toniello took it away, another has given it back. Between the two, he stands aside—forgotten!

And there, in the outer room, unseen, unmissed—out of sight, out of mind—alone, he stands; listening wildly, heart-brokenly, to that strange, wonderful song — a song which is no longer the product of skill, but a spontaneous utterance of pure emotion. It is the song of which she told him once—ah, how vividly her words came back to him as he listened to it now!

"There was a time when I sung true song, though without words; a time when my own thoughts were like harp-strings, and my heart a lute upon which all things played."

In those days she sung that song for Toniello;
and now again it is to Toniello that she sings it.
Between the two Toniellos, where may Gaetano
stand? — aside, unwanted, unnoticed! His place
knows him not.

In that moment the living man envied the dead.

Suddenly he started up, shuddering, rushed out of
the house, leaped on to his horse, and rode fierce and
fast—away, no matter where!

He was afraid of himself. He felt for a moment
something like jealousy of his own child.

Had the Dark Angel, who hovers forever over all
that lives, looked, in that moment, into Gaetano's
heart? For he suddenly folded his sombre wings,
and settled down by the tiny cot of the little Toniello.

Softly that angel touches with his cold finger the
restless children of earth; but beneath its touch the
stricken ones struggle painfully for breath, the throat
rattles, the limbs stiffen, the fluttering life departs.
Sometimes, however, the angel falls asleep, weary of
his endless work, which ceases not by night or day;
and then, with relaxing touch, the cold finger slips
from the little throat, and the child breathes again.

Over the cot of the little Toniello stoops the Angel of Destruction.

The feathers of the angel's wings are compressed
sharply into the form of a scythe. His unseen arm
is stretched over the cot, his unseen eyes are fixed
upon the child, and his unseen finger has touched
the little forehead. There, unflitting, day and night,
sits the Dark Angel. Doth he drowse and slum-

ber? doth he wake and watch? Is he weary of his work, or only patient—that he sits there so long, never flitting? Who knows?

The physicians, summoned by Gaetano, are unable to read those unseen eyes. They know of no potion to lull that angel into slumber, and it is not in human power to relax his stiffening finger.

The mother utters not a word to these men; she knows that they are powerless. Nor does she breathe one prayer to God, nor lean her aching head upon her husband's breast.

She stands at the feet of her child, and stares at the Destroying Angel, who waits at the child's head —never flitting.

Help is nowhere to be found, either on earth or in heaven; she does not even think of seeking it. She only longs wildly, impotently, to breathe her own breath into the child's suffocating throat, to offer her own throat to the unseen strangling finger, and ransom with her own life the life of her little darling.

Thus the angel and the mother stand, night and day, staring at each other across the body of the child—he at the head, she at the feet.

To and fro between them, Gaetano wanders restlessly.

The man who had suffered in silence the most poignant grief, who had braved the most pestilential climates, and endured the most violent exertions, is now completely broken down.

Three physicians have passed the night in the chateau. They watch. Gaetano talks with them falteringly, confusedly. He casts a long look upon his child, then upon his wife, and creeps away, staggering like a drunken man.

Slowly, the shadow of night wanders across the earth. Loiteringly, the dawn approaches. The morning glow begins to glimmer, casting a pale-red gleam into Gaetano's chamber.

At last the first sunbeam glitters through the window-pane, and falls on the golden hair of Paolina, who has entered softly, as silent as the beam itself.

Gaetano kneels at the *prie-dieu*, his head buried in his hands, and sobs aloud. He feels that all is over.

Paolina steals up to him, and softly strokes his arm—for the first time—as she used to stroke the arm of her father when she was a child, and Toniello's in the days of her girlhood's brief happiness.

"Gaetano!" she says, in a low voice, almost a whisper.

Gaetano springs up with a ravaged face. His feverish eyes peruse the features of his wife.

Paolina is weeping—for the first time.

Till now, he has never seen her shed tears. He knows that these are the first she has shed since her childhood.

"Dead, dead!" he thinks, shuddering.

But through Paolina's tears a sunny smile steals out.

"Gaetano," she says, "our child lives. He is saved!"

And with a wild, joyful cry from the depths of a frozen ocean suddenly thawed, she flings herself upon her husband's breast, throws her arms about his neck, and weeps aloud.

All the long woe of her desolate soul, all the restrained tears of a life-long suffering, she is weeping out on that true heart, which has become so dear to her.

He knows it when he gently lifts up her head and looks into her eyes. He has no need to ask it, but yet she tells him,

"I love you, Gaetano! I love you very dearly and deeply, only I did not know it."

And then her hand glides again, caressingly, across his arm.

"Go, now," she murmurs, "to our child, Gaetano! Embrace for me the good Dottore Corri, as well as the other physician. I will follow you, but let me linger here a moment. I wish first to pray, Gaetano —to pray to your God!"

He looses his embrace, and goes to the rescued child.

Above the *prie-dieu* hangs the dumb God upon the cross, mute and sad.

The sunbeam falls upon the stooping face of the dumb God and on the upturned forehead of the woman, whose hands are stretched out to Him in prayer. The blood-drops on the brow of the divine image glow like kingly rubies, and the tear-drops falling from the woman's eyes shine pure as orient pearls in the beam that has kindled both.

And around those two silent figures the dawn grows slowly brighter.

NOTRE DAME DES FLOTS.

NOTRE DAME DES FLOTS.

CHAPTER I.

To the west of the seaport town of Havre, a huge heap of earth rises out of the English Channel. This is Cap la Hève. Like a gloomy side-scene darkening the lighted stage of some great theatre, it juts out, stretched in the daytime along the wide gleaming sea, and in the evening across the setting sun. The dark outlines of a church pierce the bright clouds above the promontory ; and the slender spire of the church, fine and sharp as a needle, is distinctly visible, not only from Havre itself, and the Côte de Grace, whose low mountain-range cuts the horizon beyond the estuary of the Seine, but also far out at sea.

In that church is the shrine of Our Dear Lady of the Waters, the patroness of ships and the mariners, *La Dame des Flots.*

The apse behind the altar of the little church has been closed in, up to a level with the top of the side-wall, leaving open above it the recess of the pointed arch ; through which, far in the background, and almost as if hovering close under the parti-colored cross-beams of the vault, gleams the image of Our Lady, with the Infant in her arms.

Inaccessible from the recess of the choir, unapproachably receding in the misty spaces of that lofty vault, and far withdrawn from human touch, the holy effigy, as there it hangs on high, awakens an awful veneration. But the forehead that gleams so pale under that black hair, that painfully puckered mouth, that head so sorrowfully bowed, with the far-off look in the eyes of it, that seem to be watching all the shipwrecks on all the oceans of the world— these aspects of the sublime image bring it down in sympathy so close to each sad heart, and make it seem so human, that one fancies one must have somewhere seen that face before among the restlessly wandering and secretly suffering race of men.

What Pallas Athene, enthroned on the Acropolis, once was to the Greek sailor, is Our Lady of the Waters now to those who plough the seas—a light far shining through the darkness of the storm and the perils of the deep.

> "Étoile du matin, Notre Dame des Flots,
> Tu reçois tous les veux des pauvres matelots.
> De ton temple sacré, vu du loin sur les eaux,
> Délivre du peril, et marins et vaisseaux!"*

This prayer is inscribed on one of the memorial tablets which, closely crowded together, cover the surrounding walls. Most of these tablets are repre-

---

* Our Lady of the Waters! Morning star
Of us poor shipmen! from thy shrine afar,
Fair o'er the rolling waters shine, and save
The shipman and his ship from wind and wave!

sentations of ships ; from great three-masted vessels, carved in ivory, to little fishing-smacks, rudely drawn, but sometimes touching in the artlessness of the inscription under them. As, for instance—

"Petit travail, sans aucun talent, d'un mousse, offert à Notre Dame des Flots, par reconnaissance."

Or pathetic in their laconic simplicity, like the following—

"J'ai prié, et j'ai été exaucé."

And thus they rise one above the other, up to the vaulted roof. Here and there among them is the bridal-crown of some fisherman's wife, offered in homage to Our Lady. And thick about the Guardian Image leaned the last props of the poor fishermen, whole bundles of crutches, ripe harvest-sheaves, which Death has reaped.

Among these votive offerings hangs a poor wooden frame with a glass cover, wherein are placed two long tresses of thickly plaited hair. The woman to whom they once belonged must have bent her head under the burden of their bright abundance ; and when she loosed and combed them out, they must have covered her whole body as with a flowing garment. These tresses have the color of ripe corn ; and if a sunbeam glides across them, they gleam like dead gold. Nothing else is in the little casket. The wooden frame bears no name, nor does the narrow space of the wall above contain any inscription or dedication. It is a touchingly shy gift to Our Dear Lady—a gift silent and faint-hearted, yet withal so splendid that a queen could not have offered to that shrine a richer tribute.

And pathetic as the gift is the story of it, which by those who will may here be read. If to thee, reader, it seem a tale too full of woe, recall whatever thine own heart hath suffered; and in that peace of resignation which succeeds to griefs outlived, bethink thee how sorrow helps to bind together the whole human race, like a high and holy doctrine delivered unto all. But if, when thus thou lookest into the depths of thy heart, what thou seest there is only the still, clear splendor seen by the fisherman in the depths of the windless waters when the sea is calm, then lay aside this tale. For then, to myself alone shall I have told it now again, as often heretofore, when I stood within the little church upon the windy cape, looking at those golden tresses through the black frame of their wordless casket, and listening to the long low roar of the waters beneath.

*   *   *   *   *   *   *

In Normandy, not far from Louviers, was once situated a small country-seat closely secluded from the outer world. The park was bounded on one side by the winding waters of the Eure, and on the other by a waving line of low mountains. If, turning from the banks of the Eure, you followed the main avenue of the park, the dark foliage of its tall old trees gradually subsided as you advanced into the lighter tints of a lower and more scattered woodland. This in turn gave way to graceful groups of young trees and shrubs, and finally you would find yourself in a large old flower-garden. From the midst of the flower-garden, and in striking contrast to the gay colors of the ephemeral blossoms whose breath was sweet upon the air around it, rose a gloomy remnant of past ages —a rigid mass of ancient stone, gray and stern, with steep roofs and heavily walled towers.

In the right wing of this building, which was the only inhabited part of it, lived an old widowed lady —by name, Madame de Mersay. Her estate, which she managed herself, was not of wide extent. Had she ever found time, in the restless activity of her daily occupations, to look out of her bay-window, she might with those keen eyes of hers have overlooked it all. To the right, beyond the park walls, were farm buildings and a pasture-ground; straight in front a sweep of field and meadow, stretching to the foot of the low mountain - range; and to the left, the last skirt of the forest, which at that point joined the mountain-line.

This was all that Monsieur de Mersay had left to his widow; and it was exactly as much as he himself had inherited from his father.

A stiff Legitimist, firmly insisting upon the hereditary position of his family, he stood out into the latter half of the nineteenth century, like his own castle, an uncompromising anachronism, stern, but venerable. Acting with none of the new political parties, circumstances had withdrawn him from contact with the gentry of his own opinion; and it was only now and then that he ever had occasion to notice, with a wondering shake of the head, how these also were going with the altered current of the time. That was when he chanced to look at a newspaper (a chance that happened rarely), and found there in strange company the proudest names of the *anicen régime*. He could not comprehend what induced the owners of these noble names to allow penny-a-liners to inform all sorts of persons, whom the information in nowise concerned, that they had given an evening party, that they had been at the races, or had gone to Baden-Baden, or had appeared in the Bois de Boulogne with a new equipage. He could not understand why, instead of maintaining their honor with the point of their swords, they stooped to appear before the public tribunals in the undignified positions of plaintiffs and defendants; nor why, whenever they gave alms, an act so natural, and so essentially private, should be announced in francs and centimes by all the journals.

If, in one of these journals, Monsieur de Mersay chanced to find an old Legitimist name at the head of an industrial enterprise, he blushed crimson, and tore the newspaper deliberately into little bits. The world in which such things were possible was to him an unintelligible world. His ideas about this world he had learned from his father, and his ideas about the next from an old abbé. That was the sum total of his knowledge; and all that it had taught him was to preserve the escutcheon of his house unstained by the rank breath of the swarming vulgarities he shunned. His life was passed in retirement, and in doing what was right and good—the right noiselessly, the good secretly.

Thus living and acting, he had never added an acre to his patrimony, notwithstanding his incessant activity.

Daily, at early dawn, the old gentleman's giant figure might be seen moving across the misty fields, mounted on his gray Norman horse; and wherever his large hawk-nose appeared, the laborers set to work with the utmost ardor. He was a benevolent master, for he understood the orders he gave, and could himself lend a hand to the work if it were wanted. Moreover, he had the strength of two strong men, and if a wheel stuck in the furrow or the ditch, he could draw it out with one jerk of his powerful hand.

Never did the most vehement exertions of this sort set his face glowing half as red as it grew on one occasion, when Monsieur Chauvel, a manufacturer from Louviers, pointed out to him that, although his farm was situated in the centre of the most flourishing industrial districts, he was making nothing of it, in spite of the care and labor he devoted to it.

Chauvel proved to him, by an array of unanswerable figures, that a large percentage of his income was annually carried to waste by the waters of the Eure, and how their motive power might be turned to better account by a judicious application of industrial capital. To which the old gentleman replied,

"You and I, Monsieur Chauvel, can no more do the same things than we can bear the same name."

Madame de Mersay had grown up among the same antiquated views and traditions, in a chateau of Brittany, even lonelier and more isolated than that of her husband.

In her own departments of daily duty—the house, the poultry-yard, the orchard, and the fruit-garden—

her activity was not surpassed by his. The only moment when she sat still was in the morning, over her chocolate. It was then that she planned out her day's work; and it augured no lucky day if the spoon with the crest of the Mersays did not stand upright in the chocolate, thickened with rice-flour. At all other times the green ribbons of the old lady's cap were to be seen twinkling, under her cheerful, kindly face, all about the house and its precincts, where their apparition had the same influence on the maid-servants as the mighty hawk-nose of her husband on the men.

When Monsieur de Mersay died, of a fall from his horse, his widow redoubled her activity, and took into her own hands the principal direction of the farm, leaving only to an old head-servant of the property the detailed execution of her instructions.

All was as before, except that the old lady's cap-ribbons twinkled, not only about the house, but also about the fields; and that they no longer displayed the favorite color of Monsieur de Mersay, the bright green of his family arms, but were now black—a color which they never changed again. It was, however, a color that suited her face much better; for the face, too, had lost its lively hues since Mersay's death. Her dependants scarcely noticed this change in their daily and hourly intercourse with her, and only felt concerned about their mistress when the morning chocolate remained untasted, even though the spoon stood upright in it. Her activity was never relaxed, and in the example of her late husband was the main-spring that kept it going.

That example, indeed, she followed in all things, with unselfish disregard of her own interests.

Monsieur Chauvel came from Louviers on a visit of condolence to her; he was willing to buy at a high price the property which her husband had left her.

"Allow me, madam," said he, "in consideration of the friendly relations which have so long subsisted between your family and myself, to relieve you of a burden which I fear you will find it impossible to support under conditions that would severely tax all the strength and energy of a man. Moreover, you are so happy as to possess in Mademoiselle de Mersay a daughter already old enough to take her natural place in the *Grand Monde*, where her personal attractions cannot fail to command the consideration to which she is entitled by her birth and rank. Pardon my frankness. Monsieur de Mersay was so good as to honor me with his confidence in financial and other matters, and I have therefore deemed it a sacred obligation to speak to you on this subject with the unreserve of an old man, whose white hairs may, I trust, sufficiently excuse the freedom of his speech."

"I thank you, Monsieur Chauvel," replied the widow; "but pray be good enough to tell me, with the same frankness, whether you are under the impression that Monsieur de Mersay would have sold his estate, merely to introduce his daughter into the *Grand Monde?*"

"No, madam, I cannot say that."

"Then, if you please, we will not speak of it any more, sir."

Mademoiselle de Mersay, the subject of this conversation, was fair, slender, and delicate as the seraph in the old picture of the Madonna that hung above her bed. Kind-hearted she was, as the sun, to every living creature; and dreamy, as the moon, at which she was so fond of gazing with her large blue eyes —eyes that gleamed under clusters of bright curls, like two little bits of blue heaven peeping through a mass of golden cloudlets.

When this young lady wanders, in the morning, about the flower - garden of the old chateau, those golden curls hang loosely undulating down to the skirt of her dress, like waves of ripe corn rippled by the breeze; and the blue eyes glow between them, like large corn-flowers half hidden by the waving wheat. She stops and pauses over every blossom which has opened during the night, as if putting to it some question, which the blossom answers, as best it can, with its sweet odor. Above her, thousands of little leaves are whispering on the trees; beneath her, thousands of little ripples lisp and laugh along the river; around her, is the multitudinous murmur of the morning bees, and the humming of tiny wings that sparkle in the sun; and from the bushes and the hedges, the branches and the ivied eaves, sweetly tremble innumerable bird-notes.

When she pauses here and there, she stands intently listening to all these sounds, and trying hard to guess what they are saying to her. But she cannot understand it.

Then she thinks of her Uncle Godefroy; and of his sayings, and his books; wherein she learned how unspeakably large the world is, and how full of sounds, because of the millions of human beings in it, laughing and weeping, shouting and sobbing — and she herself, how lost in the midst of them all, not understanding any of their sounds!

In herself all is so still! She neither laughs nor weeps.

And all at once this thought so pains her that it takes away her breath; and she lays her hand anxiously upon her bosom.

There—she listens, standing quite still—there, she feels something beating, distinct, loud, quick, impetuous. Longer and longer she listens, and ponders. Then she begins to smile softly. She has found it at last—the sound which she also has within her, like all else around her, and the wide world itself. A poor, monotonous sound only, but it pleases her.

She has still, however, to discover what it means, and long she presses her hand against her heart. But she cannot make it out.

The meaning escapes her, like that of all the other sounds. Within her, as without, look and listen as she may, the only answer returned to her question is the echo of the question itself. But within her there is something which she cannot tell in words. It is like a shoreless sea; and floating up from the deeps of it come blossoming islands with strange flowers, such as she has never seen before, and forms that have no likeness upon earth, and melodies wondrous sweet.

Often, sitting alone in her own little room, she has sought to fix these images, not in words, but in lines and colors; but ever they floated softly away, and her fingers could not follow their fading outlines, nor her pencil find any color as warm and bright and vivid as theirs. And many an evening, alone in the ivy-arbor, she has tried timidly to sing those strange melodies; but they also changed in the song that glided from her lips, and were no longer the same.

It is evening; and a little bird has begun to sing in the rose-bush beside the arbor. The bird sings all alone. Everything is suddenly silent. The other birds, the rustling of the leaves, the murmuring of the waters—all the unintelligible sounds, the incomprehensible harmonies, without her as within — are hushed around that little bird. Is it, she wonders, that they all are listening to his song, or that he sings so loud no other voice is audible?

Yes, that is the nightingale! How sweet, and yet withal how woful, is his song—sobs and exultations, pangs and raptures, lamentations and delights, all together!

Meanwhile, the moon swims slowly up into the sky, across the dark tree-tops; and far away the land glimmers in a bluish light, like a still, soft, boundless sea, wherefrom emerge dim images, dubious and full of mystery.

And she listens, and looks, and dreams. Then she goes slowly home, and kneeling before the picture of the Madonna, dreams of Heaven. At last, nothing is awake in the little room but the moon, whose rays glide softly across the floor to the feet of the slumbering maiden. But around the maiden's head hover heavenly visions, that graciously mingle with the dreams of earth and of her own beating heart.

Blanche de Mersay had neither brother nor sister, nor playfellow of any sort. The neighboring town of Louviers was only visited for Divine Service on special holydays; and there, also, she had no intimate acquaintances. How pleasant the town looked, though, with its many gardens lying fair in the river-valley of the Eure! Its factories were partially hidden behind high green trees; buildings of great antiquity surmounted the little new houses of its manufacturing population, and the venerable Gothic cathedral towered high above a range of chimneys.

The priest of the neighboring village taught Blanche all that he himself had learned in his youth; or, at least, so much of it as he had not forgotten in the after-years of his long life. She asked him at first much more than he could answer, and many things which he had never even thought of before. The good man went home in a more and more meditative mood each time he came to the chateau.

Monsieur de Mersay would sometimes shake his head, and knit his bushy eyebrows above his hawk-nose, while listening to the chatter of his child. He took her on his knee, and passed his hand over her forehead, as if to wipe away something. The child felt, sensibly enough, the roughness of that hard, laborious old hand; but the hand was not sensible of what was behind the fine white wall it brushed so hard.

For Madame de Mersay, a rose was always a rose, and nothing but a rose. Its odor could suggest to her no idea of anything else. To her eyes, the lily was the only flower that signified something; for it belonged to the arms of the De Mersay family. Neither of the child's parents understood her; and knowing no name for something in her which was not in themselves, they said,

"Blanche has taken after Godefroy."

Godefroy was the name of Monsieur de Mersay's younger brother. He had once wandered far away over the world, because his home had become too narrow for him; and he returned, years afterwards, because the world had become too wide for him. Weary and broken-hearted, he came home only to die there, slowly; as the stricken deer trails itself with limping foot out of the light into the dark thicket.

Like Blanche, he, too, used often to pause suddenly, and linger long, as he wandered about the little garden of the old chateau, listening to some distant sound, or poring over some folded blossom, as if his gaze would burst it open; or he would stand for long hours together on the banks of the Eure, gazing at the fleeting current, or watching the slow rising of the moon.

In the house he was habitually silent, and spoke only when alone with Blanche. She did not quite understand his talk, but she liked to listen to it, because his voice sounded so gentle and kind; and when he passed his hand over her hair and brow, it was not as when her father did it. The uncle's hand was so soft and tender, that its touch always sent a faint thrill through her. At other times he would sit bending over one or other of the many books he had brought home with him, and thrusting back, from time to time, with wasted fingers, his long black hair that drooped over the page. Blanche sat beside him, and noticed that, when thus thrust backward from his temples, the roots of the long black hair were snowy-white. Sometimes she noticed also that he could smile; but it was only when he coughed and put his hand convulsively to his chest.

He showed her the pictures painted in his books; they were bright with gold and rich colors. By-and-by he taught her to read the books, which were written in an old tongue, spoken ages ago in France; and she read in them of kings, and knights, and noble dames, and charcoal-burners, and valorous deeds, and wicked witchcraft. When her uncle rose from his books, tossed back his long black hair, and stood gazing out of the window at the wan, rolling clouds, she thought he was himself like one of the knights in those old books, who had gone forth in search of distant adventures, and come home mortally wounded. And she liked him all the better for it. She could not yet understand how much she loved him.

One evening Uncle Godefroy died, with his hand on his breast, and a smile on his lips.

But Godefroy's knights continued to live on in her soul—fair and dauntless, as they rode forth in the morning twilight, with their waving locks under their plumed helmets, and their glowing hearts under their white armor, to conquer the heathen, and slay the dragon, and free noble ladies from wicked

12

spells. And, because she had no other companion, she related all their glorious exploits to her dog Lyon.

Uncle Godefroy had bequeathed to her this dog, which he had once saved from being drowned.

Lyon was a big, rough, shepherd's dog, and not at all pretty; but he had such true eyes! with which he looked up at her, never moving, while she sat under a tree in the park and told him all the wonders of the olden time. When she stopped talking to him, having come to the end of her tale, he lifted up his paw and softly touched her knee with it. By this gesture Lyon implied that she might go on speaking—he was all attention. But for the present she had no more to say, having told him all she knew. So many a time would she steal away into the corridor, where the pictures of her ancestors hung along the walls, and thoughtfully study those pictures till she had invented a story for every knight, adding every day some new adventure to his strange quest; or else she fetched one of her late uncle's books which she had not yet read, and sat with it, as still as a little mouse, in any corner of the old chateau where nobody was likely to interrupt her.

In this way she always found new matter for Lyon's instruction. But she was sorry that the old knights were now nowhere to be seen, except in their pictures. She would have liked to be tormented by an old magician, that some brave young knight might come and deliver her just in time to save her life. They had quite disappeared, however, these knights of old. Blanche had found that out, when she went with her parents to Louviers, and saw the gentry there entering the church.

Even the people of quality, even the rich manufacturers—they were none of them knights-errant, nor did they look at all knightly. It was not the coat, nor the high black hat which everybody held in his hand—she could not tell what it was, but she felt it distinctly, that none of them would go forth in search of noble adventures.

Yet, the world is so large — somewhere about it, she thought, such men must still be living; and among them, perhaps, one who would undertake great things for her sake. She knew exactly how he looked, that one in a thousand. She had described him in every detail to Lyon, so that her faithful dog should not bark at him when he came. Lyon would not have done that, however, for, from her description of him, the knight must have looked exactly like Lyon's beloved benefactor and late master, Godefroy de Mersay.

She liked also to look over the garden wall, now and then, and listen, where along the woodland might she not, some day, hear the neigh of a prancing steed approaching the chateau? or from the outskirts of the park to watch if, down the winding waters of the Eure, there came no mystic bark with a purple banderole and a golden prow.

And so the years went by, and the child became a young woman.

But still her lonely path was through the dreamland of her maiden fancies, wherein she had created for herself a world of her own, a world known only to herself. And with all the scenes and images of that strange world the tender brightness of her own fair soul was interwoven, like the silver clew that winds among the glowing depths of a fairy labyrinth.

The lingering winter imperceptibly subsided into the spring. The first rose-bud had burst open on the bush, and the nightingale began to sing, where between the branches of the trees the moon was peeping.

Blanche sat in the arbor and listened, motionless, to the bird.

She thought of the king's daughter who was changed, by a lame old witch, into a flower. But soft-hearted little wood-goblins crept out of the mosses, and clambered down from every rifted tree to comfort the king's daughter. And some of them played to her sweet tunes on blades of trembling grass till their puffed cheeks were glowing, and their little hearts nearly bursting with the effort, while others danced round her in graceful circles. So the goblin dance and minstrelsy went on, till the prince came riding through the forest; and, lured nearer and nearer by the sweet sounds that hovered round it, beheld the enchanted flower; and plucked it, and breathed it open with his warm breath, and touched it with his lips; and the spell was broken.

And Blanche thought that the enchanted flower must have been just like the rose upon the bush beside her.

For the little bird never left that flower, but sung to it, like the goblin minstrels in the fairy tale, so sweetly and sadly, that it seemed as if his little heart must burst with the fulness of its emotion.

But how, she thought, did the other wood-sprites dance round the enchanted flower?

And softly she rose on tiptoe, and began to dance in the moonlight round the rose-bush, to the music of the nightingale.

The moonlight illuminated all her fairy figure, flowed from her glittering tresses to her twinkling feet, and spread a silver carpet on the grass they tripped. And elfin as the image was the movement of the dancing girl; a soft, unearthly wavering of the flower-like form; from throat to ankle a bounteous pulsation of the slender, supple limbs; a mysterious budding and blossoming of beautiful emotions, revealed only to the dreamy light that never shone by day.

Suddenly the nightingale stopped his jubilant song, and was silent.

Blanche also stopped her dance, and looked at the rose-bush, watching for the bird to begin again. But he did not begin again; and leaning over the gate, and looking at her, stood the figure of a man.

Blushing from head to foot, she plunged into the shadow of the trees, and hastened back to the house. There, safe in her own little room, she stood, pressing both her hands against the loud beating of her heart, and wondered whether it was the prince, who had come to deliver the rose, or only some inquisitive mortal.

The night was late before she fell asleep, and then she dreamed that she herself was the enchanted rose.

But it was not the Fairy Prince that she had seen; it was only Arthur de Mersay, Godefroy's son, who came next day to visit his aunt.

The aunt and nephew had never met before, and they knew each other only by name.

When his father died, Arthur was beyond the Atlantic. The first news of his loss reached him only when he landed at Havre, on his return to France; and he had arrived in Louviers the night before this visit to the chateau. Thinking it too late to drive over to his aunt's that night, he had strolled out of the town on foot, with that longing to stretch one's legs which is familiar to all who have just landed from a long sea voyage.

The garden to which his steps had rambled along the banks of the Eure was unknown to him; he had no idea that the girl he saw dancing in the moonlight was his own cousin; and it was with a pleased surprise that he learned the name of the chateau, when the next morning it was pointed out to him as the seat of Madame de Mersay.

The moonlight fairy had been dancing all night in his head; and such was his longing to see her again in broad daylight, that he would certainly have returned to the little garden gate, even had it not led to his aunt's house, and have opened it, even if it had been the postern of a nunnery.

Arthur de Mersay was not the man to let any hinderance stand between him and his desires. He recognized the little gate as he passed through it this morning; and the rose-bush, too, where the nightingale had sung.

From the rose-bush, as he went by it, he plucked a rose, inhaled for a moment the sweetness of the flower, and then flung it away.

Blanche, who was sitting in the arbor, sprung up, frightened and vexed.

Why, if he wished to enjoy the sweetness of the rose, could he not stoop his head to the poor flower, and leave it to bloom uninjured on its stem? She would take the stranger to task for this ungentle act, and ask him by whose authority he was entitled to rob the nightingale of what belonged to it—the first rose of spring.

But now he stood before her, and she did not ask him.

The question was needless. The stranger's authority was distinctly certificated on his forehead, when, as he took off his hat to salute her, the deep sabre-scar on his temples became visible, just under the roots of his black waving hair. By other signs, moreover, the question was already answered. Blanche, with a thrill of inward awe, recognized in this stranger a being from higher worlds. His was, in all particulars, the image of the fairy prince — the long-dreamed-of knight from afar — who, from her childhood till this hour, had haunted her thoughts, waking and sleeping. Even to the minutest details, the counterpart was complete, as he tossed back his long black locks with a proud impatience; just like the hero of the tales she had so often told to Lyon, and prophetically interpreted to herself, as he used to appear when the visionary combat for her life was about to begin. And the motion of his hand seemed to Blanche exactly like that of her uncle.

The knight of her dreams had come to life; and, with a graceful salutation, he informed her that he was the son of Godefroy de Mersay!

Confused, she gave him her hand, and said,

"I am Godefroy's niece Blanche."

"I must needs believe it," he replied, retaining her hand in his, "since you tell me so."

She looked at him, puzzled.

"I saw last night," he continued, smiling, "upon the very spot where you now stand, a form unearthly fair, a form of such ravishing beauty as, till then, I had nowhere seen, and only once heard of—in Germany, the land of legends. There, I once heard a legend of a fairy who dances in the moonlight, enchanting all who have the chance to see her. But, soon as seen, she glides away from the beholder, leaving him nothing but a wounded heart, which can never again be healed. I then thought it only a pretty fairy tale; but since yesterday I know it is a truth!"

Blanche, as she freed her imprisoned hand from the young man's clasp, felt the blood rushing to her cheeks, and would have liked to run to her room as she had done the night before.

But across the entrance of the arbor Lyon was lying at full length, upon the grass. He did not bark; but he had nuzzled his head low between his outstretched forepaws, and was meditatively contemplating the stranger.

"I will lead you to my mother," she said, hurriedly.

She had fortunately seen the black cap-ribbons fluttering in the kitchen garden.

Madame de Mersay was walking slowly between the beds, and examining the young plants, which stretched forth their little heads, prudently testing the spring air. She looked up surprised as the stranger approached accompanied by her daughter. But her surprise changed at once to enthusiastic welcome when he told her his name.

He was a De Mersay, and that was enough for her.

Before he could say another word, she sounded a little silver whistle that hung from her neck, and ordered an old white-headed servant who presently answered its summons to see that her nephew's luggage was promptly fetched from Louviers, as also to prepare for him the chief guest-chamber; to which, when they had re-entered the house, she finally conducted that young gentleman herself—"for a good long stay!" said the old lady, cordially, as there she left him, after casting a housewifely glance around the room to assure herself that it was all in order.

As soon as the young man found himself alone, he began to pace restlessly up and down his sitting-room. But he looked at none of the things around him there, and did not even notice the fresh nosegay of spring flowers which had been placed upon his table. His gaze, as if eagerly bent on some distant object, was fixed straight before him.

This far-off look was habitual to Arthur de Mersay. It was the key to his character. He had ever before his eyes some distant object, ardently desired;

and in the excitement of its pursuit all that stood between that object and himself was completely obliterated from his perception.

His character was capable of only one passion; but that passion was intense, all-pervading, and irrepressible. It was the passion of acquisition. This passion was the main-spring of all his feelings and actions. Deprived of its animating force, the whole man would have fallen to pieces as an earthen image that is crumbled into atoms by the displacement of its centre of gravity. And, for that reason, the thing acquired had no lasting value for him. He threw it aside as carelessly as he had thrown away the rose that morning. The prize once possessed, all delight in it was gone, and already in the distance hovered some new attraction.

As for the goodness or reasonableness of the means employed for its attainment, he gave to the future no more thought than he vouchsafed to the past concerning the worth of what he had gained and then forsaken. His passion urged him forward with an egotism as blind, senseless, and unfeeling as the mechanical impulsion with which a billiard-ball thrusts the other balls aside, and, after hitting the mark, recoils from it—always polished, shining, elastic, nimble, and always hard—hard as a stone!

Never anywhere had he yet found rest in life. The unappeasable craving of his disposition had driven him, always with the same yearning for something afar, from the soon-exhausted excitements of Paris, first as a soldier to Algeria, and then as a traveller over all the world.

And so, for years, he had roamed from land to land—a restless, indefinite volition—not, however, like the wind, which impels the ship and turns the mill, or fans the forge and heats the iron in the stithy —still less as the light breeze, that caresses the petals of the roses, and plays with the loosened locks of laughing maidens; but rather as one of those elementary gases which, in the blind conflict of natural forces, rushes into sudden combination with the atoms of another; and then, whirled away by some new attraction, violently dissolves the evanescent bond.

In this way he had squandered his youth, his best energies, and the considerable fortune he inherited from his mother, without winning from the waste of all those treasures a moment of genuine happiness, or even of partial contentment. In the attainment of his ever-shifting aim he had never failed; but in this sterile monotony of success he felt no more satisfaction than a man who is a practised marksman might feel in always hitting the bull's-eye, which he knows he cannot miss.

And from all these successes, such as they were, his only lasting acquirement was a dull weariness of the world, and a disgust of his own existence—sometimes so intolerable, that his hand involuntarily lifted his revolver to his head; only, in the very moment of lifting it, his aim had changed again; and again, just as involuntarily, he had followed the new aim, with always the old result—desire ever insatiable, and possession never enjoyed.

Now, as he paced the floor of his apartment in

the Château de Mersay, his face assumed its old
eager expression, and the far-off look grew more and
more intensely fixed in the keen, hungry eyes. For
there, on the horizon of his fancy, was still dancing
the moonlit Fairy; and to her exquisite image his
soul went forth, in all the sudden intensity of its inveterate passion, and with all its consuming impatience of time and means.

While Arthur de Mersay was thus employed,
Blanche had gone quietly back to the rose-bush by
the ivy-arbor.

She stooped and picked up the enchanted rose,
which she found there, lying in the sand. Then
she shook it carefully, and softly blew the dust from
its petals, and carried it stealthily to her own little
room. There, she put the flower into a glass of
water which stood upon her table, and sat down before it. And thus for hours she sat alone, her elbow
on the table, her cheek propped upon her hand, musingly watching the poor little wounded blossom;
which, refreshed by the bath she had given it, seemed
to revive gradually beneath her gaze.

Meanwhile, as softly came and went the sweet
days of May, every morning in that old garden the
young couple went wandering side by side, closer
and closer daily, as their hearts drew nearer together
—one with impetuous desire, the other shyly and
dreamily, through a sunny mist of golden fancies.

Blanche now saw breathing alive before her the
phantom image which had so often baffled the effort
of her pencil to fix its fleeting outlines. To individ-
ualize her maiden fancies, she need only steal a tim-

id glance at her cousin Arthur, as he stood there, tall and strong, the black locks hanging about his pale, finely moulded face; and, across his forehead, the scar, which sometimes reddened while, with that steadfast, eager gaze of his, he told her all about his combats with the Kabyles, or his adventures in all sorts of distant lands and seas.

Nor was it only the longed-for outlines that she had found at last; but, therewith, all the magic hues, all the starry splendors of that glowing treasure which till then she had only seen shining far out of reach, like a sunken argosy, in the hushed depths of her own day-dreams.

All this, she thought, belonged to Arthur. She knew not, in the touching and beautiful simplicity of her heart, that she herself had fetched it, piece by piece, from the fairy riches of her own soul, and unconsciously clothed him in the glory of it. With all the innocence, the softness, and the warmth of her nature—all the generosity and greatness of her soul —she had invested him, as with a splendid garment. And, like precious gems on the broidered mantle of some royal saint, into that splendid garment her adoring hands had woven all the sweet and holy visions of her youth.

When, at night, she returned to her little room, and knelt at her bedside, with folded hands, before the old picture of the Madonna with the Seraph, her eyes now beheld there, instead of the sacred image to which the prayers of her childhood had been addressed, only the glowing image of Arthur; from which her gaze sunk dazzled and abashed by the radiance that trembled down from it through all her frame.

She was incapable of perceiving that it was the celestial glory of the love in her own heart which shed this halo around the form she had unconsciously created, out of the depths of its unfathomable tenderness, in the image of its immaculate ideal. She only sunk lower on her knees, till her young head almost touched the ground, as she murmured meekly and brokenly,

"It is *thou* whom I adore!"

In Arthur, on the other hand, his longing for the moonlit Fairy grew more and more overpowering, till it absorbed his thoughts, and stifled every other wish in the heart it filled to bursting.

The looks he fixed on Blanche, with all the hungry eagerness of his nature, were so imperious in their usurpation of her will that the girl was constrained to lift her eyelids, trembling and blushing from head to foot, and suffer those despotic looks to flow unresisted into her eyes and soul. And, believing that the Realm of the Beautiful and Good extended just so far as that all-penetrating gaze, and that where its radiance fell not there only were sorrow and death, she looked up into his eyes, gratefully, humbly, adoringly, in the boundless confidence of the delicious conviction that he loved her.

Blanche's mother had nothing to say against this love. She was a woman whose own life's happiness had withered away with the loss of the husband in whose heart it was rooted, and to whose affection it had opened its earliest blossoms. All her prayers had been *for* him while he lived, and *to* him ever since his death.

It was a Mersay who had made her own life unspeakably happy, and he who now wooed her daughter was also a Mersay. She need, therefore, have no fears for the security of her daughter's internal happiness. She beheld her child's future with the love-veiled looks in whose gaze was reflected all the felicity of her own past.

But for the security of the child's external welfare she had the sharp, anxious eye with which she scanned her fields when hail-storms hovered on the horizon. She at once undertook to set in order the worldly affairs of her future son-in-law, and was the more scrupulous in the matter that Arthur himself had neither any idea of the condition to which his fortune was reduced, nor any care to know it.

The result at which she arrived made her desirous that the young couple should settle at Havre.

Arthur's mother had been born there. She was the daughter of one of those merchant princes whose riches float on every sea. There it was that she had first met Godefroy de Mersay, in the salons of the Sous-Prefet. The young lady's lively fancy was at once attracted by the soft dark eyes and knightly grace of the interesting, dreamy-looking youth who had come from Paris to pore over the manuscripts of Bernardin de St. Pierre in the museum at Havre. His character pleased her by its contrast to the passionate violence of her own. She had little trouble in inducing him to forsake Bernardin's Virginie for her sake. She was an only child; and being also a

wilful and a spoiled one, she overcame with equal
ease the purse-pride of her father, whom she soon persuaded to receive with open arms, as a son-in-law,
the younger scion of a noble but impoverished family—and one, moreover, who was a scholar and poet,
quite incapable of managing the great fortune he
would receive with her hand.

Having thus attained her object, she again became
entirely her father's daughter. Because Godefroy
had but few wants, she looked upon him as a poor-
spirited fellow, and because he was soft and gentle,
he soon bored her. His ideal aspirations seemed to
her a mild sort of lunacy, and his steady, intense devotion to her, intolerably burdensome. Her father,
she said, had been right all through. She went off
to Paris, *pour se distraire un peu*, intending to pass
the winter there, as she informed her husband; and
there she remained for the rest of her life. What
little good there was in her selfish and capricious
disposition soon perished in an unceasing whirl of
dissipation.

The child born of this ill-assorted marriage was
not suffered to interfere with the excitement and
frivolity of the mother's unquiet existence. The
boy, as soon as born, was put to nurse in the country; and afterwards, as soon as he left college, the
stripling himself was prematurely plunged into the
same mad whirl.

Godefroy de Mersay meanwhile pursued his sad
and lonely path unnoticed. The tender, weak man
bore his burden uncomplainingly, as an inevitable
dispensation. He idolized his wife; and when at

last, worn out with dissipation, she breathed away her restless soul, he returned to the solitude of his home, only to die there. He had nothing more to do in the world, for his son had been quite estranged from him by his wife.

The prodigal daughter of the Havre merchant had dissipated before she died no inconsiderable portion of her large fortune. Arthur, who, though in face and figure he resembled his father, was in character and heart the exact image of his mother, had been equally prodigal, and not much of his maternal inheritance now remained. Only an estate near Havre, which was let to strangers, and a large country-house with a garden, in the town itself. The rent of the property had been fixed more than a generation ago by Arthur's maternal grandfather; and since then, as it was regularly paid, no one had thought of raising it.

Madame de Mersay drove over to Havre, and returned with the conviction that the rent ought to be doubled, and that it would be best for Arthur to take the management of the property into his own hands, so that he might henceforth have some settled and orderly occupation.

Such was the pecuniary position of Arthur at the time of his marriage, and the dowry of Blanche was not large. The moderate revenues of the De Mersay estate had long been declining. But Arthur did not mind that; he never cared for money-matters. He wished to settle at once in Paris; and indeed, he had already formed plans for the maintenance of his wife's Parisian establishment on the most magnificent scale.

13

Madame de Mersay listened with a smile to these boasts. She treated him like a child who cries for the moon, and quietly pointed out to him the impossibility of setting up house in Paris, even on the most modest footing.

He would have obstinately adhered to his plans (for the Havre prospect he regarded only as a pet hobby of his aunt's, to which he had no intention of paying serious attention) had it not been for a sudden thought which rendered the idea of married life at Paris unexpectedly distasteful to him.

This thought came into his mind one day as he watched Blanche standing in the garden and softly stroking Lyon's head. A poignant jealousy seized him at that sight—jealousy of the dog, jealousy of the whole world, and more especially of the seductions of Paris. For he thought of his mother, and how she had been hurried along by that great frivolous Parisian world into a life of distraction, incompatible with any sort of domestic affection. Before his eyes, between him and Blanche, rose the unwillingly remembered images of his own Parisian friends —idlers of the salon and the boulevard—and finally the image of his own Parisian life. And gloomy, almost menacing, in those eyes was the flash which in that moment kindled the hard, far-off look of them.

"No," he thought, "not Paris! never again Paris!"

He would have Blanche all to himself. His possession of the woman he loved should be absolute and exclusive. Every word and look of her, every thought and interest of that woman's life, must be, not only his, but his entirely, and his alone. And so, from the window he turned suddenly to Madame de Mersay, who supposed that all this while he had been carefully considering her plans about Havre, and said,

"You are right; I will not take Blanche to Paris."

Madame de Mersay embraced her nephew.

And in the month when the summer roses begin to bloom the bridal pair, beaming with happiness, stood before the altar in the cathedral of Louviers.

Arthur did not know that what he had led to that sacred altar was only his own glowing desire; and Blanche did not guess that the hand in which her own lay trembling was only that of a vision.

As she passed out of the porch of the cathedral into the church-yard she paused a moment to press her beating heart, its happiness was so great.

The marvellously carved stone-work of the old cathedral, whose delicate traceries she had so often admired, hung rich above the portal through which she had entered into her new life. It was like a mysterious curtain broidered with fairy figures, shutting out all that once had been. On this side of it began all that was now to be; and when she lifted her eyes, and saw the bright blue sky, and all the bystanders looking kindly at her, life seemed so beautiful, and all the world so dear and good, that tears of joy filled her eyes, and she could not speak in answer to Arthur's whispered question,

"Blanche, are you happy?"

She only looked gratefully up at him with her moist eyes; and her golden hair gushed from beneath her veil, as she bowed her happy head in all-sufficient response to that whisper.

CHAPTER II.

MADAME DE MERSAY continued to live at the old chateau, near the grave of her husband.

The young couple left her, some days after the wedding, for their home at Havre. During their journey, they chattered, at first, like two silly children; then they spoke of the future like two serious children; and finally they sat quite silent.

Arthur was weaving his ambitious thoughts, further and deeper every moment, into the widening woof of a vast enterprise in South America, of which the grand and original conception had been fascinating his fancy ever since his first visit to Havre for the preparation of the home to which he was now taking his bride.

The precise form which this enterprise was to assume he had not yet quite settled; he only saw, in the future, numerous ships belonging to it ploughing the Atlantic, and pouring the treasures of the New World at his feet. He had no fear of failure; his fancy presented to him a picture of all the merchant princes of Havre eagerly rallying around him in support of the enterprise which was to bear his name. Possibly it was the business-like character of his mother-in-law's preoccupations on his behalf that had thus turned his thoughts, for the first time, along the track of commercial calculations. But he did not fix them on the track itself—they were already concentrated upon the end of it; and the idea of South America had occurred to him because the last years of his life had been passed there.

While thus musing, he held Blanche's hand in his own. It was only for her sake, he said to himself, that he had thought of all this. She should be rich, and surrounded by every splendor and luxury that wealth could procure for her.

Blanche, meanwhile, as she leaned her head upon her husband's shoulder, was dreamily absorbing into the bliss of her own heart the shining repose of the beautiful valley of the Seine, which, as they passed along it, softly melted from one delightful picture into another, clear and bright as the sunny landscapes of Claude Lorraine.

The busy life of the seaport town recalled them both to earth. With a start the two dreamers awoke, the husband from his calculations, the wife from her golden reveries; and at last they were at home upon the sea-girt cliffs of Ingouville, which, covered with villas and gardens, stretch northward from the town of Havre.

When, arm-in-arm with Arthur, Blanche stepped on to the balcony of her new drawing-room, she saw beneath her, in the warm evening light, a terraced garden glowing with flowers; and lower down, at the foot of the cliffs, the bay of Havre, its shore clustered with houses, its haven thronged with masts;

and all around, and far beyond it, far as her gaze could reach, the shining levels of the great calm sea.

The sun was already deep in the west, and had begun to dip his broad red orb below the ridge of Cap la Hève; but his rays still overspread the heavens and the earth, and gleamed along a golden inlet in the east, where the waters of the Seine flowed down into the sea. About the sea itself numbers of little sails were glittering red, like festive flags in the evening glow, and upon the wide unrippled waters a red-gold glory rested. Far away upon the distant horizon the streaming smoke of a great packet-ship, outward bound, looked only like a little dark feather floating in the flushed air of sunset.

Blanche passed one hand across her eyes, as if it were all a dream, and laid the other on her heart. It was long before she could find words for what she felt there; but at last she said, speaking under her breath,

"Arthur, your father often stood just where we are standing now, in the evening glow, gazing on this enchanting picture. Uncle Godefroy often spoke to me of the sunsets he had watched from Ingouville. He called them his evening prayers. It was, he once told me, in such an hour as this—here, on this very balcony—that he first confessed his love to your mother. How all these reminiscences seem to mingle, in splendor and repose, with the unspeakable felicity of our own love, while we stand as they did, on the same spot, looking at the same scene!"

Arthur's gaze had been fixed all this while upon

one dark spot on the distant splendors of the horizon—the smoke of that outward-bound packet-ship.

"I am so glad, for your sake, Blanche," he answered, "that you like this place."

And then, with a start, he added, "Blanche de Mersay shall one day rule over yonder sea; hers shall be the ships in yonder haven, and like a queen shall she look down upon the merchant town that now lies stretched at her feet!"

Blanche looked up wonderingly at these words, which were quite unintelligible to her. Then, with a shy smile, she leaned her head timidly upon his breast and whispered,

"I want nothing, Arthur, but to love and serve you."

And truly this she did from that time forward. All the virtues which had taken steadfast root in the characters of her parents put forth their brightest blossoms in her own. From her mother she inherited the gift of making a pleasant home; from her father, an activity never tired, always cheerful. Her love taught her to guess her husband's wishes in his looks, and enabled her to anticipate their utterance.

In these active pieties of affection the full beauty and abundant loveliness of her nature found, for the first time, their complete expression. As the warmth of spring dissolves the snows of May, the devotion of the wife relaxed the maiden reserve of the girl, only to bring forth in ever-increasing opulence the bloom and fragrance of her perfect womanhood.

And for all she gave she was contented with such

small returns. His love was to her not the natural recognition of a right, but the miraculous bestowal of a grace so great that the least manifestations of it were priceless. For a kind look or a tender word she was unboundedly grateful. If Arthur picked her a flower to put in her hair, she could not find in the fulness of her heart words enough to thank him. She stood before her glass admiring the flower he had given her, with as much pride and satisfaction as any other woman, if only half as beautiful, would have felt, when she looked at her glass, in admiring herself.

"You are too good to me, Arthur!" she would exclaim on those occasions, clasping her exquisite arms about his neck; and then she would stand on tiptoe, that he might the better see how beautiful his flower looked.

In this way Blanche took and cherished, as the highest and the best in life, the nearest and least gift of the passing moment—a gift unexpected and undeserved. And in return for such gifts, she cheerfully consecrated to his service every occasion that time and place vouchsafed her.

The abiding vigilance of her affection never failed to detect and seize even the most fleeting opportunity of proving its devotion. And her hands instinctively turned to whatever work, and her feet to whatever way, chance placed from hour to hour within the reach of this unwearied purpose. All she did, and all she refrained from doing, was in submissive obedience to love's claim upon each hour as it came —a tender abandonment of her whole being to the present, and a gracious devotion to it. What thus might come to her, or become of her, by-and-by, was a consideration which found no place in her life. She heaped together, as it were, with both hands, the treasures of her heart, and poured them at the feet of her beloved, never heeding how many of them thus fell unseen and unnoticed by him. Why should she reckon her riches or stint their expenditure? She knew her heart was inexhaustible.

Arthur's nature, which, unlike his wife's, was always fretfully straining towards the future and the far, yielded at first to the charm with which, for him, she had invested the present; and its habitual impatience slumbered for a while beneath the spell of those soft hands which held the sweet hours fast.

He was like a wanderer who, hastening with eager steps from hill to hill along some mountain-range, has reached at last the summit nearest heaven. There he rests a while, well pleased. The pure air of those serene precincts fans his heated forehead cool; and in contented repose he gazes now upon the ethereal azure above him, now upon the smiling valleys below, and then upon the mountain-flowers that blossom at his feet. This lasts perhaps an hour. Then he is rested, and keenly scans the distant prospect towards which his way still lies. Fresh summits rise there, half veiled in cloud—summits still to climb, and vast mysterious gorges still to be explored! Already the spot on which he stands has lost its charm.

So fared it with the charm which the present, embodied in the sweet image of his wife, still exercised over Arthur. It lasted, but not for long. After a short while the devouring acquisitiveness of his nature had consumed all that was given to it without resistance or reserve; and he again fell a prey to that dissatisfaction with the world and himself—that lethargy of satiety into which he invariably relapsed after the attainment of his wishes.

In this condition of mind, his great South American scheme was the first stimulant to which he had recourse. He who had never known the worth of a franc, and had always cherished the maxim "L'argent peu," now began to read with eagerness the quotations of the Bourse, the foreign exchanges, and the commercial news. He became a subscriber to the *Courrier du Havre*, and studied in it the numbers, names, and freights of the local shipping. He stood for hours before an enormous map of South America, and knit his eyebrows if, during these important occupations, Blanche stole into his room.

She no longer ventured to go near him, or to take his arm and wander chatting with him about the house or through the garden. Their pleasant daily walks down to Havre or round the cape were gradually discontinued. Their delightful excursions across the bay of Honfleur, or Trouville, and even sometimes to Caen, had grown rarer by degrees, and at last they ceased altogether.

When Arthur took up his hat, and Blanche looked at him with the imploring eyes of a timid child, whose look was a mute entreaty to be allowed to go with him, he now invariably replied, in a hasty tone, and with an absent air,

" You must excuse me to-day, my angel; I am going out upon pressing and important business. Go
and see, meanwhile, if the hyacinths in the garden are
yet in bloom."

To-day it was the hyacinths, to-morrow the roses—
every day a different flower that she was asked to
look after, for the sake of varying that otherwise invariable answer. The flowers he named were, generally, those which happened to be out of season, and
faded long ago; but Blanche went through the re-
quired formality, and duly examined the dead brown
flowers lying on the ground.

The walks she was not permitted to accompany
were indeed "upon business bent," for her husband
was now looking everywhere for connections with
the principal merchants and ship-owners of the town.
These worthies honored his name with a respectful
bow, and listened to his projects with a polite smile;
but not one of them ever treated him *au serieux.*
He called them a set of narrow-minded *épiciers,* and
turned with his usual impetuosity, in search of better fortune, to the minor magnates of the mercantile
community. They also, however, regarded him only
as a petulant child, who seemed to think that he could
have the sun and moon for playthings.

Arthur never took his wife with him into these
commercial circles; nor, indeed, did he ever take her
into society of any sort. He still held fast to what
he told Blanche when she became his bride: that they
were to live only for each other, and entirely out of
the world.

Blanche herself, reared as she was in loneliness and

seclusion, had no other wish. The charming idyl of two lives thus woven into one had always been a sweet dream to her; but it was now a dream which she was often left to dream alone.

About this time the sudden death of Madame de Mersay brought about a situation in which Blanche became once more, for a while, the central object of Arthur's thoughts and occupations. The intensity of her grief was an entirely new revelation to him. It opened to his sight depths in her soul quite unknown to him, and not even intelligible to such a nature as his. Till then he had seen the image of his wife only in the sunshine of love; now it stood before him in the double light of love and sorrow.

The unwonted coloring its beauty took from this twofold aspect was not unattractive to him. But his eye soon became accustomed to it; and meanwhile his mind was already occupied less about Blanche herself than about the sale of her property.

Blanche, for her part, though she was fond of Ingouville, would have liked to live with Arthur where her father and mother had passed their lives in tranquil happiness; yet she was content, since Arthur wished it otherwise. It pained her, however, when she heard that the home of her forefathers was to be pulled down, and the old trees in the park felled and sold, to make room for mills and factories.

Arthur was obliged to go several times to Paris for the personal negotiation with Monsieur Dumont, its purchaser, of various details connected with the sale of the estate. Blanche meanwhile lived upon the few last words and looks with which he had taken hasty leave of her; and what was at first a cause, became by degrees only a pretext, for absence.

He now went oftener to Paris, and he stayed there longer every time. The Boulevards, on which he had not set foot since his voyage to South America, had assumed for Arthur de Mersay all the charm of novelty. The Bois de Boulogne appeared to him, after an absence of several years, like a newly discovered country. The old acquaintances he picked up again at Paris were as good as new ones, since they presented to him features which time had either altered or effaced from his recollection. The figure he himself cut in the midst of them seemed to him at first a little ridiculous, and he felt rather ashamed of his own provincialism. Then he wondered whether provincial life would ever move in a century as fast as the world of Paris in a year. He longed to explore this altered world in all its aspects, and he was soon whirled away by it.

After a little while the thought of Havre threw him into a cold shudder; for there, and indeed everywhere except at Paris, the spectre of Ennui lay in lurk for him, and it was only inside the walls of Paris that he thought himself safe from its pursuit. For a while he entertained a vague intention of telling Blanche to join him there; but he forgot it, as he forgot all his grand commercial projects, and everything that he had cared about before. A more potent attraction had already excited his never-resting covetousness; and towards the attainment of the object to which it allured him he was straining to the utmost all the energies it had revived in him.

This object was Mademoiselle Julie Oeillet, a member of the *corps de ballet* of the Grand Opera.

Mademoiselle Oeillet had the blue-black hair and the eyebrows and the eyes of a native of the Equatorial Desert, with the olive complexion of a Sicilian. All about her breathed of the glowing south; and in the fervid atmosphere of her presence Arthur forgot that snow-white image of the north—his wife. Between these two women the inward contrast was even greater than the outward; only here the difference was reversed. In the soul of the fair daughter of the north were all the sweets and ardors of the south; and in the swarthy child of torrid suns, all the frost and ice of the polar zone.

Mademoiselle Oeillet was no *coryphée* of the ballet, nor could she ever become one. Her body was made for the plastic repose of the antique tragedy, and not for lively movement. Her form and features served upon the stage as a restful background to a series of shifting groups, and such was the narrow sphere relentlessly proscribed by the stage management to her activity. Mademoiselle Oeillet had rebelled against this decree, and first she stormed, and then she wept, but finally she accepted it with a smile; for in the mean while she had discovered that she could play in the world a more shining part than that which was reserved for the *prima ballerina* on the stage.

At first she was satisfied with the modest *début* of Monsieur de Mersay. He did very well, to begin with. He had a handsome face, a distinguished appearance, agreeable friends, and money always ready as often as she wanted anything—and her wants were many. She allowed him to send her nosegays and bracelets, to pay her bills, to put a carriage at her disposal, to call on her in her house, and to reciprocate the inflammatory glances she vouchsafed him at the Opera. These were his privileges, but they went no farther. Mademoiselle Oeillet had an intuitive talent for the art of taking everything and granting nothing. She only liked beginnings, and knew exactly when and how to glide gracefully out of the room before the end got too near. Hope Deferred knocked all the more eagerly at her door next day.

Julie Oeillet could only read print with difficulty, but she read human character with ease. In an hour she had read Arthur de Mersay through and through, and knew that his devotion was only to be retained by constantly stimulating, and never satisfying, his covetousness. This was to her an easy task, for it coincided with the bent of her own nature. Its performance, instead of obliging her to play a part, permitted her to indulge her natural disposition unrestrained. She listened with cool indifference to Arthur's passionate declarations, answered his sighs with a laugh, and his despair with an air from Offenbach. If this threw him into a cold fit, she could always revive him from it by a gush of Syrian sunshine from that sultry heaven in her eyes which at once became overclouded and as cold as winter when the hot fit on him grew too hot.

Into the sweetest understanding she contrived to introduce an indefinable something which jarred its symmetry; she knew how to strike a discord from

the most perfect harmony, how to temper the most
excited flights of emotion by the timely application
of a prosaic word; and could drench fire or kindle
oil to precisely the temperature she wanted. Her
relations with Arthur de Mersay were a continual
conflict between blind passion on the one side and
calculating coquetry on the other, which kept him
breathless, and oblivious of everything else.

To Havre he only returned occasionally, and at
long intervals, for the few days during which Julie,
in her calculated caprices, from time to time denied
her door to him. She never withdrew these inter--
dictions, which he obeyed, grinding his teeth with
unavailing rage; and his wife became the victim of
the ill-temper in which, on these occasions only, he
rejoined her.

Blanche was all this while as if in a narcotic slumber—a sort of opium-dream from which she could
not rouse herself, though the warning alarum sounded shrill and often at her ear. She awaited Arthur's
return, at first for days, then for weeks, then for
months; and each time she had to learn anew the
lesson of absence, as if each time were the first time,
so hard that lesson was to her, and so incomprehensible!

She counted the seconds as a deserted child counts
the rain-drops on the pane, and their loitering fall
was infinitely slower than the unsatisfied beating of
her young heart. She sat at the window, starting
and looking out countless times in the course of the
endless day, whenever a wheel or a footstep sounded
near, and then searching the empty high-road with

an anxious look that was ever on the watch for what
it never found. She lay during the long nights
listening in the dark for the sound of a step that
she remembered, and heard nothing but the feverish
throbbing in her own temples.

The knowledge came to her at last of the secret
which Arthur was keeping so far away from her.
With his accustomed carelessness, he let bills, ac-
counts, and letters lie about upon his table. Julie's
letters were among them. During his absence,
Blanche, whose instinct was to make all around her
neat and orderly, used to tidy his papers for him;
and on one of these occasions her eye fell by chance
on the contents of a letter from Julie to her husband.
She looked no farther, but what she had seen went
far enough. It was a shock that took away her
breath—a pang of acute physical pain. She turned
deadly pale, and clasped both hands convulsively
upon her heart.

This lasted no longer than the stab of a knife.
But the open wound remained; and for many a long
day after that, the stricken woman wept silently, uncomplainingly, by herself, and to herself alone, in
her fresh solitude.

The heart of Blanche, however, was one of those
which must continue to dream until they cease to
beat. Even the rudest experience does not entirely
awake them from their visions; and to her this shock
was only like a cold wind blowing upon her shut
eyes, which, with a heavy effort, opened a little, and
then closed again before the reality could become
distinctly perceptible to her.

14

So the dream went on, though upon a new track less lovely than the old one, which that rude interruption had broken down. The old track blossomed like the garden of her home, and was sweet with the breath of roses and the song of nightingales, in shadowy depths of unfathomable verdure. The new one stretched barren before her, like a long, unshadowed waste of stony ground, beneath a burning glare, which she henceforth must tread, barefooted and bareheaded, as a penitent. For she laid upon herself all the fault of Arthur's estrangement from her, though she could not guess in what she had failed towards him; and she believed that, at the end of her weary penitential pilgrimage, a new garden would blossom by-and-by.

Her faith in him was still unshaken. Something of the glamour with which her heart had first adorned him was stripped off; but she thought, with self-reproach, that it was the awkwardness of her own hand that had done this. She never gave way to doubts of her ultimate success in the unceasing endeavor to fill up or bridge over the abyss which had so inexplicably opened between them, and the tenacity of her infinite trustfulness was unconfounded by the persistence with which his inveterate indifference to the treasures she threw into it was daily widening that abyss.

That she did not completely break down, however, was mainly owing to the fact that about this time she became a mother. Now, at least, there was one living human creature about whose being she might pour, in unrepulsed abundance, all the long-pent yearning love of her heart, all the overflowing fervor of her soul. And from the faded dreams of her own childhood she wove fresh dreams for her child.

When, with tears of joy, she showed his infant daughter for the first time to Arthur, who, some weeks after her confinement, had unexpectedly returned to Havre for a day or two, he looked absently at the child. Then, after a few irresolute turns up and down the room, he walked to the window, and said, looking through it, with his back to her,

"Financial affairs, full of anxiety and difficulty, will probably keep me long away from you on my return to Paris. For the short time I can stay here I shall live down-stairs. The noise of children has always made me nervous, and would now make me ill. Call this an idiosyncrasy of mine, or what you will, but I can't bear it."

Blanche turned her large eyes steadfastly towards him; and for this one time she tried to speak, and did speak, to her husband words of clear and weighty truth, while she kept her hand upon the beating heart of her child; for so weak was her power of self-assertion that she would not have had the courage to utter them had she felt the beating of her own heart; and, as it was, they died away at last in sobs.

Arthur listened silently. The scar upon his forehead turned to a deep red, while his face beneath it grew colorless.

Just so, in days long passed, had another woman, driven at last to bay, risen up and stood before him with a child in her arms—another woman, fair and wan as this one. And the words of this one were as the words of the other. They came back to him like ghostly echoes from a long-forgotten world that was no more. And the image of the living woman was so terribly like that of the dead one!

He shivered, and stared with wide-open eyes on Blanche, but did not answer her. Half an hour afterwards, however, he returned to Paris, without a word of farewell.

Three months passed away without a line from him.

At the end of that time he came back unexpectedly, and in great agitation. He entered the house in haste, without a word or a look to any one, strode restlessly through all the rooms, then through all the garden, and then back again from room to room. He examined everything with keen eyes, as if seeing it for the first time, and at last he sunk wearily into a fauteuil, and in a hard, dry voice said, without looking at Blanche,

"I am obliged to sell this place. It is too expensive, and I can no longer afford the luxury of keeping it up. The money realized from the sale of your property is unfortunately lost in an unlucky speculation, as also the greater part of your dowry. I regret it for your sake, but regret helps nothing. We must retrench our expenses."

He said all this rapidly and fluently, without changing his voice, like a school-boy who is repeating a lesson he has got by heart.

The words were cold and lifeless, but Blanche attributed them to all the emotions of a mind broken by afflicting anxiety; and as her own best consolation was the child, she hoped it might be his also. So she took him by the hand, and led him up-stairs to the little bed in which the infant lay smiling asleep. She said not a word about her lost fortune, or the home she was to lose. She only spoke to him about the smile upon their child's face. But to him her words were as lifeless as his own.

The purchaser of Ingouville was Monsieur Dumont, who had also bought the De Mersay estate near Louviers. He arrived the same day, to inspect the premises he had offered to buy. He had a large manufactory at Havre, and wanted Ingouville for a summer residence. He took advantage of Arthur's visible impatience to have the whole purchase-money paid at once, and thus got the place, without lengthy negotiations, for half its real value.

Arthur, taking for Blanche a small lodging in Havre, returned to Paris with the banker.

Some weeks after his departure, Blanche stood for the last time upon the balcony of her home at Ingouville—not this time with Arthur, who had not returned from Paris, but with her child in her arms. The last evening was like the first—in all its external aspects, at least. The broad flame of sunset spread bright and pure behind Cap la Hève; sea, land, and sky shone rosy red, and the spire of *Notre Dame des Flots* pointed, like a dark finger, to the glowing clouds that roofed the golden chambers of the west.

Blanche embraced all this glory with a farewell gaze, but she shed no tears. She was taking her happiness away with her. The little one smiled while it spread out its plump dimpled arms, as if to grasp the glory of the evening sky; and the mother, smiling also, pressed her happiness to her breast, and went.

But there was no staying in the new home. Soon she was ordered to change it for another, and a poorer one, in the remotest part of the town near the sea, where the fishermen lived. Arthur now never came to see her. The little sums he sent her from time to time were insufficient for the most indispensable wants. Gradually they grew more and more infrequent. At last he wrote to her that, being himself without a sou in the world, he could send her nothing more.

Blanche had sold by degrees all her jewels, and whatever else of life's external embellishments was left her; her only remaining personal property belonged to its strictest necessities.

In some of the idle hours of her girlhood she had once done embroidery-work for her amusement; now she did it again for her livelihood. When the last letter came from Arthur, she took her embroideries to a shop, where she succeeded in disposing of them for less than they were worth. She begged for orders, and got as many as she could execute. The delicate daughter of the De Mersays sat from morning till night, bent at her low window, and working for her daily bread. Forty sous a day she got for it, and that was her all in all.

On Sundays she took a walk with her child to the church of *Notre Dame des Flots*, upon the cape. Through all the rest of the week, day by day, hour by hour, she worked unceasingly.

And yet Blanche thought that joy enough was left

her; and when she knelt in the church of *Notre Dame des Flots*, beneath the image of the Madonna, she could not comprehend why the face of the sacred image looked so woe-begone; for Our Lady held her divine infant in her arms, and the infant smiled.

To Blanche the smile of her own child was everything; it was the ever fresh renewal of the old dreams of her youth, and the never-failing promise of their ultimate fulfilment. Those dreams replaced for her all that Arthur had promised her in the first days of their life together at Ingouville—jewels and Indian stuffs; sumptuous entertainments, resonant with music and radiant with light; operas, plays, balls, and voyages; the loud festivities of the world and the silent festivals of the heart. All this, and more—immeasurably more than all this—was to Blanche the smile of her child.

When the little girl, on awaking in the morning, played with her mother's tresses, laughingly hiding behind them all but the peeping beam of her blue eyes, the poor mother thought herself the richest woman in the world; and she began to love her own beautiful hair, because it was such a dear daily plaything for her child.

When, as the day went on, she looked up now and then from her work towards the child, or lifted her upon her lap, and the little girl threw her arms around her neck and hugged her, till the child's curls and the mother's became indistinguishable from each other (for they were both of the same color), then she thought herself the happiest woman in the world. And she took up her needle again with courage, and the room was filled with music sweeter to her than any other, for the child began to chatter with Lyon in that language which only God and mothers understand.

Lyon was both a big playfellow and a good plaything which could not be broken. He let the child pull his shaggy hair; he opened his jaws wide, that her little hands might inquisitively examine his teeth and tongue; he let her grasp his ears and feel his nose; he touched cautiously with his paws her little arm when she wanted to play at "catch-catch." And anon he was a careful guardian, solemnly following her as she crawled about, like himself, on all fours. If she stumbled in the attempt to go alone on her two little legs, Lyon was at her side, that she might cling to his hair with all her ten little fingers. And finally he made himself a soft cushion for the child, on which, when she was tired, she might lean her little head and go to sleep. He did not go to sleep himself, but lay stretched out upon the floor without once moving, while his faithful eyes twinkled with intelligence at Blanche.

"Our little one is asleep," they seemed to say. "We must make no noise."

But one misfortune brings another; the loosened sand-grain grows into the rolling ball, and this, in turn, into the devastating avalanche.

The caprice of fashion suddenly renounced the sort of embroidery that Blanche was able to work. One morning she was told at the shop that no more of it was wanted. She tried other shops, and got everywhere the same answer. When she came home, tired of her long, fruitless walks about the town, strangers were in her house. In the name of the law they claimed the scanty furniture of Monsieur de Mersay as security for a debt long overdue. Blanche did not understand what it all meant; and she pressed her little girl to her bosom, fearing that they would take the child from her too.

When the strangers went away, Lyon, who had been showing his teeth, ready at a sign from Blanche to attack them, growled after them at the door, and then all was still.

The child is asleep in the mother's arms. The mother lays her carefully in bed, and thinks, " This bed no longer belongs to me!" Then she goes to the table, which will be sold in a few days, and writes to Arthur at Paris. Then she puts on her bonnet, and walks, with weary feet that nearly fail her at every step, back into the town, and through it to the jeweller's, where she sells the little cross she has worn till now on her breast, as her mother had worn it before her, and her grandmother before that. It is her last possession !

Several days later, the letter she had written to Arthur returned to her unopened, with the words, "*Parti pour l'Angleterre*," written by a strange hand upon the cover.

Then, at last, Blanche let sink her head and hands, and sat staring at the floor in a stunned, senseless, helpless lethargy.

It was not given to her, as it is to some, to grow hard and strong, like a wind-beaten tree, in the stormy climate of a life of struggle. She never outgrew the shrinking softness of her flower-like nature. Her love for her child had indeed driven several sturdy little roots into the hard, stony soil of her life, but they gave her no support now. Turn where she might, far as sight could reach or thought wander, there was no help. Nothing before her and around her but hopeless desolation; and into that desolation she stared with wild, dry, reckless eyes.

A low sobbing aroused her.

The child was sitting beside Lyon on the floor, and looking at her mother. The little girl knew nothing of all this misery and mischance, but she was frightened by the look of the mother's face, and began to cry, till the whole of her little face was like a rose-bud drenched in rain.

The dog lay still, one arm of the child about his neck, and he, too, was looking strangely at Blanche. Like her, he had eaten nothing all day, but he did not whine.

Blanche looked up. She saw the eyes of the child and of the dog fixed upon her, and suddenly she seized her head with both her hands, and felt she must be going mad. For there, in the corner, behind the child, was hovering, white as death, a shivering spectre, thinly clad in tattered rags, with glassy eyes, gaunt cheeks, and bare, bony feet; and the spectre was clutching at the child with fleshless fingers, as if to snatch it away from her.

With a cry of terror, Blanche threw herself as a shield over her child, and stretched out her hands above its head in passionate expostulation towards this horrible apparition. Then she lifted her life's last treasure to her bosom, clasped it close, and rocked herself above it. This soothed her mind a little, and she burst at last into a flood of tears, as if she could weep out her whole soul.

After a while she looked round the room and out of the window. In the whole town of Havre she had not made a single acquaintance; for Arthur, in her happier days with him, had wished her not to mix with the local society, and ever since she had continued to order her life in accordance with her remembrance of his wishes. She had not a friend in all the world, not a human being to whom she could appeal for aid.

But One there was on high who had saved others from shipwreck — One who might still, perchance, save her also. And to the shrine where dwells Our Lady of the Waters, in the little windy church on Cap la Hève, she went forth with her child in her arms.

CHAPTER III.

It is a *jour de fête*, and the sky above keeps holiday with the earth below; for the sun is laughing gayly down at the gayety of the laughing crowd.

Blanche emerges from the gloomy suburb into the splendid Rue de Paris. As she catches sight of herself in the gigantic plate-glass mirrors of the shop-windows, the wretched mother smooths with trembling hand her child's threadbare dress. Timidly she crosses the public garden in front of the

Hôtel de Ville. Hundreds of smartly dressed people are listening there to the music of the military band; hundreds hurry past her joyously, on their way to the Aquarium; and farther up, along the Rue de Sainte-Adresse, is flowing a brilliant stream of carriages and hackney - coaches, crowded with holiday-makers. She wonders if her child will one day wander barefoot here.

On both sides of her way stand the luxurious villas and country-houses of Sainte-Adresse, surrounded by blooming gardens. And again she wonders where she is to find a bed for her child when they have been turned out of their lodging a few days hence.

Under the trees the restaurants resound with song, and laughter, and merry chatter, and the clink of glasses. Below, along the shore, the Parisians, who have come to Havre for the bathing-season, are fishing the oyster-beds of Queen Christina, and calling and laughing to each other over their sport. And Blanche thinks that to - morrow her child will be starving.

Now she has climbed the heights of Cap la Hève. The crowd disperses into groups: some gather round the shooting-booths, others about the cider-stalls, and some are strolling on to the light-house. Blanche enters the church, and kneels down before the image of the sailors' patroness, Our Lady of the Waters.

She, too, is a shipwrecked sailor, lost in life's wide ocean, without a plank to cling to. Her lips can form no words of prayer, but her heart prays passionately—not for herself; only for her child. She lifts her little one imploringly up to Her who has also a child in Her arms. But upon the human mother and her child our dear Lady looks down so wofully, and with a face so full of unutterable pain, that Blanche rises shuddering, and turns away her troubled looks. All around, upon the wall before her, she sees the names and votive offerings of those who have been saved. But they who have perished? Blanche suddenly thinks, where are *their* names inscribed? and, were they written here, would these walls be high enough to hold all the inscriptions?

And as she gazes up to the roof with a bewildered eye, all the suffering that is in store for her child gathers and heaps itself suddenly before her. She does not merely feel, she sees it. The mass of its growing misery rises higher and higher; it rolls above her head, which rests submerged beneath it; it mounts the walls, it reaches the groinings of the arch, it crams and bursts the vaulted roof above.

Blanche, with a sense of suffocation, groped her way along the wall to the door, and went out, wondering if it had yet touched the sky. There, outside the church, she stood a long while, gazing up into heaven; and then, shaking her head drearily, she wandered away with the child from the loud, many-colored swarm of holiday-makers, to the lonely edge of the downs above the sea.

The cannon of the Coast Battery stand peacefully beside each other in the grass. On the last of the row sits a young wife, stitching a baby-frock, and smiling sometimes at her little girl, who is playing in the grass beside her. Leaning against the wall of the signal-house stands the coast-guard officer on duty for the day. His eyes blink in the flood of sunshine from the sea; but he opens them now and then to steal a look at his wife and child. A couple of swallows are darting about the air in search of food for their young ones, who thrust their broad heads greedily out of their nest in the signal-tower. Above, in the blue, trills a lark. The bird is out of sight, but its song sounds clear from the sky, whence it is sending messages of love to its brooding mate below.

And Blanche looks far across the sea, to where, beyond the horizon, the English coast is hidden from her sight. Suddenly a child's voice sings shrill, out of the grass close by,

"*Malbrook s'en va-t-en guerre.*"

Then the song stops, and she hears nothing but the carolling of the lark and the sighing of the sea. As she lifts her eyes, the young father, thinking himself unobserved, has just stepped backward and embraced his wife and child.

Blanche turns and stares again across the rolling waves, in the direction of England. Her nerves are overwrought, her strength is going, and all around her reels and hovers in a glaring mist. With delirious eyes she gazes up again into the blue sky, and, with a voice that startles the coast-guard officer back to his post, cries out,

"Is it all empty up there, and no one in heaven or on earth to save my child?"

And she listens, and stares, and listens. But the radiant stillness of heaven returns no answer to her cry, and over sea and land hangs fast the azure vault in vast impenetrable peace.

She drooped her head, her lips twitched and trembled.

"No one up there in heaven," she muttered, faintly, "and none on earth to care for my little girl! None," she added, with a soft sob, "but I alone!"

Deeper and deeper drooped the mother's head, till the child in her arms was covered with her golden tresses.

Then a sudden thought struck her. What was it that the poor old water-carrier had once told her? That somebody had been asking whether the woman with the golden hair could not be induced to sell it?— that a rich gentleman was trying to buy hair of that peculiar color, and would give a great price for it?

Blanche had allowed the poor woman to chatter on, not wishing to hurt her feelings, but had paid no attention to her words, not understanding the drift of them. The possibility of selling her hair had never before occurred to her. Now, however, as these salable golden tresses lay spread out before her eyes in the lap of her child, the words of the water-carrier returned to her recollection with a sudden significance, swift and clear as a flash of lightning.

She rose hastily, re-entered the church, and knelt once more before the Madonna, in grateful thanksgiving for that ray of hope. This time she did not look up, but held her eyes down and her head bent in self-reproach at having doubted for one moment. And thus she could not see that Our Lady of the

Waters was still looking down at her, as before, with the same expression of unutterable woe.

Blanche returned to the town with hope in her heart.

The poor water-carrier directed her next day to the lodging of the man who had asked about her hair. He told her he had been for a long time commissioned to find hair for sale of that peculiar golden tint which hers possessed, but that till now all his researches had been in vain. After endless expressions of astonishment and admiration at the treasure she carried on her head, he declared that she must present herself with it to the gentleman who had given him the commission. This gentleman was the wealthy banker and manufacturer, Monsieur Dumont, who was to be found every afternoon at his country-seat at Ingouville.

Dumont! That was the name of the purchaser and possessor of the home of her earlier married life at Ingouville, and of her girlhood, near Louviers.

Blanche, without a moment's hesitation, continued her way up the steep road over the cliff to Ingouville.

She rang timidly at the door of the house in which the happiest hours of her life had been passed. The porter rudely refused her admittance. She went away through the garden ; she knew a little entrance there, leading into the house through the flower-beds, where she used once to gather flowers for Arthur every morning. She found it open, slipped through it, and crept up the stairs she had first mounted leaning on her husband's arm.

How well she remembered it all—the old house, the old days, the old feelings! Her heart was fit to burst, and she had not even her child with her, to clasp to it and give it courage.

A servant met her, and without asking her name, told her to wait in the anteroom.

"One of the factory lot," he muttered to himself as he left her there.

In the adjoining room, from which she was only separated by a *portière*, she heard the sound of a man's voice speaking fast in broken tones of agonized entreaty.

"Monsieur Dumont," said the voice, "I have worked hard all these years in your factory, and now my children are starving!"

"I dare say," replied the voice of the banker, calmly, "considering that you have not done a stroke of work for eight weeks."

"But I have been ill, monsieur, grievously ill—you know that very well!"

"How am I to know it? and what has this to do with the matter? Do you mean to say that I am the cause of your illness?"

"*Monsieur Dumont! mon bon Monsieur Dumont!* I do beseech and implore you, for pity's sake, advance me two months' wages, and I'll go back to my work to-morrow."

"But what security can you give me that you'll be able to go on working? How can I tell that you are quite recovered? You don't look like it; you may fall ill again—you may die!"

"Monsieur, my savings are all gone. Everything

15

we possess is sold. Ah, monsieur, for the love of God, be not so hard! I have six children!"

"I dare say. And is that my fault, too? I know people who would be glad to have six children. I tell you I cannot lend you the money. I have no money, and, what is more, I have no time to waste."

Blanche pressed her hands to her throbbing temples. She could not have believed it possible that God had made human hearts as hard as this. But she braced herself for the ordeal, and entered the banker's room as the poor workman staggered out of it. *She*, at least, was not come to borrow, but to sell.

The banker was writing.

"Who are you?" he asked, without looking up from his desk.

"I have been told," she replied, "that you want to buy hair of a certain color, and I am come to offer you mine for sale."

Dumont waited to hear what the woman would say next. But she said no more; so, turning carelessly in his chair, he looked up at her. Suddenly the tall, strong figure of the man was jerked, as by an electric shock, and he started to his feet with a keen glance at Blanche.

"Madam," said he, "your hair is indeed beautiful, incomparably beautiful, and perhaps unique. Will a check for two thousand francs satisfy you? Well, I will write it out at once. Be so good—"

The banker paused. A strange, nervous contraction rapidly crossed his brown, Provençal face, but it quickly resumed its hard and cold expression.

"Pray sit down!" he continued. "I think, madam, that I have already had the pleasure of speaking with you once before, though only for a moment. That was enough, however, for the lasting recollection of such features as yours. It was in this house, in this very room, I think, when I came here about the purchase of the place. Have I not the honor of speaking to Madame de Mersay?"

Blanche bowed.

"I pity you, madam."

"Sir," said Blanche, rising, "I came here to sell you my hair."

"Pray have the goodness to sit down, madam, and honor me with your patience for a moment. Money-maker as I am, I am aware that it does not become me to express any opinion in reference to your personal situation, even if it be only in the way of sympathy and regret. But the pity I expressed just now has reference to matters which must soon become public, and which concern myself no less than you, madam. Suffer me to mention first so much of them as concerns myself. Monsieur de Mersay incurred heavy debts long before the sale of this property, and he has largely increased them since. I have lent him money without hesitation, relying on the security he pledged me. That security was his wife's fortune. Madam, you have just now offered me the wonderful treasure bestowed on you by nature; I trust that this is the only sacrifice—"

"Monsieur Dumont," interrupted Blanche, proudly, "rest assured that your money will be repaid you. It is not my husband who will ever suffer the name of De Mersay to be sullied by a public prosecution for the recovery of a legitimate debt. Whatever may be the liabilities he has contracted towards you, he will assuredly find the means of discharging them; and it is doubtless for this purpose that he has now gone to England."

The same nervous contraction as before overspread the dark face of Dumont. It was a singular expression, which his friends used to call "Dumont's smile."

"I know about Monsieur de Mersay's journey to England," he replied, "and I know very well what is the object of it. In not mentioning that object to you, madam, I believe that I shall best observe the consideration which is due to you. But if you suppose that Monsieur de Mersay would shrink from involving his name in a comparatively innocent civil suit, you are — forgive me — under a pious illusion. You have a great and a generous faith in you. I am sorry to be obliged to disturb it, but it is in your own interest."

Saying this, Monsieur Dumont opened a drawer in his writing-table, and took out of it a bundle of papers. He held them out before Blanche's eyes.

"Madam," said he, "these papers aver that Monsieur de Mersay, for the pleasure of seeing an obscure ballet-dancer adorned with a costly necklace, has soiled an ancient name by the perpetration of a vulgar crime. These checks are all forged, and I have in my possession not only the proofs of the forgery, but also the identification of the forger."

Blanche sprang up, trembling all over.

"No, no!" she cried, loudly; "this is impossible! it is a damnable calumny!"

" In a few days," said Dumont, coldly, " the judgment of a court of justice will, I trust, have satisfied
your own judgment that the son of Provençal peas-
ants, who has raised himself in the world by honest
work, does not calumniate the offspring of Norman
knighthood in calling Monsieur de Mersay a swindler
and a forger.   I have had at heart, madam, no other
interest than your own in thus placing you in a position to take the necessary steps for protecting yourself and your family, by separating your destiny from
that of Monsieur de Mersay.   But in punishing this
man I have a personal interest, and I avow it.   I hate
the aristocracy—even a peasant's son has his antipathies—and I wage an inexorable war against aristo-
crats whenever and wherever I can.   Against wom-
en, however, I never fight, and against you, madam,
least of all, for you resemble one who—   No matter!
Calumny has never been my weapon, for I find
money the all-sufficient instrument of my purposes.
Money! money! money!   Money is power, money
is revenge, retribution, justice!   Slowly and painfully have I forged this mighty instrument; for long
laborious and penurious years scraping together *sous*,
as now I sweep together millions.   I have said that
even a peasant's son has his antipathies—ay, for even
a peasant's son has a history.   Allow me, madam, to
tell you a story which I happen to know by heart.
It is the story of a young Provençal peasant.   I knew
him years ago.   He had then a heart as glowing as
any in Provence.   But a fine aristocratic young officer, fresh from Algiers, condescended to be at the
pains of teaching this young fool that persons in his

class have no right whatever to a heart.　As for me, if at any moment I grow weary of the bitter war my life is passed in waging, I have only to think of a grave in Provence — a grave beneath which lies mouldering the broken heart of a young girl, betrayed, abandoned, lost, ruined, by that fine young aristocrat!　She was as beautiful, madam, as you are yourself, and like — O God, how like you!　You might have been twin-sisters.　She came from a race of northern emigrants.　She had your white forehead, and the same soft golden hair above it.　When I look upon your face, it all seems to me like a dream. But forgive me, I—forgot myself!　You doubtless wonder why I presume to tell you this story.　Well, I will be brief.　I speak only of facts—the hardest and the driest.　It is not for me to speak to you of feelings, and there are some which cannot be told. Have you ever observed, madam, in the museum of this town, among the geological remains of antediluvian epochs, the fossilized flora of a perished world —things that were once flowers and are now stones? Well, such is the end of my story; for it is only a record of fossilization—the story of a heart turned into stone.

"And now," said the banker, rising, and pointing to the window, "look yonder, madam.　Do you see, on the horizon, a thin cloud of smoke just above the sea-line?　That is the English steamer.　Monsieur de Mersay has probably by this time concluded his negotiations about Mademoiselle Oeillet's London engagement, and in two hours hence that steamer will have entered the port of Havre, where the agents of the police are waiting to arrest one of her passengers. By-the-way, I forgot to tell you, madam, that the name of the peasant's son was Dumont, and that of the aristocratic young officer, Arthur de Mersay."

Blanche sat stunned and speechless, her lips and her whole face as white as death. At last, with a shuddering effort, she flung out her hands towards Dumont, and clasping them, exclaimed,

"Mercy! mercy for that unfortunate man!"

"I fear," said the banker, "that you have not quite understood my little story."

"For the sake of my child," cried the wretched woman, "mercy! pardon!"

"Madam," he replied, "there was also a child in that story of Provence. I forgot to mention this. The child is lying in the same grave as its mother."

Blanche fell upon her knees before him.

"It is not for *him* that I pray," she said, "nor yet for *me*. I would bear it willingly for him and for myself. But my poor, helpless child—that she should be branded for a crime she has not committed! that the chain on the hand of the father should eat into the heart of the daughter! and that her sinless steps should be through a world where every one will point to her as the offspring of a criminal! Her smile killed forever! her life blighted before it begins! her dear, frank eyes forbidden to look up into any human face without shame and fear! Ah! Monsieur Dumont, you will not thus condemn the innocent? The child has never wronged you, sir. You have not seen her—have not seen her smile; you do not know, you cannot tell; ah, if you could only see her smile, you would not be so hard!"

She crept nearer to him and took his hand.

"Monsieur Dumont! Monsieur Dumont! let me bring my little girl to you! Only wait till you have seen her. She has such beautiful hair! It is the color that you like—the same golden color, only so much more beautiful; and her smile, and her voice —ah, if you could hear her voice!"

Dumont looked down at Blanche as she knelt at his feet; and wasted and stricken as she was—wasted with the long vigil of a hopeless grief, and stricken with a mortal pang—never had she looked more beautiful. Even then, in the agony of that moment, she could not speak of her child without a celestial smile that suffused her whole face. As he watched it shining through her tears, he thought again of the lonely grave far away in Provence, and the dead girl whom the living woman so strangely resembled, and how she, too, had smiled just so, through all her misery and shame while her child still lived. He thought of all this; and in the vision on which he gazed without speaking, past and present were inextricably mingled. The fair white brow, the golden hair above it, the beauty and the anguish—all the same as of old, a re-enacted tragedy!

Dumont snatched away the hand which Blanche was desperately clasping. He turned from her roughly, tore the forged checks to pieces, thrust the fragments into her hand, and exclaimed in a hoarse voice,

"Now go, madam! Leave me!"

But Blanche seized his hand once more, and covered it with tears and kisses.

"Monsieur Dumont," she said, "my child will live to requite you, and God in heaven will reward you too. But I cannot go yet. My child owes to you her rescue from starvation to-morrow, and from shame forever. And I owe to you yet more—and this is all I have to give!"

She rose from her knees and loosened her hair. It rolled down over her neck and breast, down over her whole figure, like a golden raiment, thick, soft, and glossy as silk.

Dumont sprang to her side.

"The check was for your child," he cried. "I no longer want your hair. Don't! don't! I couldn't bear it!"

He was about to seize her hand, but something threw itself between them both; for Lyon, who had followed Blanche unperceived, sprang upon Dumont. The banker seized the dog by the throat, dragged him to the door, and flung him out of the room. But before he could prevent her, Blanche had cut her hair short to the roots. When he rejoined her, it lay across the whole table, which it covered entirely, hanging over the edge, down to the carpet.

"Monsieur Dumont," said Blanche, "my child shall learn to pray for you with me. You have prolonged her life by buying my hair. How I can ever sufficiently thank you," she added, in a faltering voice, as she looked at the forged checks, "for thus sparing my husband, I know not. It is so little that I can do, however much I long to do! But if, with these hands, I could dig out of the grave the woman you loved, restore her to you alive, and lay myself down instead of her where now she lies, I would do it with all my heart!"

Into the eyes and features of Dumont came a sudden glow.

"Madam," he said, taking her hand, "you could—"

But there he stopped; and flinging her hand violently from him, he turned away with a fierce cry,

"Go, go! For God's sake, leave me!"

And she went.

The evening breeze came sighing from the sea, and as it wandered through the trees they shuddered and shook down their leaves upon the woman who was hastening along the garden. She, too, shivered in the breeze from the sea, and tightened the poor kerchief she had tied about her cropped head. Her look was turned to the sea, where the smoke-cloud of a steamer, nearing the coast, waved over the blue sky like a long gray ribbon, and her hand pressed convulsively a little parcel of torn papers.

At the same moment, watching from the balcony of the house she had just left, stood a man who knew not what to do. Should he rush after that woman, clasp her to his breast, and carry her back in his arms? or should he seize his revolver and shoot her dead while she is still within reach?

CHAPTER IV.

As Blanche descended the steep road from Ingouville, she often stopped, trembling from head to foot,
and leaned for support against the walls through
which it wound. For she could not help looking
now and then at the papers she held in her hand,
and the sight of them made her faint and sick. On
her way through the town she changed her check
and bought some food. When she reached her poor
lodging, the old water-carrier, who had stayed to
look after the child during her absence, was scared
by the ghastly change in her appearance; but being
assured by Blanche that there was nothing the matter with her, she went away, shaking her head.

The child was asleep, and smiled in her slumber.
The sight of the child's smile brightened the mother's face, as when the light of a candle shines on the
face of a corpse.

"They will not kill my darling's smile," she said
to herself, and knelt down at the bedside, with her
eyes fixed on the face of the sleeping child till all
was dark. Then she lighted a candle, and continued
her gloating, doting watch over that rescued treasure. About midnight Lyon crept close to her, put
his head on her arm, and looked up into her face,
with eyes that said plainly, "It is time for us to go

to sleep." But Blanche remained in the same attitude all night, never once closing her eyes.

When morning came, and the sun shone into the room, the child awoke, and looked at her mother with a puzzled, dissatisfied face. She plucked at the unfamiliar kerchief which the poor mother had tied about her shorn head, and not finding underneath it her customary plaything—the lost locks—began to cry. Lyon heard the child crying, and sprang upon the bed. He had long, crisp hair, and the child thrust all her little fingers into it, laughed through her tears, and thought no more of the pale woman with the cropped head, who retreated humbly, and yielded her place to the dog.

It was enough for her that her child was laughing again.

Just about the same hour, Monsieur Dumont was being admitted to the apartment of Mademoiselle Julie Oeillet. He had arrived in Paris by the night train from Havre, and a servant carried after him a large bandbox. The *danseuse* was not yet out of bed, and the banker waited in the boudoir till she joined him there in a most fascinating *peignoir*.

"You are a wicked man, Monsieur Dumont," said Julie, pouting, "to break in upon people's rest at this unnatural hour of the morning. It is robbing and murdering sleep."

"Mademoiselle Oeillet," replied Dumont, "for your sake I have just passed a whole night in the train without sleeping at all."

"And for aught I care," said the lady, "you might as well have passed it comfortably in your bed; nor did I get up for your sake, but for that of the big bandbox in whose company my maid tells me you have arrived."

"Well, guess what is in it?"

"An infant elephant, to judge by its size."

"No; guess again."

"Monsieur Dumont, I have not yet breakfasted, and am in no humor to guess riddles."

"Mademoiselle," said the banker, "you have often had the goodness to inform me that till now the supreme longing of your life has been for a peruke of a particular indescribable color, only seen in your dreams—a color indispensable to your satisfactory appearance in the part of a wood-nymph. You have everywhere sought for hair of this ideal color, as if the happiness of your existence depended upon it, and you have repeatedly assured me that you would grudge no price for it. But hitherto you have been unable to find it. Well, will you now be so good as to look into that bandbox?"

The dancer lifted herself in the correct conventional attitude on the tips of her toes, and cautiously dipped her nose over the side of the bandbox. But the next moment she plunged both her hands into it, and was laughing and crying with frantic delight. Then she sprang up, whisked and bounded about the room, lifted the bandbox, put it down again, danced round it, and, as she passed the banker, seized his arm and exclaimed,

"*Bon!* I keep my promise. No price is too high for me! How many kisses will you have for it, black Dumont? When? where? how? Shall I dance before you for fifteen minutes and then embrace you, *mon petit Dumont!* or what else? Quick! your price?"

"Ten thousand thanks, mademoiselle. But my price is not nearly so high as all that. You will merely cease to receive Monsieur de Mersay."

"*Tu me fais pitié, mon Otellon!*" laughed the *danseuse.*

"Pardon me," replied the banker, "it is you, mademoiselle, who are to be pitied, if you do not follow my advice. In the first place, it is the only price at which the bandbox is for sale. In the next place, I have called this morning to inform you that Mersay is completely ruined. Is it your intention to undertake a course of performances for his benefit?"

"*Vous vous emportez, monsieur!* I am in love with Monsieur de Mersay."

"Indeed? What a pity! and you don't believe me? Well, then, I have further the honor to inform you, mademoiselle, that yesterday the hair in that bandbox was growing on the head of Madame de Mersay, and that she has just parted with it to save herself and her child from starvation. You see, then, that this poor lady's husband is really and truly a beggar."

The dancer turned and dived once more deep into the bandbox. She thought that she herself would rather have died of hunger than part with such an adornment. Mersay was a handsome man; Mersay was her devoted slave; but as she looked at the hair she believed that Dumont must have told her the truth. Mersay was charming, but he was ruined;

and her eye wandered to the millionaire. She rang the bell.

"Another plate! Monsieur Dumont breakfasts with me."

"Mademoiselle," said the banker, "this fair hair will become your mourning for Monsieur de Mersay to perfection. Are twenty thousand francs enough for the mourning?... Well, you have only to apply for it quarterly at my counting-house. The amount of the first quarter lies already under the plate you have had the amiability to order for me, but of which I regret to say I cannot avail myself, as I must get back to Havre immediately."

When Arthur de Mersay returned to Paris with the London contracts, and humbly rang at the door of the *danseuse*, he was informed that Mademoiselle Oeillet was no longer living there. He hastened to her new house, a little luxurious hotel, and was refused admittance. He came again the same evening and got the same answer. After repeated visits, all equally in vain, the porter told him that mademoiselle had given the strictest orders not to admit Monsieur de Mersay under any pretext whatever, as she did not wish to see him any more. His master, whom he named—a certain foreign nobleman well-known for his immense fortune and dissolute life—had placed the hotel, the servants, and himself at the disposal of mademoiselle, whose orders he was intrusted to obey.

All De Mersay's entreaties were in vain, and his letters were returned unopened.

Then Arthur went back to Havre. Pale as death,

he entered his wife's wretched little home. He
never once looked at her, and therefore he did not
notice how shyly Blanche shrank from the light, nor
why she wore that tight-fitting cap, from which not
a tress of hair escaped. Nor did he touch the food
she put before him. For some time he sat still, in a
gloomy reverie, without speaking, and whenever the
child or the dog approached him, he pushed them
away fiercely. Then he called for pen and paper,
and began to write.

Blanche left the room for a moment to fetch a
glass of water. Suddenly she heard the report of a
fire-arm, and rushed back. Arthur sat leaning back
in his chair, a dead man. A revolver lay near him
on the ground, a letter was open before him on the
table. It was addressed to Mademoiselle Julie Oeillet, and contained only these words—

"Unable to live without thee, I die.—ARTHUR."

They were the very words with which, in the days
of her courtship, he had once threatened Blanche if
she would not accept him!

Why he came from Paris to write this letter, and
kill himself under the eyes of his wife, remained a
mystery. But Blanche, when all was over, sent the
letter to its address.

Mademoiselle Oeillet answered—not by letter, but
by a large bandbox, addressed to Blanche.

This woman, who every time before going on the
stage used to cross and sprinkle herself with holy
water, was afraid that misfortune might befall her if
she performed in that blond wig. For the whole

afternoon of the day on which she received De Mersay's posthumous letter, she had a bad headache!

Blanche made up the hair, which thus came back to her, into a votive offering to *Notre Dame des Flots*.

Some time after Arthur's death she received a letter from Dumont asking her to become his wife.

"You know not," said the letter, "what it is to have carried in one's breast for years and years nothing but a stone, and then suddenly to feel again a heart there! I love you devotedly, as I once loved her whom you resemble. All of me that is not buried in her grave—all of me that unconsciously, to myself, has survived the petrifying process of the long, miserable years since then—all this belongs to you, and is irrevocably yours."

Blanche replied that her resemblance to the dead girl would soon be complete, for she knew she had not long to live. "Even if I had two hearts," she said, "instead of the one that is already dying away, you have merited a better lot than to weep over two graves."

And after that Blanche heard no more of Dumont.

Suddenly, however, she was overwhelmed with commissions for light embroideries, for which high prices were spontaneously offered. One day she received from a solicitor at Paris, whose name was unknown to her, a considerable sum of money, which the solicitor's letter declared to be the residue of her dowry, after payment of all Monsieur de Mersay's debts.

It was as if a careful eye kept watch over her at

16

every step, and Blanche thought it was the eye of Heaven, which, delighting in her child, had care of the little one's future.

For herself she wanted nothing; and if the child, leaning on her bosom, had not often wonderingly said to her, "*Maman*, what is it that beats so here in your breast?" she would have believed that her heart was standing quite still.

Slowly she faded away.

Only in response to the merry laughter of her little girl did there ever come a wan gleam into the weary eyes, and a faint smile to the pale lips, and a soft glow upon the faded cheek. They were the dying signals of a fearful joy; for terrible, indeed, was the hourly conflict between the body of the woman, pining for rest in the grave, and the heart of the mother willing to live on for her child's sake.

But Blanche's hair never grew long again. And when she breathed her last, smiling still because her child was smiling, it was only little short golden locks that curled over the fair dead forehead.

The child smiled, even when the mother was lying in her coffin, and played merrily with the flowers which a stranger had brought and strewn over the dead.

This stranger was a man with a dark brown face and deep mournful eyes. He stood for hours looking in silence at the dead, before the coffin was taken away; and afterwards he was also present when it was lowered into the grave.

The child, still smiling, did as she saw the others do, and threw down upon the coffin a little clod of

earth which the stranger had put into her hand.
Then the man took that little hand in his, and led
the child away to a carriage which waited at the gate
of the church-yard. She clapped her hands and
shouted with pleasure when the horses started off at
a brisk pace; but suddenly she remembered Lyon,
who had remained in the church-yard, and she began to call for him, and to cry so loud that the
strange gentleman ordered the coachman to drive
back.

Lyon was lying on the grave, and moaning. They
could not get him away. The stranger told the
sexton to employ some workmen to remove the dog
by force, if necessary, and bring him to Ingouville.
This they did; but the dog, as soon as he was free,
sprang from the balcony into the garden, and rushed
back to the grave, from which he could not again
be removed. And there at last he died.

The child, as she grew older, was sent for a short
while to a well-known boarding-school at Paris, where
she was educated at the expense of her adopted
father, Monsieur Dumont. He was kept duly informed of all that concerned his little ward, but he
himself never went to Paris. He had sold all his
estates, and gone to live again in his native village
in Provence. Later on, another *pension* was found
for the completion of the education of this young
lady, who, while there, received news of the sudden death of Monsieur Dumont, and the announcement that, with the exception of a few legacies, he
had bequeathed to her the whole of his immense
fortune.

The rich heiress was soon surrounded by suitors. Her beauty attracted all eyes, and her name opened to her all doors in the best circles of French society. About her millions and her parentage the gossip of Paris created a whole cycle of romantic legends; according to which her father had shot himself, in consequence of the heartless frivolity of his wife, whom he passionately loved. Every one lamented the tragic and untimely death of that intelligent and handsome young man, who, but for his wife's misconduct, might have had such a splendid future.

This is what Mademoiselle de Mersay heard on all sides about her parentage. She could neither contradict nor corroborate the tale, for she had not the least recollection of her early childhood. But it made her often think sadly and tenderly of her poor, dear father.

At this moment she is the finest, as well as the fairest, of all the fine ladies in Paris; where the whole world is lost in admiration of her beauty, her taste, her extravagance, and above all, the magnificent abundance of her glorious, unique, indescribable corn-colored hair. She is never so enchanting—all the world asserts—as when she smiles; for her smile has in it something wonderfully sweet and soft. But nobody knows, and least of all herself, what a price this smile has cost. The only human being who knew this is no more; but even she could not have told the cost of this smile, for in her opinion no price was too dear for it.

And the smile is not for her—the dead, forgotten

mother! She does not see it. She is sleeping somewhere in the church-yard at Havre, but no one exactly knows where.

Many a year has passed away since the death of
Dumont, who put no stone upon that woman's grave,
but only planted roses round it, like those which,
years before, he had planted round another grave in
the village church-yard of Provence. And as since
Dumont's death no one has looked after this nameless grave, it is now quite indistinguishable.

Perhaps the dead woman's daughter trod smiling
over it, when, upon her wedding-tour, she stopped
at Havre to give orders about the magnificent marble monument she has erected there to the memory
of her father.

It happened that on that occasion she strolled into
the little church of *Notre Dame des Flots*, and saw
there, hanging on the wall, in their poor black wood-
en frame, among the votive tablets offered to Our
Lady of the Waters, some wonderful tresses of hair,
in color and abundance exactly like her own. She
looked at them with surprise and curiosity, and a
strange, uncomfortable feeling came across her as
she wondered who could have been the woman to
whom those tresses once belonged, and what could
have induced that woman to sacrifice such a splendid gift of nature. Nervously she lifted her hand
to her own beautiful head, and hastened out of the
church, which all at once appeared to her dismal and
haunted. Her husband, and the friends who accompanied them, joked and rallied her a good deal about
this odd little fit of superstitious sentiment; but she

could not smile any more that day, though she knew not why.

The wooden frame has since become stained and broken, the paint has peeled off it, the glass is loosened, the dust has got thick behind it; and the last time I stood in the little church, the hair itself had begun to fade. Soon this offering will be removed to make way for others. The walls of the little church are not spacious enough to record the sorrows and sufferings of every mourner, as the endless generations go and come.

And this is the end of one poor heart's romantic dream—a mournful end! But to how few of our dearest dreams does this world vouchsafe a joyful fulfilment! Not all can end unhurt and happy; and least of all those who have a tender heart and a disposition to sacrifice themselves for others.

Therefore is it, that from her high and lonely shrine in the little church upon the windy cliff, where the great sea waves came rolling and moaning from the north round Cap la Hève, Our Lady of the Waters looks down on all below with a face so sad, so unutterably sad!

A JOURNEY TO THE
GROSSGLOCKNER MOUNTAIN.

A JOURNEY TO THE
GROSSGLOCKNER MOUNTAIN.

A PERFUME, faint and fleeting, that is gone as soon as come, sometimes conjures into motion, wave upon wave within us, a sudden sea of reminiscences.

To some it comes on the breath of a rose-bud, or a whiff of woodland air; to others, in the scent of the pine-log burning on a cottage hearth, or the fragrance of a goblet of noble wine : for each the magic incense has a different savor, but to all alike it comes as the coming of the spring, that wakes to life a whole dead world. Faded pictures glow again in all their pristine colors; weary eyes, long closed, reopen; lips, long silent, begin to speak; dear ones, long forgotten, wander as of old beside us; we see them, we hear them, we feel the soothing pressure of their hands in ours; and the dead are alive once more.

This is a sensation I invariably experience whenever, in after-dinner musings, I happen to scent upon the air the aroma of Syrian tobacco. For then it seems to me as if my old friend Radenburg were still sitting in the corner near me, silently smoking his *chibouque*, or rousing himself out of a reverie to answer some intrusive question of mine.

How distinctly do I see again the tall figure of the man, and his sunburnt face! A man at the prime of life, just thirty years of age, but having in his features and his manners the quiet gravity of a man much older. And even a ghostly fragment of the man's life comes floating to me on those soft gray fumes that unfold themselves like the faded pages of some hoary volume, inscribed with the record of long past events.

Radenburg moved through life so unobtrusively that, by his fellow-travellers along its crowded thoroughfare, he was but little noticed. He never put himself forward. He had no hankering after a ministerial portfolio or an academic chair, nor even any care to increase his private means. It was not from lack of ability, however. In the scientific world his attainments as a naturalist were well known and highly esteemed. Not a few of his contemporaries in that department of science had privately benefited by his researches; but the results of those researches he had no inclination to publish in any form; and the Chair of Natural History, to which he had been called at an unusually early age, he quitted shortly afterwards, to join an expedition to Africa. He did not resume it on his return, but continued his studies only for the silent satisfaction of his own mind, and with unselfish benefit to all who applied to him for information or advice. On the whole, he lived a life of noble, though quiet activity, in the unostentatious pursuit and enjoyment of what is good and beautiful.

In society his position was that of an agreeable and

clever man, whom everybody welcomed as a guest, but whom nobody ever thought of as a promising subject for matrimonial projects; although, in age, disposition, and person, he seemed just the sort of man to make any woman happy. One after another, the wiliest mothers of marriageable daughters had been obliged to give him up as a bad job, baffled by his passionless good-humor, and the undistinguishing amiability of his behavior, whether to young ladies or married women; for both maidens and matrons had attempted his capture with the same disappointing result. To all alike he was equally attentive, and equally indifferent.

This equable placidity, which became him exceedingly well—for it was in complete harmony with all the rest of the man—would certainly have seemed to any observer of his own sex only the normal condition of the man's natural temperament. But the women ascribed it rather to the effect of some external chill than to a natural deficiency of internal warmth; and with their fine instinct in matters of sentiment, they observed that my friend's invariable amiability was but a superficial gleam of winter sunshine, and that the mark on the thermometer beyond which his temperature never rose, and rarely sunk, was only a few degrees above zero.

By degrees, however, finding in him no other capacity suited to their requirements, they had accustomed themselves to regard him as one of those useful human beings who, in a quiet way, contribute to the comfort of houses not their own; who are generally recognized as belonging to the lady of the house, without being suspected of claiming over her any reciprocal proprietary rights; who serve to enliven many a vacant hour with the charm of their conversation, and temper many a family affliction with the solace of their sympathy; who are always present, and always ready, to take a fourth hand at whist if it is wanted; and who benevolently keep the children quiet by entertaining them with *bonbons* and fairy tales.

To hosts and guests alike such persons are the indispensable conditions of a thoroughly pleasant *salon*. They constitute a sort of household furniture, convenient for general use, but not inconveniently attractive of general notice. Their place in the family is scarcely perceived so long as it is filled. It is only when that place is empty forever that, missing something, both husband and wife, and, above all, the children, cannot keep their looks away from the vacant seat; for then, every day, and every hour of the day, they all feel the want of what is gone. And because my friend pursued so good-humoredly and inoffensively his course through life, spectators of it more distant than myself found nothing noticeable in the ways of him; which neither shed before them any very shining light, nor left behind them any deep shadow.

To the few, however, who were more intimately acquainted with Radenburg, or by whom his character had been more attentively studied, it was apparent that this equable demeanor was only an exceedingly well-made coat which he wore in society; and that the even temperature of his manner was the result of a vigilant self-control, which it sometimes cost him a considerable exertion to maintain. There were unguarded moments, revealing to an observant eye the inward struggle whereby this external equanimity was achieved, and what strength of will was exhausted in the hourly effort of it. There were times, too, when the combat was suspended by the fatigue of the combatant—when an immense lassitude completely overcame him, and every nerve and faculty of the man subsided into a state of resigned abeyance, in which both the desire and the capacity of enjoyment were extinguished.

But he rarely succumbed to these fits of depression; and, when they came upon him, he shook them off quickly with a resolute resumption of his habitual smile. One saw that he had a determined will to keep his mind clear, as it were, of every course into which he did not wish others to suppose it capable of wandering. Nor did any element of violence ever enter into the arena of this secret conflict. There were no attempts to drown the voice of the adversary in paroxysms of loud mirth or wild gayety. It was an honest, steady wrestling of the man with himself—a dreadful hand-to-hand struggle, which looked, nevertheless, so like a friendly embrace that only a keen listener could hear the labored breathing of the wrestler.

And thus there was in the whole demeanor of this man that high tone which belongs to men of calm and composed character, but with a *nuance* distinguishable only by a well-trained ear; as when the string of a viol is broken, and the violinist goes on courageously playing his score upon a lower one.

I was the more impressed by this appearance of restrained composure in the character of my friend when I met him again in after-life, from my remembrance of the impulsive, open-hearted gayety which had been particularly noticeable in him during his college days. In those days we were drawn together by similarities of taste and disposition. Afterwards our paths in life diverged; and I had not seen him for several years, when an accidental meeting renewed the friendship of our youth, which subsequent intercourse confirmed and deepened by a common interest in many things.

Radenburg's sister possessed a delightful villa in one of those summer resorts which are within easy reach of ——. She was fond of receiving her friends there, and they were all delighted to come whenever she asked them; for she was still an exceedingly handsome woman, and her young daughter was already a very lovely creature. Moreover, both mother and daughter had the most charming manners, and were as amiable and intelligent as they were good-looking.

In the course of one unusually hot summer, a rather mixed gathering of guests from town was assembled at this villa, and I happened to be one of them. My own visit, however, was more particularly to Radenburg, who had come to stay with his sister for the rest of the season.

It was close upon the dinner hour. The ladies of the house had gone to their toilet, and Radenburg was not yet returned from one of his daily botanical excursions. We guests were sitting or lying on the lawn under the shady trees, with our faces all hungrily turned to the north side of the house, where the cool dining-room opened on to the terrace. The country air sharpens the appetite; and, as we had been breathing it all the morning, we were now nearly famished. There was also a thirsty influence in the scene around us. Every leaflet hung breathless in the glowing heat, as if longing for refreshment; the flowers drooped their heads; and stretched under a bush, with his tongue lolling out of his mouth, Raspe, our hostess's white poodle, was audibly panting.

It was horribly wearisome. Every one was silent, and yawning. The stillness was rather emphasized than relieved by an occasional hungry sigh from one of the guests, or an impatient snort from Raspe at some fly which had settled on his nose, and which he was too lazy to snap at. When the sigh and the snort subsided, the only sounds upon the silence were a distant chirping in the hedges and a restless tapping on the gravel path. Both these sounds were monotonous and incessant; both went on with a sort of *rabbia;* both were short, sharp, and yet continuous —an endless *staccato* without pause; each by itself was irritating, and both together were maddening.

The chirping was from the crickets, the tapping from the tiny *bottines* of Countess Achenberg.

This little countess was as fair and slight as a sylph. Her flesh seemed diaphanous; her beauty was all in expression, and her fine and delicate figure had the effect of an apparition which might at any moment vanish away while you looked at it. Meanwhile, it was full of a restless, though fitful vitality. She liked to be moving about when every one else was quiet; and to chatter, irrepressibly and charmingly, whenever there was a general indisposition to talk. On the other hand, however, in the midst of the most animated company, she would curl herself up in an easy-chair as still as a dozing kitten, and listen to the most brilliant conversation with eyes half shut, as if unconscious of all around her.

Her physician had no idea how she contrived to live on, so long after her life had been given up by himself and his colleagues. He shook his head dubiously, and even resentfully, every time he saw her. And indeed her face consisted almost entirely of two immense blue eyes, to which all the rest of it was only a kind of delicate filagree setting. This lady's illegitimately prolonged life was to his mind a sort of blasphemy against the sacred infallibility of the laws of Nature. Savonarola, however, would have probably said of her that in her case the fleshy veil had been worn away by the spirit into a refined medium, transparent to its inner light. For, in repose, she looked like one of those affecting little images of mediæval saints which one sees enshrined under a Gothic baldachin. But whenever she roused herself—as she was continually doing, with a sudden impulse—out of these states of immobility, all their rigidness melted at once into a vivacity of outline and movement as quick and sparkling as sunbeams on a rivulet; and forthwith the Gothic saint was transformed into a very captivating woman, singularly graceful and lively.

Nor could any one then doubt the thoroughly modern texture of the fine nervous system whose sensitive fibres had been stiffened but a moment before into the saintly outlines of the rigid mediæval image. These vibrating nerves it must have been that had frayed so thin and fine the fleshly veil; and they alone seemed now to sustain in fitful animation the spiritualized body that remained. What it was, however, that kept these restless nerves themselves still going, and imparted to them such surprising elasticity and endurance, remained to the physician a riddle and a rebuke. There was, moreover, in the general tone of this lady's character a certain note which in others would have been, perhaps, unpleasantly eccentric; but in her it was only as if a strain of tender tone were being played upon a violin that has been newly strung.

Suddenly the countess stopped short in her restless pacing of the gravel-walk, and glanced at our circle. It was a glance which had on all of us the effect of an untimely flourish of fiddles in the midst of a general pause. A thrill went through the whole hungry group. Imagine a bear who is expected to growl sagaciously, or even dance, when he is sulking for his food. But it was no use. One had to dance to the tune of those big eyes whenever they pleased. And the only question was which of us should be their first victim; for it is a well-known fact that whoever speaks first after a general silence is sure to say something silly.

17

"I should like to know," said one of our party, a thin, sallow man, "why Radenburg always leaves us so suddenly, and without any sort of reason."

The speaker was a would-be dramatic poet; and in these disappearances of Radenburg he had evidently begun to sniff the plot of a tragedy he had for years been in search of. Apart from this dramatic hobby of his, he was really a most inoffensive creature; and if he would have allowed us to cut his long hair a good deal shorter, and prevent him from continually sucking his pencil, I am sure we should all have been ready to do him these little kindnesses with the best will in the world. As it was, I think that, in a passive sort of way, we were grateful to him for having started a general subject of conversation adapted to the depressed condition of our faculties.

The *motif* given, the variations followed; and "Yes, why?" grunted a stout millionaire, whose servant always carried his umbrella behind him, and whose social habit was to let other people talk for him.

"Yes, why?" repeated the millionaire.

"He is a poet!" said the millionaire's daughter—a rose-bud only just transplanted from an educational forcing-house into the open air of society.

"My brother-in-law, Conrad Radenburg," said our host, "is on one of his customary excursions into the insect world. He has in hand the discovery of a tremendous secret of the *coleoptera* or *lepidoptera*, or something of that sort, and is always at it. His room here is already a den of insectivorous plants."

"That is an explanation of the mystery," replied

the dramaturgist, "entirely inconsistent with, and, as I conceive, emphatically contradicted by, the deeply tragical expression I have noticed in his face on these occasions. It is not the face of an eager naturalist, but the countenance of Saul when the dark spirit was on him."

"*Quelle ingénieuse invention!*" laughed, from under her pretty mustache, the Baroness Boden; a brunette as seductive as she was coquettish, with the archest of downy upper lips, the roundest of arms, the softest of hands, the pertest little foot, and the longest retinue of devoted slaves.

"*Ce bon Radenburg!*" she continued, "why cannot he take his afternoon doze like any one else? He assumes these mysterious airs to make himself interesting."

"Perhaps he suffers from headaches," suggested an old lady companion with blue spectacles, thoughtfully sticking her needle into a horrible little bit of brimstone - colored embroidery on which it was employed.

And so the conversation rambled on inanely, till it became a sort of round game of idiotic guesses, to which every one in turn contributed some new banality; except, indeed, the old lady, who never changed her card, but stuck to the headache.

Gräfin Achenberg, who had been listening to the conversation without uttering a word, suddenly turned towards me with a quick jerk.

"And you," she said, "who are his friend?"

I felt those big eyes of hers upon me as if two burning stars were boring their beams into my forehead.

"I don't know," said I. "But since all you ladies have failed to reclaim him, I take it for granted that he is incurable, and that whatever be his *idée fixe*, no power on earth will move him from it."

The Gräfin turned sharply round without another word, and continued her promenade.

Over the faces of the other ladies fleeted, at the same time, a curiously complicated and slightly ominous expression, which, however, was happily converted into a general smile of satisfaction by the welcome announcement of dinner.

Radenburg, who meanwhile had returned in time to join us at table, sat between an inquisitive spinster of forty and the millionaire's daughter. They both treated him like a pet doll. The elder lady, in her pertinacious efforts to "pluck out the heart of his mystery," bored a deal of dry sawdust out of him, and the younger one clothed the supposed poet in all the finery of her young imagination. Radenburg submitted passively to the boring and costuming, like a well-conducted doll that moves hands, feet, and eyes, and even says "yes" and "no" when pinched in the proper place. By the time that dessert was served, however, he had begun to grow restive; and no sooner had we risen from table than he artfully endeavored to effect his retreat.

But the elderly spinster was not to be evaded, and promptly placing her arm in his, "I want," said she, "to ask your advice, Herr von Radenburg."

"My advice?" faltered Radenburg, looking the picture of dismay; "must you have it at once?"

"If you please," said the lady, as she calmly carried him off along the terrace, and down one of the alleys in the garden.

Soon, however, Radenburg was seen re-emerging from the alley all alone. There was a general and significant simper among the ladies as my friend loitered back to the house, innocently contemplating the tips of his toes while he went along.

This interesting study of his was suddenly interrupted by a hand on his arm ; and a very pretty hand too, exceedingly well-shaped and dazzlingly white, for it belonged to Baroness Boden.

"Radenburg, a word with you in confidence !" said the baroness, familiarly, as she opened upon him her half-closed eyes, which were of the color of cats' eyes. Their opaline gleam, and the glittering teeth which her smile simultaneously unsheathed from under the delicately curved and downy upper lip, put me in mind, as I watched her, of those beautiful beasts of prey whose graceful movements have a cruel purpose. The white hand which had just arrested my friend's loitering steps was attached to an arm equally white, and deliciously rounded. With a scarcely perceptible movement, this white arm coiled itself round Radenburg's, and lay there in a snake-like repose.

The enchantress paused a moment, swept with a swift, confident glance the whole group who were watching her from the terrace, and then bore away the victim, carefully lifting, as she went, the frill of her dainty petticoat just enough to reveal an exquisite foot and ankle.

The ladies on the terrace all looked like the chorus

in an opera when the hero has departed to his doom. In the dark shadows of the trees under which Radenburg had disappeared with the baroness, mortal was the combat about to be waged between the power of woman and the obstinacy of man; and armed in all the fascinations of their sex was the champion who had undertaken to maintain its cause.

Conceive, then, their consternation when the destined victim presently reappeared in the broad sunshine, apparently unscathed! There was a dead silence all round; and as slowly as Banquo's ghost, Radenburg stalked on towards the house—unaccompanied!

In this solemn moment up rose the old lady with the blue spectacles. Laying aside her brimstone-colored embroidery, she advanced towards Radenburg, fumbled in her reticule, and fished out of it a little bottle which she placed in his hand.

There was something awful in the tone of her voice as she said to him,

"A sovereign cure for headache—ten drops on a lump of sugar!"

Meanwhile the millionaire's rose-bud daughter had stolen up to the other side of him. She said nothing, but she looked her prettiest, as with a blush she placed a flower in his button-hole.

Radenburg bowed silently, right and left, to the two ladies, and fled as fast as his feet could carry him.

The old lady and the young one were left looking at each other, like the first and last man in Hebel's poem—

> "They meet, and there silently, face to face,
>   Stand staring, brother at brother;
> The first and the last of the human race,
>   With nothing to say to each other!"

Then they both plunged into the shadows of the alley; and one by one the other ladies left the terrace, and dispersed, like threatening clouds, about the garden.

Countess Achenberg alone remained, curled up in her arm-chair, near the gentlemen, who were smoking on a retired part of the terrace, to which they had betaken themselves immediately after dinner. She had noticed every detail of this little comedy (that I felt sure of) with those big eyes of hers, which were now bent upon the ground in one of her fits of self-absorption; and knowing that at such moments she did not like to be disturbed, I descended the steps of the terrace and strolled through the garden towards an arbor at the outskirts of the alley, in which some of the other ladies were sitting.

Outside this arbor all was clear and sunny, but not so were the fair faces within it; and not caring to confront the storm I saw brewing there, I hastily retraced my steps back to the terrace. Here I found the smokers discussing politics over their coffee. It was just before the Franco-German War, and consequently the social atmosphere was here, also, in a rather stormy condition; so I again beat a retreat. But I felt horribly bored and restless; and as there is nothing which a generous man is more willing to share with a friend than ennui, I at last instinctively re-entered the house, mounted the stairs to Radenburg's room, and knocked without compunction at his door.

My knock elicited first an angry growl, which was quickly followed by a fine clicking sound like the snapping of a lock or the cocking of a pistol, and then a reluctant "Come in!"

The room, as I entered, was so full of tobacco-smoke that I had some difficulty in discovering its inmate through the clouds that surrounded him. He was lying on a *chaise longue*, his coffee on a little table beside it, and one end of an enormously long Turkish pipe in his mouth. He turned towards me a dreamy, absent look, which slowly changed into one of reproachful surprise, as he exclaimed,

" And *thou* too?"

He was right; and the question sounded to my conscience like "*Et tu, Brute?*"

There in one corner lay the poor little rose-bud; in another the unfortunate bottle with its precious drops; and I felt with shame that I deserved to occupy a third. I retreated without answering a word; but just as my hand was on the door, he called after me,

"Do you smoke Syrian tobacco? I have no other."

"Yes," said I.

"Then," said he, "sit down and take a *chibouque*."

I threw myself into an arm-chair, and for a while we smoked our Latakia in silence.

Radenburg's eyes were fixed upon a casket which was placed on the table beside him. There was something peculiar in the shape of the little key which stood in the lock of it. I remembered that Radenburg always wore this key attached to his watch-chain; and it struck me that the clicking sound I had heard, before he bade me come in, must have been caused by the hasty shutting and locking of the casket.

Before my friend spoke again, the clouds of smoke between us had become so thick that I could no longer discern his features; and his dreamy voice came to me out of an impenetrable mist.

"Have you ever been up the Grossglockner Mountain?" asked the voice.

"No," said I.

"Then," replied the voice, "you shall ascend it with me. Don't be afraid. I know you are no lover of alpine adventures. The expedition shall be only in thought. I make it every day with my *chibouque*. You can impart this information to our inquisitive friends down-stairs. The rest of my time is at their service, and I am always glad when I can be of the least use or amusement to others; but this one hour of the day they must really be good enough to spare me, for—"

He stopped suddenly, and then added, in a hesitating tone, "No matter, 'tis no business of theirs, but you shall know it if you will."

Radenburg paused again. For some time he went on smoking in a profound silence, which I did not venture to disturb. The fragrant cloud that concealed him from my sight grew denser and denser. At last the voice came again out of the mist, and in tones even dreamier than before.

"There was, once upon a time," said the voice, "a girl, fair and shy, and a boy, reserved and taciturn. They both lived just outside the mediæval fosse and many-towered rampart which enclosed the crowded buildings of an ancient city. The city was old; but the life in it, still young and vigorous, had boldly overleaped the rampart and the ditch, from which a broad, long street had thus adventured forth, all by itself, across the green glacis and the meadows beyond—a street of houses surrounded by large gardens.

"Right against the dark old tower of the rampart stood a villa, completely overgrown with a luxuriant variety of bright creepers; and in this villa the girl lived with her mother, a widowed lady, of old but impoverished family. Just opposite the villa lived the boy, in a large, high-gabled house.

"All the windows of the villa were closely curtained against the light, with the exception of one, opening on to a balcony, where, between the parted draperies, a fine female profile was sometimes illuminated by the rays of the setting sun. Without that illumination it would scarcely have been distinguishable from the whiteness of the curtains through which, moonlike, it borrowed its faint lustre from the sun. It was generally bent over a book, brushed by its drooping ringlets; and here and there about the green framework of creeping plants which formed a background to its fine, slight outlines, hung the sullen blossoms of a luxuriant passion-flower. By the garden-gate of the villa was always crouching a little pug-dog, whose eyes with a woful stare said as plainly as eyes can say, 'The world is a vale of tears!'   The pug-dog had round his neck a velvet ribbon, colored like the passion-flowers on the screen behind the balcony, and the draperies drawn across the other casements of the villa; and the soft violet tone of all these tints harmonized with the face of the woman above at the window, and the child below in the garden.

"There, under a weeping willow, stands a stone chair, fantastically carved, and in the chair is sitting the child, a little girl, whose delicate face glimmers through a cloud of soft curls.   The fair young face has a pensive and refined expression; and the child sits there as motionless as a little marble goddess, set for a garden ornament on her quaintly carved pedestal, in a bower of blossoming verdure.   The whole image and its harmonious surroundings have a tender charm, which fails, however, to attract a single glance from the boy at the other garden-gate on the opposite side of the street.   Whenever he looks up from what he is about, it is only to stare at the corner window of the house behind him.   This, like all the other windows of that house, is thrown wide open to the fresh air and sunlight; and by the window-sill is seated a buxom, comely dame, with a cheerful face and a beaming smile.   She is mending a very big rent in a very small pair of breeches; and over her homely task, as if it had for her some irresistibly humorous association, the good soul privately breaks now and then into a little cordial chuckle, which she hastens to hide away under a mien of dignified maternal reproof whenever the boy in the garden below looks up to that corner window.

"Many a time, perchance, ere the day is over, wilt thou again have occasion to renew both the inward chuckle and the outward expression of reproof, thou good, kind - hearted mother! That little pickle of thine is, meanwhile, busily engaged in the examination of a small wooden tray on which he has pinned a multitude of dead butterflies. Beside him, on the ground, is a large bottle crammed with all manner of crawling and creeping creatures, and a handkerchief, tightly knotted together by its four corners into a bulging bag, which heaves and struggles with a snaky movement from within, and seems to be making a huge effort to wriggle itself away sidewise across the lawn. The young naturalist is beginning to feel hungry, but he is restrained by 'sundry scruples from entering the house with his hard-won treasures; and he keeps one hand awkwardly tucked behind him, as if to conceal some unlucky rent in that part of his garments.

"The little goddess of the weeping willow has also at last begun to show signs of restlessness. She is not hungry, but she is bored to death. She, with her silken curls and her violet frock, is not allowed to associate with the children in the street, and for many a day, perhaps, she may have cast longing glances now and then across to the lad in the opposite garden. He does not seem inclined to come and play with her, nor, indeed, does he look at all a fit playmate for such a dainty little damsel; for he is always poring over his horrid insect-cases, and he is ragged and soiled from scrambling into all sorts of holes and corners, and up the trees and through the bushes, in search of their ugly contents. But then, at least, he is something different from her only other playthings—the melancholy pug, and the monotonous parrot, and the baronial coronet worked in hair, and framed under glass, which, whether prized as a family relic or admired as a work of art, was only interesting to an acquired taste.

"Just at this moment the little maiden, by good or ill luck, detected a creature of unknown name and unpleasant appearance comfortably curled up on the arm of her marble throne; and forthwith she set up a very human cry for help.

"The cry itself would not have elicited any response from the boy in the opposite garden, for he was accustomed, and perfectly indifferent, to every variety of noise which the street was capable of producing. But the cry was an articulate one, in which the two words, 'A snake! a snake!' were distinctly audible; and by those two words he was instantly and powerfully attracted. In three bounds he crossed the street; with the fourth he upset the pug-dog; and the next moment he had climbed the rail, cleared the hedge, and smashed a hydrangea.

"As he stretched out his hand, however, to seize the monster, he burst into a fit of rude and uncontrollable laughter.

"'You stupid!' cried the boy, 'that's not a snake, it's only a common slug.'

"The little maiden stood trembling all over; and as she bent forward, with a shuddering mixture of fear and curiosity, to look at the thing in his hand, she stammered out,

"'Oh, you dirty, dirty boy!'

"She must, however, have felt a secret admiration for the courage with which he had laid hold of the repulsive creature, for the next day she used all her little arts to tempt him back again. For this purpose she placed herself on her carved throne, raised herself up on tiptoe, and made a sign to him with her finger; but she was so hidden by the intervening boughs of the weeping willow that the boy could only see a bit of her violet dress. She did not know his name, and so she called out to him,

"'Dirty boy, there's another animal here.'

"And he came. The 'dirty boy' did not make any impression on him, the 'other animal' did.

"She led him on tiptoe to a rose-bush, and pointed to one of its blossoms, in which a green and gold beetle had ensconced itself. The boy quietly popped the unlucky little creature into a bottle of spirits which he had in his pocket, and turned to her with a disappointed and rather contemptuous face.

"'It's nothing out of the way,' said the boy; 'only a rose-beetle of the common kind—*vulgaris*, you know.'

"While the rose-beetle was going through its death-struggle in the bottle, the little girl stood pale and speechless with horror. At last she exclaimed,

"'Oh, you naughty, naughty boy!'

"The wretch only laughed, and went off with his victim.

"He now possessed two names which the goddess of the weeping willow had deigned to bestow upon him; and who knows how many more she might have graciously found for him, if they had not, some little while later, had a long talk together, followed by a short dispute, which she triumphantly closed, by observing,

"'My mother makes poems, and your father only makes houses!'

"At these words he turned his back on her, and went home slowly.

"The little girl clinched her right hand, struck its little fist passionately into the palm of her left, and made up her mind, as firm as a rock, not to think anything more about him. There were plenty of other boys in the new street, and she would show him at once that she no longer cared for him the least little bit in the world.

"So she placed herself between two pyramids of clipped box, and stared resolutely down the street, where the little boys were turning somersaults, spinning tops, or playing at robbers and soldiers, while the little girls sat demurely on the door-steps, nursing their dolls or prattling to each other. She looked at it all musingly for a long while, but somehow or other it didn't interest her; and while she still stood listening to the voices from the street she was furtively trying to catch a glimpse of the 'naughty boy' in the garden opposite.

"She now began to feel very sorry that she had hurt his feelings; and after hesitating for a few moments, she went shyly round to the garden-gate. There she stopped a while, still hesitating, and then she suddenly ran across the street. That he might not turn his back upon her again, she had taken the precaution to carry with her a peace-offering. It was a bit of green glass, which she regarded as a rare curiosity, for it had a wonderful effect when you looked through it.

"The peace-offering was so far successful that the naughty boy did not again turn his back on her. He let her remain at his side while he leisurely tested the effects of the glass by looking through it at the house and garden. All this while she stood breathless, clasping her little hands behind her back; but when he had finished his experiment, and turned round to her with a dissatisfied look, she let her arms fall at her side, and ground a hole into the gravel with her heel.

"'It is too stupid!' said the boy, 'and there's no truth in it. Our red house-roof, your horrible pug-dog, and your own pug-nose are all grass-green!'

"This was outrageous. And she had meant so well by him!

"Weeping, she crept home to her garden-chair. And after that the grass grew undisturbed over the foot-paths to the two garden-gates. One of them was untraversed by the girl, and the other by the boy.

"And so the time passed on.

"But one summer morning the boy stood again at the garden-gate of the opposite house. He held the green glass before his face, and was looking through it. Thus looking, he attentively examined everything except the garden-chair opposite and its lonely little inmate; for whenever the glass turned in that direction he quickly withdrew it. And the little goddess sat quite still on her garden throne. This he could not help noticing plainly enough, as every now and then her unwelcome image reappeared in the green glass. In the afternoon the boy posted himself in the street, still with the green glass before his eyes. He looked through the glass inquiringly at the pavement, then at the garden rails on the opposite side, and finally at the pug-dog behind them. The pug-dog, thus contemplated, looked more profoundly melancholy than ever; for he was completely green—a color which did not at all become him. The boy seemed unable to take his eyes off this phenomenon, but he felt that he was too far away to examine it satisfactorily; so he slowly crossed the street, opened the garden-gate, and planted himself directly in front of the animal. The pug-dog opened wide his melancholy eyes, and stared pensively at the boy. Through the green glass the boy also stared pensively at the pug-dog. Just then, however, he felt his neck enclasped by two soft, warm, slender arms, and the next moment he was heartily embracing his little friend.

"From that day forth the two children loved each other sincerely, and lived only for one another.

"Later on the boy went away to school, and afterwards to college; but from the distant city to which his life was then transplanted, his thoughts were ever wandering back, through the garden-gate, to the little girl under the weeping willow. When he came home for his holidays, no sooner had the coach set him down at the inn than he hastened through the town, and passed out by its opposite gate-way down

18

the new street, with a heart beating as if it must burst at every step that brought him nearer to that beloved garden.

"His first look was ever to the green-mantled villa — *her* home; and it was only second looks that then turned, with second thoughts, to the high-gabled house which was his own. There he could see his father's white hair and his mother's dark locks mingled together, and their four loving eyes turned towards the gate of the town with looks that seemed to say, 'Is he coming?' Then their white poodle, a sedate and venerable animal who had long survived the vivacity of youth, sprang out to greet him with unwonted capers and a spasmodic wag of his stumpy tail; then the father's stalwart figure appeared, filling up the door-way through which the mother had already passed out into the garden; and as she clasped her boy to her faithful heart, over her stooping shoulders, one on each side, peeped two blooming girls — the boy's sisters, who, as sisters do, had outstripped their brother in the short journey from childhood to youth.

"But opposite, across the street—ah, there by the open garden-gate, in her old place, between the two pyramids of box, stood *she*, the goddess of the weeping willow! Her arms hung down; each side of her violet dress the small white hands fluttered nervously, and her little head bent sideways towards her right shoulder. There was nothing graceful, or even becoming, in her attitude, but something, nevertheless, which spoke in deeply penetrating tones to the boy's heart. It was an inexpressibly touching embarrassment that pervaded the whole figure as she stood there so shy and still and painfully constrained; like some angel in an old German picture, who would fain fly or wander away, but must needs stand waiting motionless upon the watch. The arrested feet, the drooping arms, the bent head, the longing eyes, all were saying in the same tone, 'What can I do without thee? Come to me! come to me!'

"And the boy broke loose from his family, and came.

"She stood still and waited. He hastened forward and stood still too. Then her arms went round his neck, and her large eyes grew larger and larger as they looked into his, and she murmured,

"'Thou art here at last!'"

Here the voice of Radenburg faltered, and his story came to a sudden stop.

"You knew that boy," he continued, after a moment's silence, "in our happy college days, and you know how hard he worked to attain distinction and an independent position; for that boy was myself. Our college contemporaries used to talk of my impatient ambition, but I was only thinking all the while of the girl under the willow-tree, and her dear eyes, with the longing prayer in them,

"'Come back to me! come soon!'

"And at length the longed-for day arrived when come I could; a day for which I had labored hard, and waited patiently, when I might rejoin her, never more to part; for the object of all my efforts was attained. At home they were not expecting my return. They knew nothing of my success. I wished to surprise them. The train left at noon. I was up betimes that day, had breakfasted early, and was restlessly pacing my chamber, too impatient to sit still. The postman brought me a circular. I threw it, unnoticed, on the table. What announcement of any kind could interest me that morning? But afterwards, as I was lighting a cigar, a spark from it fell on the paper, which began to smoulder; and taking it up to shake out the little cinder, I was startled by the first words of its lithographed lines which I chanced to catch sight of.

"The circular was a *faire part de mariage*, wherein a certain baroness of my native town announced to all the world the engagement of her daughter Marie to a count, whose titles and estates were enumerated at a length which nearly filled the whole page. I knew this count very well, and had often met him. He was an amiable, corpulent man, about forty years of age, and a widower without children. Alas! I also knew his bride. Those deep, large, longing eyes, how well I knew them! The loving clasp of those dear arms about my neck, how intensely I could feel it still! And that violet dress! Violet was the color she habitually wore. For which reason, perhaps, everything around me now suddenly assumed that hue. Even the lithographed circular was dyed in it. The last thing I remember was the violet appearance of my own hand as the paper fell from it.

"When I recovered consciousness they told me I had long been ill, and in a thoroughly miserable condition. That was untrue. It was only when I came back to myself that my condition was thoroughly miserable. I remember the day when, for the first time since my recovery, I was allowed to sit at the open window. It was a mild, dull day, not sunny, but still and soft. I took up the circular, which was lying on my knee. I had not forgotten its contents. I knew them by heart; but with the perversity which impels the sufferer's finger to the sore spot, I wished to study them again, word by word. In doing so, I now perceived in them something which had escaped my notice. It was a little pencil-line faintly traced under the name of the baroness, and at the end of it was an M.

"The line was a strange one; soft as a delicate secret, tremulously traced, and all uneven—as if the poor heart's violent beating had unsteadied the hand that drew it, and then broken off and begun again lower down, as if the eyes that guided the unsteady hand had lost their way—blinded by tears! That little sign told me as plainly as words the plainest could have said—'It was my mother's doing, but I—'"

After another short silence, "This," continued Radenburg, "is the only bit of her handwriting that I possess. It was as if, with her own hand, she had written the epitaph of her heart, and sent it to me thus. Since then I have wandered about the world, and trifled with my life as with a useless thing. Yet useless as it was, a charm seemed in it against which nothing could prevail. I tried to concentrate my thoughts, now on this thing, now on that; hoping that here or there some particle of my being might find an interest in the world, and cleave to it as the drifting seed to the jutting rock. In vain! Look where I would, it was ever and ever the same picture that I saw. In the midst of a broad plain, a many-towered city. Just beyond its walls, a house muffled in creepers. And in that house a pale woman, who traced, with tearful eyes and trembling hand, the line, so faint yet so impassable, which, from all that was once mine and hers together, divided all that was no longer hers or mine—a life in which it was no longer lawful even to think of each other!

"But enough of this. I never willingly speak of the past at all; and that is why, perhaps, it has set me talking too much now. The dam once broken, I cannot stem the flood that carries me away. I must not forget, however, that I have promised to take you with me up the Grossglockner Mountain.

"One evening in the early autumn, my wanderings, which had always the pretext of a scientific object, had brought me, as it happened, through the Möllthal to Heilingbluth, a little village in the highest part of the Carinthian Mountains. Having secured my lodgings at the pretty little inn there, I strolled out to look at the old Gothic church; and, when I had sufficiently examined its internal architecture, I stepped out of the porch into the old church-yard. The shades of evening had already fallen over the village below, and the darkness, moving slowly up the steep hill-side, completely covered the whole lower range of the mountain chain. But above the sky was clear and bright, and in a lucid space of pure ether gleamed a solitary, many-tinted mountain-peak. It was the snowy summit of the Glockner, in all the splendor of an alpine after-glow.

"'That is the last summit on which the sunset lingers; the others are already wrapped in night,' said a low voice in front of me.

"I knew the voice, and I knew the speaker—a woman who, seated on the hill-side, was gazing at the glowing mountain before us. And I knew the man at her side. I shuddered, seeing them together; and unable to endure the torturing sight, I returned to the inn, and shut myself up in my room there.

"I was gazing, in a sort of trance, out of the window into the darkness beyond, when the maid, entering with lights, offered me the visitors' book. I could scarcely realize that she was, indeed, the wife of another; but there in the book I found it written in her own hand—the same pointed M that stood at the end of the pencil-mark on the circular. And although, in the pang of the first unprepared moment, I had thought it impossible to bear what the sight of her recalled, I now longed with a fervent eagerness to see her once again.

"Entering the bright little *salle à manger*, I found them both there. The count recognized me at once, and heartily shook me by the hand. His wife stood perfectly still, and said not a word. She was very pale; her hands drooped listlessly at her side, her head was slightly bent over her right shoulder, and her large pining eyes were fixed upon me. As of old, she stood still and waited; only she looked paler than of old, and her eyes had lost something of their old lustre. I approached her, and she gave me her hand. It was icy cold. We met as strangers—not as those who had known and loved each other.

"The count and countess had planned for the next morning an ascent of the *Parterre*, the glacier of the 'Grossglocken. He pressed me to join them in it.

"'I am a little awkward at climbing,' said he, with a cheery glance at his figure, which had grown much more corpulent since I had last seen him.

"'You must for once in a way,' he added, 'condescend to sacrifice your scientific researches to a lady's caprice or a friend's necessity, and lend a helping hand to my wife. In expeditions of this sort it is all I can do to take care of myself, and in fact I had much rather remain on level ground. But what can I do? *Ce que femme veut*, you know!'

"She had moved meanwhile to the window, and stood there looking out, though there was nothing to be seen outside but the starless blackness of the night. Then she began to pace the room up and down with restless steps, like a person in a fever, whom the burning heat within goads wearily from place to place. This was something quite new to me; but the count, as if it were a habit of his wife's which had become familiar to him, did not seem to notice it. He laughed and chatted gayly till we said good-night.

"But that was no good-night for me.

"When I came down next morning, in the twilight of the early dawn, the two guides were already at the door of the inn, laden with plaids and provisions. After a little while she came out quickly, and at once mounted her horse. The count followed slowly on foot. He and I had agreed the night before that we would not go on horseback; I, because I was accustomed to walking, and he, because he wanted to reduce his corpulence a little.

" The day was still dawning, and the little village fast asleep as we passed through it silently. We were surrounded by a thick, torpid fog. Above, before, and behind us nothing was visible but the gray mist, into which the countess and her horse at one moment disappeared as if by magic, and the next moment emerged from it like a ghost arising out of the depths of the earth. My companion was not in his usual cheery humor. It was evident that early rising did not agree with him, and he seemed still half asleep. Walking appeared to fatigue him much; the fog added to his discomfort; his honest face distinctly expressed his wish to be in bed; he was gloomy and taciturn.

"Just where the ascent began, we came up with the lady and her guide on the stony slope of the mountain path. I now walked beside her horse, which cautiously picked its way over the loose shingles. The fog was still heavy, but less motionless. It seemed to be gradually breaking up.

"The countess watched the shifting motions of the mist, and said to me, 'It looks as if a sculptor stood hidden yonder in the background, shaping with invisible hand grotesque weird figures from the flaky substance of the fog. Wildly his fancy kneads it into wondrous forms; then, dissatisfied with his work, he flings them from him, and anon he fashions from their shattered fragments other images still stranger than the last. Do you notice that giant phantom high above us yonder towards the left?'

"'Yes,' said I, 'it has long flowing gray hair.'

"'And a cap,' she continued—'a high cap drawn low over its forehead. Look, now. The giant has lifted his mighty arm, as if to hurl across the valley the enormous ball he is holding in his hand.'

"'Ay, but whither?'

"'Oh, to the little wight here to the right just before us.'

"'What, that one who has three arms?'

"'Yes, three arms, so he has. And with one of them he is preparing to throw another ball at the giant. How craftily he stoops down! Do you see how fast he diminishes in size? There! he has disappeared altogether!'

"And she rode on fast, to see what had become of the crafty gnome.

"The fog wove a transparent veil between us, through which I saw her glimmering on before me. It seemed to me that she was no longer alive, and that it was not a living woman, but the ghost of my dead love, I saw there, luring me into the mist in which it moved. Her floating hair gleamed white, and white the ghostly skirt of her long dress. Then the gray mist wrapped her in its folds, and hid her completely from my sight beneath its heavy pall.

"I rushed after her. A great longing seized me to hear, if only once more, the sound of her dear

voice. She had reined in her horse, and was waiting for me.

"'He has hidden himself,' she said, 'in the round
tower which our mist-mason has built for him yonder.'

"'Ah, that mist - mason,' I answered, still out of
breath, 'must have once visited our native town, and
seen there the tower on its ancient rampart. His
work is exactly like our dear old tower.'

"She was silent, and steadily perused the fog landscape. Her face was like that of a beautiful dead
woman. All its lineaments were unchanged, but so
motionless and rigid that it seemed as if no smile
could ever thaw, or tear-drop melt, the hoar-frost fall-
en on its beauty in a single night.

"'I feel chilly!' she said at length.

"I took a shawl and wrapped it round her shoulders.

"'Where is Emil?' she asked.

"I told her that the count was resting a little, and
had sent on his guide to say we were not to wait for
him; he would follow presently at his own pace.

"She was silent again; and in silence we both continued to watch the changing cloud-towers before
us.

"At last she said, in a low voice, as if speaking to
herself, 'The old tower in our garden! That, too,
is gone.'

"'Oh no!' said I, 'it stands there still. I saw it
last year.'

"'But the new proprietor,' she answered, surprised,
'told my mother, when he bought the villa, that he

meant to pull it down at once. What made him change his mind?'

"'I did.'

"'You!'

"'Yes,' I said; 'it was such an old friend of mine, that tower. I should have missed something in the world if it had gone. And as I could not otherwise prevent its destruction, I—well, I bought the villa and the garden—the whole property, in short, from the person to whom your mother sold it.'

"'I did not know that you were so devoted to antiquities,' she replied, in a low, tremulous voice, almost inaudible.

"I noticed only the trembling of her voice, and not that she wished to change the subject.

"'It was not that,' I went on. 'The old tower is a memorial monument of my youth—nay, it is more; for beneath that gravestone my youth lies dead. Gravestones only speak well and kindly of the dead. I would not, for all the world, have missed what this one says; and I went back to read what it records for me alone, with the feelings of a man who turns to contemplate the little earthen mounds which are a graveyard's chronicles, or peers into that tomb wherein he has buried all the past—his own heart. In the house opposite that tower where once, with loving eyes, my parents smiled upon my childish occupations, strangers were now watching their own children at play, and by the garden rail of the villa, below the tower, a little girl whom I had never seen before sat singing a lullaby to her doll. How long will it be before these little ones also, in their turn,

go forth into the wide world, and the loving eyes
that watch them now are closed in death like those
that watched me then ?   It is ever the same old story.
And the old tower knows it all, and tells it still.
How many hundreds of times, as it looked down upon
us, has it looked down on other children, who have
since grown up and passed away forever?   How
many hundreds of times will the same thing happen
again ?   The human life below it changes with the
changing years, but not the tower above.   The children playing in its shadow come and go, but it remains.   As the rising follows the setting sun, one
generation follows another.   Bringing hopes and
leaving memories, each comes and goes, as the others
came and went.   And year by year spring renews
what winter withered, and the flowers blossom again
—in the same way, only not with the same blossom.
But it is all the same to the old tower.   As sunrise
after sunset, spring after winter, blossoms after snows
—so, to it, are the children of to-day, who play about
it where those of yesterday shall play no more.   And
I could not but remember that we, too, in our childhood had looked with hopeful eyes upon the same
old ruin.'

"I was no longer able to restrain the rushing flood
of reminiscences which the thought of the old tower
had set flowing.   She at first listened with marked
impatience to my words; and already she had made
three or four abortive efforts to urge on her horse,
and break away from the spell that was deepening
round us.   But I heeded them not.   The floodgates
were opened, and I could not close them, for all the

past rushed through them in an irrepressible cataract. Little by little, as, wave upon wave of memory, the whirling stream rushed on, she, too, yielded to the current that was carrying us both away with it.

"When I reminded her of the titles of 'Dirty boy' and 'Naughty boy,' which she had deigned to bestow on me in the first days of our friendship, she smiled.

"It was the first smile I had seen on her dear face since we had met again, and at the sight of it I felt as if I had still something to live for.

"All our great joys and little sorrows, every word we had once spoken to each other, the whole sweet idyl of our childhood, passed in that moment through my soul, and from my lips. She listened in silence, but no longer unwillingly, her eyes still fixed upon the moving mists. And when I reminded her of our quarrel about her boast that her mother made poems, and my father only houses, a clear, silvery laugh rang light and sweet through the curtaining vapors round us.

"She remembered it all, word for word, as well as I did. And I drank with thirsting soul, drank deep to intoxication, the long-missed music of her voice, as, laughing, she rejoined,

"'Yes, and that was the cause of the dreadful judgment by which I, in my turn, was put to confusion. *"Our red house-roof, your horrible pug-dog, and your own pug-nose, are all grass-green!"*'

"'Ah,' said I, 'but what was the cause of the two children's subsequent reconciliation? What was it

that forced us by-and-by to make up our quarrel?
Was it the song of the birds and the scent of the
flowers, so hoveringly interwoven, song and scent,
with that soft tissue of sunbeams—the balmy air of
the glad green garden, where all around us the buds
and leaves were interchanging with each other a
thousand gentle greetings? or was it those tender
threads which the gossamer spiders had so finely spun
from house to house, that silently exhorted our young
hearts to follow their example? or was it something
else? One thing only is certain; that reconciliation
was inevitable and irresistible. We could not long
remain estranged from each other. And then, how
fondly were the girl's arms thrown about the boy's
neck, and how fervently the boy embraced his little
friend! I believe the two children wept bitterly to
think that anything should ever have come between
them, so dearly did they love each other!'

"'I should like to rest a little,' said the Gräfin,
softly. She smiled no longer, and I saw that her
face had grown fearfully pale, and that she was
trembling all over.

"I sprang forward; and as I lifted her from her
horse, my feelings completely overcame me.

"'Marie!' I cried, clasping her to my heart—'Marie! Marie!'

"She struggled like a frightened child, sprang out
of my arms, and was already hanging over the preci-
pice. Had I not instantly seized her arm and
dragged her back, she would have dashed herself to
death.

"She shrank from me, and stood under the rock

that beetled over the narrow path, staring at me, deadly pale, with flashing eyes. But the flash of those eyes was cold as the light that glitters on an icicle, and she looked at me vacantly, as if she had never seen me before. Beneath that look my own drooped abashed, and the arm with which I had held her sank nerveless at my side. I reeled back, and leaned against the mountain-shelf, like a drunken man who has been staggered by a sudden sobering blow.

"She walked slowly on, without speaking, followed by the guide, who had overtaken us, and was now leading her horse behind her.

"I went after them, looking neither to the right nor to the left, and seeing before me nothing but the shifting movements of the mist, that, as they shut and opened, alternately veiled from my sight, and then again revealed, each time more distant, her receding image.

"But she never once paused, or turned to look behind her. And as a man who walks in sleep, I followed her footsteps unconscious of my own.

"Dreaming still, I reached at last our mountain goal; and still to me like the recollection of a dreadful dream is all that happened after that.

"Even as I speak of it now the dreary vision reappears. The great white glacier, with the double peaks of the Glockner rising above it; the little woodman's hut, where we were to have stopped only for refreshment; the count, in his recovered good-humor, laughing and jesting with the two guides and the shepherd over their meal; and then the hurricane and driving rain that suddenly surprised us there, and rendered our return impossible.

"I remember that all through the storm I sat outside the hut in the pouring rain, and that the night which darkened round me there was not gloomier than my own thoughts.

"On returning to the hut, I found the count stretched full length upon a heap of hay, and fast asleep. The shepherd was seated at the door of the hut smoking, and he smiled to himself as I entered. I thought he took me for an eccentric Englishman. There was scarcely room enough for a third person, but I threw myself down upon the hay beside the count, and the shepherd presently followed my example. Soon he, too, was fast asleep.

"I know not how long a time I had passed in a horrible wakefulness between these two sound sleepers, when I was startled by a piercing cry from the little inner cabin, where a bed had been made up for the countess. I awakened the count, who laughed at my frightened face, but, yielding to my entreaties, went to assure himself that nothing was the matter.

"He soon returned, and asked the shepherd to fetch some water. It was with no laughing face that he said to me,

"'I fear my wife has taken cold. She is—unwell.'

"The shepherd, meanwhile, who had gone out with a lighted torch to look for the water, now came back, bringing it; and as soon as the count had left us again, he turned to me and said, shaking his head,

"'I was afraid of this.'

19

"'What do you mean?' I cried, with increasing alarm.

"'Well,' said the man, 'this evening, while you were out in the storm, the lady asked for you. The other gentleman was asleep, and she seemed anxious; so I told her I would go and look for you. When I had got but a little distance from the hut, I saw where you were; but just as I turned to go back, I was surprised to see the lady herself, lightly clad as she was, standing out in the rain, and looking all about her. I pointed out to her the stone on which you were sitting; for, being so white, it was just visible through the darkness. And then she returned to the hut. But, instead of going at once to her room, she stood at the door-way in her wet clothes till she saw you coming.'

"Just as the shepherd said this, the count opened the door and called me into the cabin.

"She was lying on a plaid which had been spread for her over the hay, and I saw at once that she was in a high fever.

"The count stood by her, perfectly helpless; and this, perhaps, gave me more presence of mind. The shepherd was a young giant; and though the night was pitch-dark, and the storm unabated, he, at my request, agreed to set out instantly to Heilingbluth, whence he was to despatch a mounted messenger to Winklern, or elsewhere, for the nearest doctor. The doctor was to wait for us at Heilingbluth, and the shepherd to rejoin us at the hut with all possible expedition, bringing with him two strong men. He declared himself quite ready to undertake this dangerous enterprise even before I had said a word about his reward.

"'I am so sorry for the poor little lady!' said he; and forth he strode, strong of step and stout of heart, into the vast black night.

"I then waked up the two guides, who had found a bedroom for themselves in a big hay-stack not far from the hut. With their assistance I managed to construct, out of such bits of timber as we could find, a sort of sedan-chair, tolerably comfortable; and in this, as soon as the dawn broke, we carried our patient down the mountain towards Heilingbluth.

"The count rode silently on just in front, and I as silently walked just behind the bearers. The clouds hung low, but the rain had stopped. The whole landscape was shrouded in a gloomy gray color. The Möll, rushing from its unseen sources in the glacier, rolled beside us all the way with a dismal, dirge-like sound, and I seemed to myself to be walking in a funeral procession.

"Near the Briccius Chapel we found the shepherd, and the two men he had brought with him now relieved the other bearers. And so, at last, we got her down to Heilingbluth.

"After some hours of the most intense anxiety, the doctor arrived. He was a kindly-looking old man, with snow-white hair, and a mild, smiling face, which had assumed an expression of ominous gravity when he rejoined us after his visit to the sick-room.

"'An inflammation of the lungs!' he said, in reply to my breathless inquiry; and I could see by his face that he had formed the worst opinion of the case.

"Famous physicians were summoned from a distance. They came, and consulted together; and having declared that they could do no more than the old doctor had already done, they went away.

"Then followed long, weary days of endless distress, when daily I looked in vain for a favorable change in the countenance of the old doctor. He was a very old man; he must have stood by the sickbeds of two generations; and yet he always seemed greatly affected and troubled when he entered my room after leaving hers. He said little, but on those occasions I noticed that he eyed me searchingly and thoughtfully, as if I, also, were one of his patients.

"Once when I vehemently seized his arm, and asked, in a tone of agony, 'Must she die?' he looked earnestly into my eyes before answering. I believe that the kind-hearted old man read my soul like an open book.

"'Must?' he said, slowly. 'No! If she wished to live, she would not die.'

"The evening of the same day the doctor entered my room, accompanied by the count, whose distress throughout the whole of this wretched time had been so great as to render him quite incapable of doing or saying anything. The count sank helplessly into a chair, while the old doctor walked without speaking to the window, and looked silently at the mountains outside. I had risen at their entrance, but I could scarcely breathe, so great was my anxiety and fear to learn the worst. Suddenly I felt the grasp of the count's hand upon my arm.

"'It is the doctor's wish,' said he, 'that you should see her. A crisis, he says, is close at hand. She has called for you several times. Go to her, dear friend, I beseech you!'"

"He pressed both my hands, and burst into tears. I turned to the old doctor, and asked if he had any instructions to give me. The old man was so affected that he could not speak. But he looked at me earnestly, just as he had done that morning, and his eyes seemed to repeat what his lips had then said.

"So I went.

"She was lying quite calm and still. Her eyes were closed, and her face was hueless.

"'Marie!' I whispered.

"She opened her eyes and looked at me. It was the soft, tender look of her childhood, the same deep, longing look as of old — a look which said plainer than words can say, 'Come, then, come to me quickly. I have waited so long for thy coming!'

"I bent over her, and to her poor white face the old smile of childlike welcome returned — the old smile, which seemed to say, 'Thou art here at last!' She lifted her feeble hands, put her arms about my neck, drew my head softly down to her breast, pressed her lips upon my own, and kissed me again and again with unrestrained tenderness. Then she took my head in both her hands, held it before her eyes, and gazed at me a long while without speaking.

"At last she murmured faintly, 'Good-by, dear!'

"The weak hands unlocked their clasp, the tired eyelids closed, and the smile died slowly away.

"'Don't go!' I sobbed. 'Don't leave me, Marie!'

"But she lay quite still.

"Then, through that dreadful stillness, I seemed to hear again the words which the old doctor had said to me that morning,

"'*If she wished to live, she would not die.*'

"And I spoke to her again—broken words, that came in sobs out of the depths of my heart as I bent above her.

"'Marie,' I sobbed, 'have you, then, forgotten the days of our childhood?—forgotten that if you go, I go, and that only while you stay, I stay? Not for your sake, Marie, but for mine—for my sake only still, as it was so often in those old days! Had you ever before the heart to deny me anything? For my sake, dear, for my sake only, stay!'

"'Oh, you naughty boy!' she said. And the old smile broke out again, and the tears were trickling softly down her cheek."

Radenburg was suddenly silent again. I looked hard at him.

"The smoke went into my eyes," he said, in a hoarse voice; and I saw that down his own cheek, also, a tear was trickling softly.

After a while he resumed in a steadier tone.

"Our journey is done," he said. "We have made the ascent of the Grossglockner Mountain, and the ascent is over. Every day at this hour I renew that journey. A foolish habit, is it not? Here in this casket I keep her portrait. Her husband gave it me in remembrance of the sad days we passed together at Heilingbluth. The smoke rises from my *chibouque*, and encircles her dear head with clouds, as did the mountain mist that day when she and I ascended the Glockner together. It shapes itself into giant images, and piles itself up in phantom-towers, and takes the forms of distant mountain peaks. And sometimes the ghastly vapor envelops her so completely that I see her through it only as a wandering shadow; and then again it disperses, and she emerges from the mist, every feature of her gentle face distinct and lovely and loving, as of old. 'Thou art here at last!' it seems to say to me again. And around us both the soft caressing vapor flings its flaky mantle, separating us from the loud wide world outside, and opening to us secret labyrinths through cloud-land, where we wander once again together, telling each other stories—stories of the buried lives which we ourselves once lived in the days forever gone—and interpreting, by a key that is ours alone, the mystic image-writing of the mist. Every movement of that cherished form I see again as when I saw it first; every sound of that dear voice I hear once more as first I heard it; and looking and listening thus entranced, I dream awake with eyes wide open."

"And she died, then?" I asked, hesitatingly, when he ceased speaking. For he remained silent, as if he had told me all there was to tell.

Radenburg rose, took the key out of the casket, and attached it again to his watch-chain. Then he went to the window and stood there, looking down upon the terrace below. After a while, without turning round, he spoke again, with his back to me, and his face to the window.

"Died?" he said. "Perhaps. Who knows? It is all the same to me. If she died, it was for my sake. Her death came to her from watching for me in the midnight storm, and she died because, for my sake, she wished to die. And if she lived, it was for my sake also—though not for me. For she lived a true and faithful wife. Between her life and death there is for me no difference left—both dear, both dead! And it is this that has given rest to my heart and resignation to my soul. I may always think of her, now that I can only think of her as of a shy child seated motionless upon a marble throne beneath a bower of passion-flowers. Whenever I see any little girl sitting all alone by herself, I think of that little girl all by herself in the lonesome past that nothing can now disturb. Her childlike eyes gaze down on me whenever I wander alone in the forest and look up into the blue heaven above me. Ay, and even when I do but think of heaven, and of what fathomless depths there are in the still, unchanging, all-embracing watch with which, wherever I go, its presence follows me about the world—a presence so constant and so fair, yet so far away, so unattainable! Ever the heaven is there above me, and never is its heavenliness defaced by what is here around me. It looks down to-day on the resignation of the man, as it looked in the days that are no more upon the hopefulness of the boy. And just so, forever there, where first I saw it in my childhood, yet forever with me still, and forever the same as of old, is the changeless image of that lonely child in the bowery garden under the ruined tower.

"Here, too, in the cloud-land that rises around me on the fumes of this solitary pipe, when with her I wander away among the gray, rolling vapors — farther and farther through the misty shadows that deepen and darken towards the scene of that last struggle on the painful sick-bed in the little mountain inn—it is still ever the same image that I see and follow—the child's image, not the woman's! It was not the wife of another who, in that lifelong farewell, so tenderly embraced me. It was the child whose childhood was all my own, with her holy child-eyes, and her pure child-lips, and her divine child-heart. And when she lay upon my breast for one dear moment, it was the fairy song of our childhood whose enchantment trembled through our souls—the same pure song which our hearts had first sung together under the old tower. We heard it then for the last time, as we had heard it for the first—pure and sweet, with the music of a sinless joy, only that then the music was sad as well as sweet; and again it died away, as how often had it died away before, whenever for my sake her true heart condemned itself to suffer and endure. '*Oh, you naughty boy!*' she murmured, smiling through her tears when I implored her to live for my sake. And any one who has never heard those words from her dear lips may well smile at such a dying out of childhood's song."

Radenburg said no more; nor did he move away from the window, where he remained, with his hands clasped behind him, silently looking down upon the trees in the garden below.

In silence, too, I pressed his hand, and without a word I stole out of the room.

I returned to the garden, pondering how the life of two persons would shape itself out if one of them lived, only for the other's sake, a life otherwise unwillingly prolonged. The one, I mused, wrestles with death only to insure the life of the other, and life's mightiest impulse, that of self-preservation, becomes only the instrument of a purpose mightier still—the preservation of another. Sanctified to itself must such a life become by all that has made dependent on the issue of its hourly trial the salvation of another life that is dearer to it than its own, when in every moment of dejection and defeat the warning voice cries to the aching heart, "If thou diest, he must die!" and the weary one returns to the struggle, triumphing over sickness and suffering, and death itself, in the thought that whispers, "The longer this struggle lasts, the longer his reprieve!"

And then I mused again over my poor friend's story, and I said to myself, " What is it in the human heart that, when you search it to the depths, is always so unspeakably sad, and yet so unspeakably beautiful ?"

As I strolled along, thus musing, my steps unconsciously led me back to the deserted terrace, and I saw that some one was still sitting there all alone.

It was Countess Achenberg. She had not noticed my approach, and consequently she did not look up when I took possession of a garden seat beside her. She was sitting in the same place, and in the same attitude, as when I had left her two hours ago.

A light breeze had sprung up. It softly stirred the leaves upon the garden trees about us, and gracefully swayed the long, delicate tufts of Indian grass under the veranda, as it crept into the trellised vine. The aloes on the balustrade, however, remained motionless, and so did the solitary woman who was sitting under them, while the breeze fluttered about her.

Lightly the fluttering breeze played over that motionless figure, and blowing softly up the terrace, breathed upon my face with a faint, sweet odor. Whence had it brought this perfume? Was it stolen from some flowering shrub in the garden, or wafted from the hair of the silent woman at my side? or was its home in the warmth of the little white hand that lay so languid in her quiet lap? or was it a sweet effusion from the whole figure of the woman which, overshadowed by the spreading canopy of rigid aloe-shafts—a spiky baldachin of sombre hue—seemed to have relapsed again into the solemn fixity of a sacred image?

Whatever the source of it, this perfume seemed to me like the breath of some delicate flower which, when the rains are over and the winds are still, softly opens to heaven all its hushed and fragrant heart in a stillness of unclouded light.

Penetrated in every pore by the beauty and fragrance of it, I gazed upon the fragile human flower before me. But sweet and lovely as it was, I felt that of all who must be sensible of its charm, not one would ever wish to pluck that beautiful blossom. Such a wish would have been sacrilege. The beauty on which I gazed was so unmistakably a beauty dedicated to the grave! "Farewell," not "welcome," was the word its sweetness breathed. The perfume I inhaled was not the freshness of a growing flower, but the fragrance of a fading one—the last sweet emanation of a beautiful soul that was slowly and proudly withering away with the secret of its suffering unbetrayed—a soul which only lingered still in those large eyes (life's last outposts), like the gallant leader of a vanquished host, to cover the retreat of its defeated forces. Why she thus willed to live on, who could say? Her life seemed so joyless, so fatigued! But one felt, as one looked at her, that if she chose, she had only to close those eyes in which the light of life still lingered, and to cease to live, without an effort.

I knew that she must have been sitting thus, motionless, for two long mortal hours and more; and the painful contemplation of this dreary trance so affected and oppressed me that I felt an irresistible impulse to endeavor at any price to arouse her from it, even at the risk of appearing intrusive and importunate.

A walking-stick lying on the table near her significantly warned me that some other guest had probably been making such an attempt, with a failure so ignominious that he had left part of his equip-

ment behind him in the confusion of his retreat.
But I remembered that she had shown some interest in the general discussion which had taken place
under the trees while we were waiting for dinner,
and I fancied that by recurrence to the subject of
that discussion I might possibly extract a smile from
her.

"Countess," I said, drawing my chair a little nearer to hers, "you asked me this afternoon if I, as
Radenburg's friend, was acquainted with his secret.
Well, it happens that I am; and I will tell it you.
Every day at a certain hour he makes the ascent of
the Grossglockner Mountain."

My heart stopped beating under the look she gave
me as I said those words. Her large, childlike eyes
opened wide, and stared at me with an expression I
cannot describe. On their long, soft lashes two big
heavy tears were trembling. She had risen suddenly from her seat. Her arms hung flat at her side,
and her beautiful head was slightly slanted towards
her right shoulder. Over her lips fluttered a strange
quivering movement that was neither a smile nor
a sigh, though in it was something kindred to each.
The expression of it was both sweet and painful—
like that dying away of a soul's song, of which Radenburg had said to me that he only could imagine
the effect of it who had heard it from her own lips.
And his words rushed back to my memory like a
revelation—"*Did she die? Perhaps. Who knows?
But if she lived, it was for my sake—though not for
me—for she lived a true and faithful wife.*"
I held my breath, listening for the childish words

of childhood's renewed farewell, "*Oh, you naughty boy!*" But she said nothing.

The silence remained unbroken; and the cry of her heart, whatever it was, had died out unheard in that inaudible movement of her lips.

All I could see was that the two big tears had slipped from the heavy lashes on which, but a moment before, I had seen them suspended, and were slowly trickling down the pale cheeks of the little countess.

THE END.

BEN-HUR: A TALE OF THE CHRIST.

By LEW. WALLACE. New Edition. pp. 552. 16mo, Cloth, $1 50.

Anything so startling, new, and distinctive as the leading feature of this romance does not often appear in works of fiction. . . . Some of Mr. Wallace's writing is remarkable for its pathetic eloquence. The scenes described in the New Testament are rewritten with the power and skill of an accomplished master of style.—*N. Y. Times.*

Its real basis is a description of the life of the Jews and Romans at the beginning of the Christian era, and this is both forcible and brilliant. . . . We are carried through a surprising variety of scenes; we witness a sea-fight, a chariot-race, the internal economy of a Roman galley, domestic interiors at Antioch, at Jerusalem, and among the tribes of the desert; palaces, prisons, the haunts of dissipated Roman youth, the houses of pious families of Israel. There is plenty of exciting incident; everything is animated, vivid, and glowing.—*N. Y. Tribune.*

From the opening of the volume to the very close the reader's interest will be kept at the highest pitch, and the novel will be pronounced by all one of the greatest novels of the day.—*Boston Post.*

It is full of poetic beauty, as though born of an Eastern sage, and there is sufficient of Oriental customs, geography, nomenclature, etc., to greatly strengthen the semblance.—*Boston Commonwealth.*

"Ben-Hur" is interesting, and its characterization is fine and strong. Meanwhile .t evinces careful study of the period in which the scene is laid, and will help those who read it with reasonable attention to realize the nature and conditions of Hebrew life in Jerusalem and Roman life at Antioch at the time of our Saviour's advent.—*Examiner*, N. Y.

It is really Scripture history of Christ's time clothed gracefully and delicately in the flowing and loose drapery of modern fiction. . . . Few late works of fiction excel it in genuine ability and interest.—*N. Y. Graphic.*

One of the most remarkable and delightful books. It is as real and warm as life itself, and as attractive as the grandest and most heroic chapters of history.—*Indianapolis Journal.*

The book is one of unquestionable power, and will be read with unwonted interest by many readers who are weary of the conventional novel and romance.—*Boston Journal.*

PUBLISHED BY HARPER & BROTHERS, NEW YORK.

☞ *The above work sent by mail, postage prepaid, to any part of the United States or Canada, on receipt of the price.*

CONSTANCE F. WOOLSON'S NOVELS.

EAST ANGELS. 16mo, Cloth, $1 25.

ANNE. Illustrated. 16mo, Cloth, $1 25.

FOR THE MAJOR. 16mo, Cloth, $1 00.

CASTLE NOWHERE. 16mo, Cloth, $1 00. (*A New Edition.*)

RODMAN THE KEEPER. Southern Sketches. 16mo, Cloth, $1 00. (*A New Edition.*)

There is a certain bright cheerfulness in Miss Woolson's writing which invests all her characters with lovable qualities.—*Jewish Advocate*, N. Y.

Miss Woolson is among our few successful writers of interesting magazine stories, and her skill and power are perceptible in the delineation of her heroines no less than in the suggestive pictures of local life.—*Jewish Messenger*, N. Y.

Constance Fenimore Woolson may easily become the novelist laureate.—*Boston Globe.*

Miss Woolson has a graceful fancy, a ready wit, a polished style, and conspicuous dramatic power; while her skill in the development of a story is very remarkable.—*London Life.*

Miss Woolson never once follows the beaten track of the orthodox novelist, but strikes a new and richly loaded vein which, so far, is all her own; and thus we feel, on reading one of her works, a fresh sensation, and we put down the book with a sigh to think our pleasant task of reading it is finished. The author's lines must have fallen to her in very pleasant places; or she has, perhaps, within herself the wealth of womanly love and tenderness she pours so freely into all she writes. Such books as hers do much to elevate the moral tone of the day—a quality sadly wanting in novels of the time.—*Whitehall Review*, London.